"WHAT HAPPENED TO YOU, CORD?

"All those scars ..."

"Just a lot of hard living. I was tossed off the lap of luxury a long time ago."

She glanced up at the harshness of his tone and realized that he'd finished shaving. For the first time she saw his face without the beard, and her mouth went dry.

He'd left his moustache, and he had the face of a warrior, a man who laughed at danger. She'd thought that his beard made him look like more of a desperado than he really was; now she realized that the reverse had been true. The beard had disguised the ruthlessness of his face.

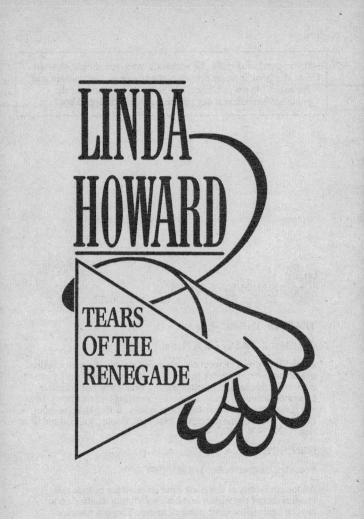

LINDA HOWARD

TEARS OF THE RENEGADE

 Silhouette® Books

Published by Silhouette Books New York

SILHOUETTE BOOKS
300 East 42nd St., New York, N.Y. 10017

TEARS OF THE RENEGADE

ISBN: 0-373-48272-8

Published Silhouette Books 1985, 1993

All the characters in this book have no existence outside the
imagination of the author and have no relation whatsoever to
anyone bearing the same name or names. They are not even
distantly inspired by any individual known or unknown to the
author, and all incidents are pure invention.

®: Trademark used under license and registered in the United States
Patent and Trademark Office and in other countries.

Printed in the U.S.A.

To Vanessa and Gail for their dedicated nagging

Chapter 1

IT WAS LATE, ALREADY AFTER ELEVEN O'CLOCK, WHEN THE broad-shouldered man appeared in the open French doors. He stood there, perfectly at ease, watching the party with a sort of secret amusement. Susan noticed him immediately, though she seemed to be the only one who did so, and she studied him with faint surprise because she'd never seen him before. She would have remembered if she had; he wasn't the sort of man that anyone forgot.

He was tall and muscular, his white dinner jacket hugging his powerful shoulders with just enough precision to proclaim exquisite tailoring, yet what set him apart wasn't the almost dissolute sophistication that sat so easily on him; it was his face. He had the bold look of a desperado, an impression heightened by the level dark brows that shadowed eyes of a pale, crystalline blue. Lodestone eyes, she thought, feeling their effect even though he wasn't looking at her. A funny little quiver danced down her spine, and her senses were suddenly heightened—the music was more vibrant, the colors more intense, the heady perfume of the early spring night stronger. Every instinct within her was abruptly awakened as she stared at the stranger with a sort of primitive recognition. Women have always known which men are dangerous, and this man radiated danger.

It was there in his eyes, the self-assurance of a man who was willing to take risks, and willing to accept the consequences. An almost weary experience had hardened his features, and Susan knew, looking at him, that he would be a man no one would lightly cross. Danger rode those broad shoulders like a visible mantle. He wasn't quite . . . civilized. He looked like a modern-day pirate, from those bold eyes to the short, neatly trimmed dark beard and moustache that hid the lines of his jaw and upper lip; but she knew that they would be strong lines. Her eyes traveled to his hair, dark and thick and vibrant, styled in a casual perfection that most men would have paid a fortune to obtain, just long enough to brush his collar in the back with a hint of curl.

At first no one seemed to notice him, which was surprising, because to Susan he stood out like a tiger in a roomful of tabbies. Then, gradually, people began to look at him, and to her further astonishment a stunned, almost hostile silence began to fall, spreading quickly over the room, a contagious pall that leaped from one person to another. Suddenly uneasy, she looked at her brother-in-law, Preston, who was the host and almost within touching distance of the newly arrived guest. Why didn't he welcome the man? But instead Preston had gone stiff, his face pale, staring at the stranger with the same sort of frozen horror one would eye a cobra coiled at one's feet.

The tidal wave of silence had spread to include the entire huge room now, even the musicians on the raised dais falling silent. Under the glittering prisms of the chandeliers, people were turning, staring, shock rippling over their faces. A shiver of alarm went down Susan's slender back;

what was going on? Who was he? Something awful was going to happen. She sensed it, saw Preston tensing for a scene, and knew that she wasn't going to let it happen. Whoever he was, he was a guest of the Blackstones, and no one was going to be rude to him, not even Preston Blackstone. Instinctively she moved, stepping into the middle of the scene, murmuring "Excuse me" to people as she slipped past them. All attention turned to her as if drawn by a magnet, for her movement was the only movement in the room. The stranger turned his gaze on her, too; he watched her, and he waited, those strange lodestone eyes narrowing as he examined the slim, graceful woman whose features were as pure and serene as a cameo, clothed in a fragile cream silk dress that swirled about her ankles as she walked. A three-strand pearl choker encircled her delicate throat; with her soft dark hair drawn up on top of her head and a few tendrils curling about her temples, she was a dream, a mirage, as illusive as angel's breath. She looked as pure as a Victorian virgin, glowingly set apart from everyone else in the room, untouched and untouchable; and, to the man who watched her approach, an irresistible challenge.

Susan was unaware of the male intent that suddenly gleamed in the depths of his pale blue eyes. She was concerned only with avoiding the nastiness that had been brewing, something she didn't understand but nevertheless wanted to prevent. If anyone had a score to settle with this man, they could do it at another time and in another place. She nodded a silent command to the band as she walked, and obediently the music began again, hesitantly at first, then gaining in volume. By that time, Susan had reached the man, and she held her hand out to him. "Hello," she said, her low, musical voice carrying effortlessly to the people who listened openly, gaping at her. "I'm Susan Blackstone; won't you dance with me?"

Her hand was taken in long, hard fingers, but there was

no handshake. Instead, her hand was simply held, and a slightly rough thumb rubbed over the back of her fingers, feeling the softness, the slender bones. A level brow quirked upward over the blue eyes that were even more compelling at close range, for now she could see that the pale blue was ringed by deep midnight. Staring into those eyes, she forgot that they were simply standing there while he held her hand until he used his grip on her to pull her into his embrace as he swung her into a dance, causing the skirt of her dress to wrap about his long legs as they moved.

At first he simply held her, his strength moving her across the dance floor with such ease that her feet barely touched down. No one else was dancing, and Susan looked at several people, her level gaze issuing a quiet, gentle command that was obeyed without exception. Slowly they were joined by other dancers, and the man looked down at the woman he held in his arms.

Susan felt the strength in the hand on her lower back as the fingers slowly spread and exerted a gentle pressure that was nevertheless inexorable. She found herself closer to him, her breasts lightly brushing against his hard chest, and she suddenly felt overwarm, the heat from his body enveloping her. The simple, graceful steps he was using in the dance were abruptly difficult to follow, and she forced herself to concentrate to keep from stepping on his toes.

A quivering, spring-loaded tension began coiling in her stomach, and her hand trembled in his. He squeezed her fingers warmly and said into her ear, "Don't be afraid; I won't hurt you."

His voice was a soft, deep rumble, as she had known it would be, and again that strange little shiver rippled through her. She lifted her head and found how close he had been when one of the soft curls at her temple became entangled in his beard, then slid free. She was almost dazed when she found herself looking directly at the chiseled strength of his lips, and she wondered with raw hunger if his mouth would be firm or soft, if he would taste as heady as he looked. With an inner groan, she jerked her thoughts away from the contemplation of how he would taste, what it would be like to kiss him. It was difficult to move her gaze higher, but she managed it, then wished that she hadn't; staring into those unusual eyes was almost more than her composure could bear. Why was she reacting like a teenager? She was an adult, and even as a teenager she had been calm, nothing like the woman who now found herself quaking inside at a mere glance.

But she was seared by that glance, which surveyed, approved, asked, expected and . . . knew. He was one of those rare men who knew women, and were all the more dangerous for their knowledge. She responded to the danger alarm that all women possess by lifting her head with the innate dignity that characterized her every movement, and met that bold look. She said quietly, "What an odd thing to say," and she was proud that her voice hadn't trembled.

"Is it?" His voice was even softer than before, deeper, increasingly intimate. "Then you can't know what I'm thinking."

"No," she said, and left it at that, not picking up on the innuendo that she knew was there.

"You will," he promised, his tone nothing now but a low rasp that touched every nerve in her body. As he spoke, the arm about her waist tightened to pull her closer, not so close that she would have felt obliged to protest, but still she was suddenly, mutely aware of the rippling muscles in his thighs as his legs moved against hers. Her fingers clenched restlessly on his shoulder as she fought the abrupt urge to slide them inside his collar, to feel his bare skin and discover for herself if her fingers would be singed by the fire of him. Shocked at herself, she kept her eyes determinedly on the shoulder seam of his jacket and tried not to think of the strength she could feel in the hand that clasped hers, or in the one that pressed so lightly on the small of her back . . . lightly; but she had the sudden thought that if she tried to move away from him, that hand would prevent the action.

"Your shoulders look like satin," he murmured roughly; before she could guess his intentions, his head dipped and his mouth, warm and hard, touched the soft, bare curve of her shoulder. A fine madness seized her and she quivered, her eyes drifting shut. God, he was making love to her on the dance floor, and she didn't even know his name! But everything in her was responding to him, totally independent of her control; she couldn't even control her thoughts, which kept leaping ahead to more dangerous subjects, wondering how his mouth would feel if it kept sliding down her body. . . .

"Stop that," she said, to herself as well as to him, but her voice was lacking any element of command; instead it was soft and shivery, the way she felt. Her skin felt as if it were on fire, but voluptuous shivers almost like a chill kept tickling her spine.

"Why?" he asked, his mouth making a sleek glissade from her shoulder to the sensitive hollow just below her ear.

"People are watching," she murmured weakly, sagging against him as her body went limp from the flaming delight that went off like a rocket inside her. His arm tightened about her waist to hold her up, but the intensified sensations of being pressed to him only made her that much weaker. She drew a ragged breath; locked against him as she was, there was no mistaking the blatant male arousal of his body, and she lifted stunned, drowning eyes to him. He was watching her through narrowed eyes, the intense, laser quality of his gaze burning into her. There was no embarrassment or apology in his expression; he was a man, and reacted as such. Susan found, to her dazed astonishment, that the deeply feminine center of her didn't want an apology. She wanted instead to drop her head to his shoulder and collapse into his lean, knowledgeable hands;

but she was acutely aware not only of the people watching him, but also that if she followed her very feminine inclination, he was likely to respond by carrying her away like a pirate stealing a lady who had taken his fancy. No matter how he made her feel, this man was still a stranger to her.

"I don't even know who you are," she gasped quietly, her nails digging into his shoulder.

"Would knowing my name make any difference?" He blew gently on one of the tendrils that lay on her temple, watching the silky hair lift and fall. "But if it makes you feel better, sweetheart, we're keeping it in the family."

He was teasing, his teeth glistening whitely as he smiled, and Susan caught her breath, holding it for a moment before she could control her voice again. "I don't understand," she admitted, lifting her face to him.

"Take another deep breath like that, and it won't matter if you understand or not," he muttered, making her searingly aware of how her breasts had flattened against the hard planes of flesh beneath the white jacket. His diamond-faceted gaze dipped to the softness of her mouth as he explained, "I'm a Blackstone, too, though they probably don't claim me."

Susan stared at him in bewilderment. "But I don't know you. Who are you?"

Again those animal-white teeth were revealed in a wicked grin that lifted the corners of his moustache. "Haven't you heard any gossip? The term 'black sheep' was probably invented especially for me."

Still she stared at him without comprehension, the graceful line of her throat vulnerable to his hungry scrutiny as she kept her head lifted the necessary inches to look at him. "But I don't know of any black sheep. What's your name?"

"Cord Blackstone," he replied readily enough. "First cousin to Vance and Preston Blackstone; only son of Elias and Marjorie Blackstone; born November third, probably nine months to the day after Dad returned from his tour of duty in Europe, though I never could get Mother to admit it,'' he finished, that wicked, fascinating grin flashing again like a beacon on a dark night. ''But what about you, sweetheart? If you're a Blackstone, you're not a natural one. I'd remember any blood relative who looked like you. So, which of my esteemed cousins are you married to?''

''Vance,'' she said, an echo of pain shadowing her delicate features for a moment. It was a credit to her strength of will that she was able to say evenly, ''He's dead, you know,'' but nothing could mask the desolation that suddenly dimmed the luminous quality of her eyes.

The hard arms about her squeezed gently. ''Yes, I'd heard. I'm sorry,'' he said with rough simplicity. ''Damn, what a waste. Vance was a good man.''

''Yes, he was.'' There was nothing more that she could say, because she still hadn't come to terms with the senseless, unlikely accident that had taken Vance's life. Death had struck so swiftly, taken so much from her, that she had automatically protected herself by keeping people at a small but significant distance since then.

''What happened to him?'' the silky voice asked, and she was a little stunned that he'd asked. Didn't he even know how Vance had died?

''He was gored by a bull,'' she finally replied. ''In the thigh . . . a major artery was torn. He bled to death before we could get him to a hospital.'' He had died in her arms, his life seeping away from him in a red tide, yet his face had been so peaceful. He had fixed his blue eyes on her and kept them there, as if he knew that he was dying and wanted his last sight on earth to be of her face. There had been a serene, heartbreaking smile on his lips as the brilliance of his gaze slowly dimmed and faded away forever. . . .

Her fingers tightened on Cord Blackstone's shoulder, digging in, and he held her closer. In an odd way, she felt some of the pain easing, as if he had buffered it with his big, hard body. Looking up, she saw a reflection in those pale eyes of his own harsh memories, and with a flash of intuition she realized that he was a man who had seen violent deaths before, who had held someone, a friend perhaps, in his arms while death approached and conquered. He understood what she had been through. Because he understood, the burden was abruptly easier to bear.

Susan had learned, over the years, how to continue with everyday things even in the face of crippling pain. Now she forced herself away from the horror of the memory and looked around, recalling herself to her duties. She noticed that far too many people were still standing around, staring at them and whispering. She caught the bandleader's eye and gave another discreet nod, a signal for him to slide straight into another number. Then she let her eyes linger on her guests, singling them out in turn, and under the demand in her clear gaze the dance floor began to fill, the whispers to fade, and the party once more resumed its normal noise level. There wasn't a guest there who would willingly offend her, and she knew it.

"That's a neat trick," he observed huskily, having followed it from beginning to end, and his voice reflected his appreciation. "Did they teach that in the finishing school you attended?"

A little smile played over her soft mouth before she glanced up at him, allowing him to divert her. "What makes you think I went to a finishing school?" she challenged.

His bold gaze slipped down the front of her gown to seek out and visually touch her rounded breasts. "Because you're so obviously . . . finished. I can't see anything that Mother Nature left undone." His hard, warm fingers slid briefly down her back. "God, how soft your skin is," he finished on a whisper.

A faint flush colored her cheeks at the husky note of

intimacy that had entered his voice, though she was pleased in a deeply feminine way that he had noticed the texture of her skin. Oh, he was dangerous, all right, and the most dangerous thing about him was that he could make a woman take a risk even knowing how dangerous he was.

After a moment when she remained silent, he prodded, "Well? Am I right or not?"

"Almost," she admitted, lifting her chin to smile at him. There was a soft, glowing quality to her smile that lit her face with gentle radiance, and his heavy-lidded eyes dropped even more in a signal that someone who knew him well would have recognized immediately. But Susan didn't know him well, and she was unaware of how close she was skating to thin ice. "I attended Adderley's in Virginia for four months, until my mother had a stroke and I left school to care for her."

"No point in wasting any more money for them to gild the lily," he drawled, letting his eyes drift over her serene features, then down her slender, graceful throat to linger once again, with open delight, on her fragrant, silky curves. Susan felt an unexpected heat flood her body at this man's undisguised admiration; he looked as if he wanted to lean down and bury his face between her breasts, and she quivered with the surprising longing to have him do just that. He was more than dangerous; he was lethal!

She had to say something to break the heady spell that was enveloping her, and she used the most immediate topic of conversation. "When did you arrive?"

"Just this afternoon." The curl of his lip told her that he knew what she was doing, but was allowing her to get away with it. Lazily he puckered his lips and blew again at the fine tendril of dark hair that entranced him as it lay on the fragile skin of her temple, where the delicate blue veining lay just under the translucent skin. Susan felt her entire body pulsate, the warm scent of his breath affecting her as strongly as if he'd lifted his hand and caressed her. Almost blindly she looked at him, compelling herself to concentrate on what he was saying, but the movement of those chiseled lips was even more enticing than the scent of him.

"I heard that Cousin Preston was having a party," he was saying in a lazy drawl that had never lost its Southern music. "So I thought I'd honor old times by insulting him and crashing the shindig."

Susan had to smile at the incongruity of describing this elegant affair as a "shindig," especially when he himself was dressed as if he had just stepped out of a Monte Carlo casino . . . where he would probably be more at home than he was here. "Did you used to make a habit of crashing parties?" she murmured.

"If I thought it would annoy Preston, I did," he replied, laughing a little at the memories. "Preston and I have always been on opposite sides of the fence," he explained with a careless smile that told her how little the matter bothered him. "Vance was the only one I ever got along with, but then, he never seemed to care what kind of trouble I was in. Vance wasn't one to worship at the altar of the Blackstone name."

That was true; Vance had conformed on the surface to the demands made on him because his name was Blackstone, but Susan had always known that he did so with a secret twinkle in his eyes. Sometimes she didn't think that her mother-in-law, Imogene, would ever forgive Vance for his mutiny against the Blackstone dynasty when he married Susan, though of course Imogene would never have been so crass as to admit it; a Blackstone didn't indulge in shrewish behavior. Then Susan felt faintly ashamed of herself, because Vance's family had treated her with respect.

Still, she felt a warm sense of comradeship with this man, because he had known Vance as she had, had realized his true nature, and she gave him a smile that sparked a

glow in her own deep blue eyes. His arms tightened around
her in an involuntary movement, as if he wanted to crush
her against him.

"You've got the Blackstone coloring," he muttered,
staring at her. "Dark hair and blue eyes, but you're so soft
there's no way in hell you could be a real Blackstone.
There's no hardness in you at all, is there?"

Puzzled, she stared back at him with a tiny frown
puckering her brow. "What do you mean by hardness?"

"I don't think you'd understand if I told you," he replied
cryptically, then added, "were you handpicked to be
Vance's wife?"

"No." She smiled at the memory. "He picked me
himself."

He gave a silent whistle. "Imogene will never recover
from the shock," he said irreverently, and flashed that
mocking grin at her again.

Despite herself, Susan felt the corners of her mouth
tilting up in an answering smile. She was enjoying herself,
talking to this dangerous, roguish man with the strangely
compelling eyes, and she was surprised because she hadn't
really enjoyed herself in such a long time . . . since
Vance's death, in fact. There had been too many years and
too many tears between her smiles, but suddenly things
seemed different; she felt different inside herself. At first,
she'd thought that she'd never recover from Vance's death,
but five years had passed, and now she realized that she was
looking forward to life again. She was enjoying being held
in this man's strong arms and listening to his deep voice
. . . and yes, she enjoyed the look in his eyes, enjoyed the
sure feminine knowledge that he wanted her.

She didn't want to examine her reaction to him; she felt
as if she had been dead, too, and was only now coming
alive, and she wanted to revel in the change, not analyze it.

She was in danger of drowning in sensation, and she
recognized the inner weakness that was overtaking her, but

felt helpless to resist it. He must have sensed, with a primal intuition that was as alarming as the aura of danger that surrounded him, that she was close to surrendering to the temptation to play with fire. He leaned down and nuzzled his mouth against the delicate shell of her ear, sending every nerve in her body into delirium. "Go outside with me," he enticed, dipping his tongue into her ear and tracing the outer curve of it with electrifying precision.

Susan's entire body reverberated with the shock of it, but his action cleared her mind of the clouds of desire that had been fogging it. Totally flustered, her cheeks suddenly pink, she stopped dead. "Mr. Blackstone!"

"Cord," he corrected, laughing openly now. "After all, we're at least kissing cousins, wouldn't you say?"

She didn't know what to say, and fortunately she was saved from forming an answer that probably wouldn't have been coherent anyway, because Preston chose that moment to intervene. She had been vaguely aware, as she circled the room in Cord's arms, that Preston had been watching every move his cousin made, but she hadn't noticed him approaching. Putting his hand on Susan's arm, he stared at his cousin with frosty blue eyes. "Has he said anything to upset you, Susan?"

Again she was thrown into a quandary. If she said yes, there would probably be a scene, and she was determined to avoid that. On the other hand, how could she say no, when it would so obviously be a lie? A spark of genius prompted her to reply with quiet dignity, "We were talking about Vance."

"I see." It was perfectly reasonable to Preston that, even after five years, Susan should be upset when speaking of her dead husband. He accepted her statement as an explanation instead of the red herring it was, and gave all of his attention to his cousin, who was standing there totally relaxed, a faintly bored smile on his lips.

"Mother is waiting in the library," Preston said stiffly.

"We assume you have some reason for afflicting us with your company."

"I do." Cord agreed easily with Preston's insult, still smiling as he ignored the red flag being waved at him. He lifted one eyebrow. "Lead the way. Somehow, I don't trust you at my back."

Preston stiffened, and Susan forestalled the angry outburst she saw coming by placing her hand lightly on Cord's arm and saying, "Let's not keep Mrs. Blackstone waiting."

As she had known he would, Preston shifted his attention to her. "There's no reason for you to come along, Susan. You might as well stay here with the guests."

"I'd like to have her there." Cord had instantly contradicted his cousin, and in a manner that made Susan certain he'd spoken merely to irritate Preston. "She's family, isn't she? She might as well hear it all first hand, rather than the watered-down and doctored version that she'd get from you and Imogene."

For a moment Preston looked as if he would debate the point; then he turned abruptly and walked away. Preston was a Blackstone; he might want to punch Cord in the mouth, but he wouldn't make a public scene. Cord following him at a slight distance, his hand dropping to rest lightly on Susan's waist. He grinned down at her. "I wanted to make sure you didn't get away from me."

Susan was a grown woman, not a teenager. Moreover, she was a woman who for five years had managed large and varied business concerns with cool acumen; she was twenty-nine years old, and she told herself that she should long ago have passed out of the blushing stage. Yet this man, with the dashing air of a rake and those bold, challenging eyes, could make her blush with a mere glance. Excitement such as she had never felt before was racing through her, setting her heart pounding, and she actually felt giddy. She knew what love was like, and it wasn't this. She had loved Vance, loved him so strongly that his death had nearly destroyed her, so she realized at once that this wasn't the same emotion. This was primitive attraction, heady and feverish, and it was based entirely on sex. Vance Blackstone had been Love; Cord Blackstone meant only Lust.

But recognizing it for what it was didn't lessen its impact as she walked sedately beside him, so vibrantly aware of the hand on her back that he might as well have been touching her naked body. She wasn't the type for an affair. She was a throwback to the Victorian era, as Vance had once teased her by saying. She had been lovingly but strictly brought up, and she was the lady that her mother had meant her to be, from the top of her head down to her pink toes. Susan had never even thought of rebelling, because she was by nature exactly what she was: a lady. She had known love and would never settle for less than that, not even for the heady delights offered by the black sheep of the Blackstone family.

Just before they entered the library where Imogene waited, Cord leaned down to her. "If you won't go outside with me, then I'll take you home and we can neck on the front porch like teenagers."

She flashed him an indignant glance that made him laugh softly to himself, but she was prevented from answering him because at that moment they passed through the door and she realized that he had perfectly timed his remark. He had a genius for throwing people off-balance, and he had done it again; despite herself, she felt the heat of intensified color in her face.

Imogene regarded her thoughtfully for a moment, her gray eyes sharpening for a fraction of a second as her gaze flickered from Susan to Cord, then back to Susan's flushed face. Then she controlled her expression, and the gray eyes resumed their normal cool steadiness. "Susan, do you feel well? You look flushed."

"I became a little warm during the dancing." Susan was

aware that once again she was throwing out a statement that would be regarded as an answer, but was in fact only a smokescreen. If she didn't watch it, Cord Blackstone would turn her into a world-class liar before the night was out!

The tall man beside her directed her to a robin's egg blue loveseat and sprawled his graceful length beside her, earning himself a glare—which rolled right off of his toughened hide—from both Preston and Imogene. Smiling at his aunt, he drawled a greeting. "Hello, Aunt Imogene. How's the family fortune?"

He was good at waving his own red flags, Susan noticed. Imogene settled back in her chair and coolly ignored the distraction. "Why have you come back?"

"Why shouldn't I come back? This is my home, remember? I even own part of the land. I've been roaming around for quite a while now, and I'm ready to put down my roots. What better place for that than home? I thought I'd move into the cabin on Jubilee Creek."

"That shack!" Preston's voice was full of disdain.

Cord shrugged. "You can't account for tastes. I prefer shacks to mausoleums." He grinned, looking around himself at the formal furniture, the original oil paintings, the priceless vases and miniatures that adorned the shelves. Though called a library, the room actually contained few books, and all of them had been bought, Susan sometimes suspected, with an eye on the color of the dustjackets to make certain the books harmonized with the color scheme of the room.

Preston eyed his cousin with cold, silent hatred for a moment, an expanse of time which became heavy with resentment. "How much will it cost us?"

From the corner of her eye, Susan could see the lift of that mocking eyebrow. "Cost you for what?"

"For you to leave this part of the country again."

Cord smiled, a particularly wolfish smile that should

have warned Preston. "You don't have enough money, Cousin."

Imogene lifted her hand, forestalling Preston's heated reply. She had a cooler head and was better at negotiating than her son was. "Don't be foolish . . . or hasty," she counseled. "You *do* realize that we're prepared to offer you a substantial sum in exchange for your absence?"

"Not interested," he said lazily, still smiling.

"But a man with your . . . lifestyle must have debts that need settling. Then there's the fact that I have many friends who owe me for favors, and who could be counted on to make your stay unpleasant, at the least."

"Oh, I don't think so, Aunt Imogene." Cord was utterly relaxed, his long legs stretched out before him. "The first surprise in store for you is that I don't need the money. The second is that if any of your 'friends' decide to help you by making things difficult for me, I have friends of my own who I can call on, and believe me, my friends make yours look like angels."

Imogene sniffed. "I'm sure they do, considering."

For the first time Susan felt compelled to intervene. Fighting upset her; she was quiet and naturally peaceful, but with an inner strength that allowed her to throw herself into the breach. Her gentle voice immediately drew everyone's attention, though it was to her mother-in-law that she spoke. "Imogene, look at him; look at his clothes." She waved her slender hand to indicate the man lounging beside her. "He's telling the truth. He doesn't need any money. And I think that when he mentions his friends, he isn't talking about back-alley buddies."

Cord regarded her with open, if somewhat mocking, admiration. "At last, a Blackstone with perception, though of course you weren't born to the name, so maybe that explains it. She's right, Imogene, though I'm sure you don't like hearing it. I don't need the Blackstone money because I have money of my own. I plan to live in the cabin because I like my privacy, not because I can't afford any better. Now, I suggest that we manage to control our differences, because I intend to stay here. If you want to air the family dirty laundry, then go ahead. It won't bother me; you'll be the only one to suffer from that."

Imogene gave a curious little sigh. "You've always been difficult, Cord, even when you were a child. My objection to you is based on your past actions, not on you personally. You've dragged your family through enough mud to last for four lifetimes, and I find that hard to forgive, and I find it equally as hard to trust you to behave with some degree of civility."

"It's been a long time," he said obliquely. "I've spent a lot of time in Europe, and too long in South America; it makes a man appreciate his home."

"Does it? I wonder. Forgive me if I suspect an ulterior motive, but then, your past gives me little choice. Very well, we'll call a truce . . . for the time being."

"A truce." He winked at her, and to Susan's surprise, Imogene blushed. So he had that effect on every female! But he was a fool if he believed that Imogene would go along with a truce. She might appear to give in, but that was *all* it was: appearance. Imogene never gave in; she merely changed tactics. If she couldn't bribe or threaten him, then she would try other measures, though for the moment Susan couldn't think of anything else that could be brought to bear on the man.

He was rising to his feet, his hand under Susan's elbow, urging her up also. "You've been away from your guests long enough," he told Imogene politely. "I give you my solemn promise that I won't cause any scandals tonight, so relax and enjoy yourself." Pulling Susan along with him like a puppy, he crossed the floor to Imogene and bent down to kiss his aunt. Imogene sat perfectly still under the touch of his lips, though her color rose even higher. Then he straightened, his eyes dancing. "Come along, Susan," he commanded.

"Just a moment," Preston intervened, stepping before them. Imogene might have called a truce, but Preston hadn't. "We've agreed to no open hostilities; we haven't agreed to associate with you. Susan isn't going anywhere with you."

"Oh? I think that's up to the lady. Susan?" Cord turned to her, making his wishes known by the curl of his fingers on her arm.

Susan hesitated. She wanted to go with Cord. She wanted to laugh with him, to see the wicked twinkle in his eyes, feel the magic of being held in his arms. But she couldn't trust him, and for the first time in her life, she didn't trust herself. Because she wanted so badly to go with him, she had to deny him. Slowly, regretfully, she shook her head. "No. I think it would be better if I didn't go with you."

His blue eyes narrowed, and suddenly they were no longer laughing, but wore the sheen of anger. He dropped his hand from her arm. "Perhaps you're right," he said coldly, and left her without another word.

The silence in the library was total, the three occupants motionless. Then Imogene sighed again. "Thank heavens you didn't go with him, dear. He's charming, I know, but beneath all of that charm, he hates this entire family. He'll do anything, *anything*, he can to harm us. You don't know him, but it's in your best interest if you avoid him." Having delivered her graceful warning, Imogene shrugged. "Ah, well, I suppose we'll have to suffer through this until he gets bored and drifts off to hunt other amusements. He was right about one thing, the wretch; I do have to get back to my guests." She rose and left the room, her mist gray gown swaying elegantly about her feet as she walked. Imogene was still a beautiful woman; she hardly looked old enough to be the mother of the man who stood beside Susan. Imogene didn't age; she endured.

After a moment, Preston took Susan's hand, his in-grained sense of courtesy taking control of him again. His confrontation with his cousin had been the only occasion when Susan could remember seeing Preston be anything but polite, even when he was disagreeing with someone. "Let's relax for a moment before we rejoin them. Would you like a drink?" he suggested.

"No, thank you." Susan allowed him to seat her on the loveseat again, and she watched as he poured himself a neat whiskey and sat down beside her, a small frown puckering his brow as he regarded the glass in his hand. Something was on his mind; she knew his mannerisms as well as she knew her own. She waited, not pushing him. She and Preston had become close since Vance's death, and she felt strongly affectionate toward him. He looked so much like Vance, so much like all the Blackstones, with his dark hair and blue eyes and lopsided smile. Preston lacked Vance's sense of humor, but he was a formidable opponent in business. He was stubborn; slower than Vance to react, but more determined when he did.

"You're a lovely woman, Susan," he said abruptly.

Startled, she stared at him. She knew she looked good tonight; she had debated over wearing the cream silk dress, for her tastes since Vance's death had been somber, but she had remembered that the medieval color of mourning had been white, not black, and only she knew when she put on the white dress that she did so with a small but poignant remnant of grief. She had dressed for Vance tonight, wearing the pearls that he had given her, spraying herself with his favorite perfume. But for a few mad moments she had gloried in the knowledge that she looked good, not for Vance's sake, but because of the admiration she had seen in another pair of eyes, strange lodestone eyes. What would have happened if she had gone with Cord Blackstone tonight, instead of playing it safe?

Preston's eyes softened as he looked at her. "You're no

match for him. If you let him, he'll use you to hurt us; then he'll leave you on the trash pile and walk away without looking back. Stay away from him; he's poison.''

Susan regarded him steadily. ''Preston, I'm a woman, not a child; I'm capable of making my own decisions. I can see why you wouldn't like your cousin, since he's so totally different from you. But he hasn't done anything to harm me, and I won't snub him.''

He gave a rueful smile at her firm, reasonable tone. ''I've heard that voice in enough board meetings over the past five years to know you've dug in your heels and won't budge without a good reason. But you don't know what he's like. You're a lady; you've never been exposed to the sort of things that are commonplace to him. He's lived the life of an alley cat, not because he had no choice, no way out, but because he preferred that type of life. He broke his mother's heart, making her so ashamed of him that he wasn't welcome in her home.''

''Exactly what did he do that was so terrible?'' Deliberately, she kept her tone light, not wanting Preston to see how deeply she was interested in the answer, how deeply she was disturbed by Cord Blackstone.

''What didn't he do?'' Sarcasm edged Preston's answer. ''Fights, drinking, women, gambling . . . but the final straw was the scandal when he was caught with Grant Keller's wife.''

Susan choked. Grant Keller was dignity personified, and so was his wife. Preston looked at her and couldn't prevent a grin. ''Not this Mrs. Keller; the former Mrs. Keller was entirely different. She was thirty-six, and Cord was twenty-one when they left town together.''

''That was a long time ago,'' Susan pointed out.

''Fourteen years, but people have long memories. I saw Grant Keller's face when he recognized Cord tonight, and he looked murderous.''

Susan was certain there was more to the story, but she

was reluctant to pry any deeper. The old scandal in no way explained Preston's very personal hatred for Cord. For right now, though, she was suddenly very tired and didn't want to pursue the subject. All the excitement that had lit her up while she was dancing with Cord had faded. Rising, she smoothed her skirt. "Will you take me home? I'm exhausted."

"Of course," he said immediately, as she had known he would. Preston was entirely predictable, always solicitous of her. At times, the cushion of gallantry that protected her gave her a warm sense of security, but at other times she felt restricted. Tonight, the feeling of restriction deepened until she felt as if she were being smothered. She wanted to breathe freely, to be unobserved.

It was only a fifteen-minute drive to her home, and soon she was blessedly alone, sitting on the dark front porch in the wooden porch swing, listening to the music of a southern night. She had waited until Preston left before she came out to sit in the darkness, her right foot gently pushing her back and forth to the accompanying squeak of the chains that held the swing. A light breeze rustled through the trees and kissed her face, and she closed her eyes. As she often did, she tried to summon up Vance's face, to reassure herself with the mental picture of his violet blue eyes and lopsided grin, but to her alarm, the face that formed wasn't his. Instead she saw pale blue eyes above the short black beard of a desperado; they were the reckless eyes of a man who dared anything. A shiver ran down her spine as she recalled the touch of his warm mouth on her shoulder, and her skin tingled as if his lips were still pressed there.

Thank heavens she had had the good sense to ask Preston to bring her home instead of going with that man as he had asked. Preston was at least safe, and Cord Blackstone had probably never heard the word.

Chapter 2

THE BLACKSTONE SOCIAL CIRCLE RANGED IN A SORT OF open arc from Mobile to New Orleans, with the Gulfport-Biloxi area as the center of their far-flung web of moneyed and blue-blooded acquaintances. With such a wide area and so many friends of such varied interests, Susan was amazed that the sole topic of conversation seemed to be Cord Blackstone's return. She lost count of the number of women, many of them married, who drilled her on why he was back, how long he was staying, whether he was married, whether he had been married, and endless variations on those questions, none of which she could answer. What could she tell them? That she had danced two dances with him and gotten drunk on his smile?

She hadn't seen him since the night of his return, and she made a point of not asking about him. She told herself that it was best to leave well enough alone and let her interest in him die a natural death. All she had to do was do nothing and refuse to feed the strange attraction. It wasn't as if he

were chasing her all over south Mississippi; he hadn't
called, hadn't sought her out as she had half feared, half
wanted him to do.

But her resolution to forget about him was stymied at
every turn; even Preston seldom talked of anything except
his cousin. She decided that all Cord had to do to irritate
Preston was to breathe. Through Preston, she learned that
Cord was working on the old cabin at Jubilee Creek,
replacing the roof and the sagging old porch, putting in new
windows. Preston had tried to find out where Cord had
borrowed the money to repair the cabin, and found instead,
to his chagrin, that there was no loan involved. Cord was
paying for everything in cash, and had opened a sizable
checking account at the largest bank in Biloxi. Preston and
Imogene spent hours speculating on how he had acquired
the money, and what his purpose was in returning to
Mississippi. Susan wondered why they found it so hard to
accept that he had simply returned home. As people grew
older, it wasn't unusual for them to want to return to the
area where they had grown up. It seemed silly to her that
they attached such sinister motives to his smallest action,
but then she realized that she was guilty of the same thing.
She'd all but convinced herself that, if she had allowed him
to drive her home that night, he would have taken her to bed
over any protests she might have made . . . if any.

If any. That was the hard part for her to accept. Would
she have made any protest, even a token one? What had
happened to her? One moment her life had been as serene as
a quiet pool on a lazy summer day, and she had been
satisfied, except for the hollowness left by Vance's death.
Then Cord Blackstone had walked in out of the night and
everything had shifted, the world had been thrown out of
kilter. Now, suddenly, she wanted to run away, or at least
smash something . . . do anything, anything at all, that was
totally out of character.

And it was all because of Cord. He was a man who lived

by his own rules, a man who lived recklessly and dangerously, but with a vital intensity that made every other man
seem insipid when compared to him. By contrast, she was a
field mouse who was comfortable only with security, yet
now the very security that she had always treasured was
chafing at her. The priorities that she had set for herself now
seemed valueless in comparison with the wild freedom that
Cord enjoyed.

She had been a quiet child, then a quiet girl, never
according her parents any of the worries that most parents
had concerning their children. Susan's personality was
serene, naturally kind and courteous, and the old-fashioned,
genteel upbringing she'd had merely reinforced those quali-
ties. By both nature and practice she was a lady, in every
sense of the word.

Her life hadn't been without pain or difficulty. Without
resentment, she had left school to help care for her mother
when a stroke left the older woman partially paralyzed.
Another stroke later was fatal, and Susan quietly supported
her father during their grief. Her father remarried within the
year, with Susan's blessing, and retired to south Florida;
she remained in New Orleans, which had been her father's
last teaching post, and reorganized her life. She took a
secretarial job and dated occasionally, but never seriously,
until Vance Blackstone saw her gracing her desk at work
and decided right then that she should be gracing his home.
Vance hadn't swept her off her feet; he had gently gained
her confidence, gradually increasing the frequency of their
dates until she was seeing no one but him; then he had
proposed marriage by giving her one perfect rosebud with
an exquisite diamond ring nestled in the heart of it.

Imogene hadn't been thrilled that her son had selected his
wife from outside the elite circle of their social group, but
not even Imogene could really find fault with Susan. Susan
was, as everyone phrased it, "a perfect lady." She was
accepted as Vance's wife, and for three years she had been

blessed with happiness. Vance was a considerate lover and husband, and he never let her forget that she was the most important thing in his life, far more important than the Blackstone empire and traditions. He demonstrated his faith in her by leaving everything to her in his will, including control of his share of the family businesses. Devastated by his sudden death, the terms of the will had meant nothing to Susan. Nothing was important to her without Vance.

But time passed, and time healed. Imogene and Preston, at first furious when they learned that she intended to oversee her share of the businesses instead of turning them over to Preston as they had expected, had gradually forgotten their anger as Susan handled herself well, both privately and publicly. She wasn't a woman on an ego trip, nor was she prone to make irresponsible decisions. She had both feet firmly on the ground . . . or she *had* had, until another Blackstone had entered her life.

As the days passed, she told herself over and over how silly she was being. Why moon over a man who hadn't shown the slightest interest in her since the night they had met? He had just been trying to irritate Preston by playing up to her, that was all. But as soon as that thought registered in her mind, a memory would surface, that of a hard, aroused male body pressing against her, and she knew that Cord hadn't been playing.

She couldn't get his face out of her mind. Odd that she hadn't noticed the family resemblance, but for all the blue eyes and dark hair, nothing about Cord had seemed familiar to her. When she looked at Preston, she was always reminded strongly of Vance; Cord Blackstone resembled no one but himself, with his black brigand's beard and wicked eyes. His personality overshadowed the similarities of coloring and facial structure.

Stop thinking about him! she told herself sternly one night as she dressed to attend a party with Preston. She had been looking at herself in the mirror, checking to see if her dress fit as it should, and had suddenly found herself wondering if Cord would like the dress, if he would find her attractive in it. With rare irritation, she whirled away from the mirror. She had to get him out of her mind! It had been almost three weeks since she'd met him, and it was obvious that she was in a tizzy over nothing, because in those three weeks he'd made no effort to see her again.

It was just as well; they were totally unsuited. She was a gentle spring shower; he was thunder and lightning. She had let a simple flirtation go to her head, and it was time she realized that there was nothing to it.

Glancing out a window at the gloomy sky, she reached into the closet for a coat. The capricious weather of the Gulf states had reminded everyone that it was still only March, despite the balmy weather they had been enjoying for most of the month. The temperature would be close to freezing before she came home, so she chose the warmest coat she owned, as well as wearing a long-sleeved dress.

Preston was always exactly on time, so Susan went down a few minutes early to chat with her cook and housekeeper, Emily Ferris. "I'll be leaving in a few minutes; why don't you go home early today?" she suggested.

"I might at that." Emily looked out the window, watching the wind whip the giant oak tree at the edge of the yard. "This is the kind of day that makes me want to wrap up in a blanket and sleep in front of a fire. Do you have a coat?" she asked sternly, looking at Susan's slender form.

Susan laughed. "Yes, I have a coat." Emily watched over her like a mother hen, but mothering came naturally to Emily, who had five children of her own. The youngest had left the nest a year ago, and since then, Susan had received the full intensity of Emily's protection. She didn't mind; Emily was as steady as a rock, and had been in Susan's employ since she had married Vance. It was in Emily's arms that Susan had wept her most violent tears after Vance's death.

"I'll leave the heat on, so the house won't be cold when you come in," Emily promised. "Where're you going tonight?"

"To the Gages'. I believe William is planning to run for governor next year, and he's lining up support and campaign contributors."

"Hummph," Emily snorted. "What does a Gage know about politics? Don't tell me that Preston's going to support him?"

Susan lifted one elegant eyebrow. "You know Preston; he's very cautious. He'll have to look at every candidate before he makes up his mind." She knew from experience that every politician in the state would be burying the Blackstones under an avalanche of invitations. Susan had tried to stay out of politics, but Imogene and Preston were heavily courted, and Preston invariably asked her to accompany him whenever he attended a party with either political overtones or undertones.

She heard the doorbell at the precise instant the clock chimed the hour, and with a smile she went to greet Preston.

He helped her with her coat, arranging the collar snugly around her throat.

"It's getting really cold," he muttered. "So much for spring."

"Don't be so impatient." She smiled. "It's still only March. It's just that these last few weeks spoiled everyone, but you knew it couldn't last."

It began to rain as they drove to the Gages' house, a slow, sullen rain that turned the late afternoon into night. Preston was a careful, confident driver, and he made the thirty-mile drive in good time. Caroline Gage met them at the door. "Preston, Susan, I'm glad you could come! Would you like a drink before dinner? William's playing bartender in the den."

Despite Caroline's easy manner, Susan caught a hint of

tension in the older woman's expression and wondered if Caroline wasn't enthusiastic about her husband's foray into politics. Following Preston into the den, she found the room already crowded with friends and acquaintances, the usual social crowd. Preston was promptly hailed by William Gage, and with a smile for Susan he allowed himself to be drawn aside.

Susan refused anything to drink, since she hadn't eaten anything, and wandered around talking to her friends. She was popular with both men and women, and it took her quite a while to make a circle of the room. It was almost time for dinner and she glanced at her hostess, frowning when she saw Caroline watching the door, anxiety clearly evident on her face. Was some special guest late?

The doorbell chimed and Caroline paled, but didn't pause as she went to greet her late-arriving guests. Susan watched the door curiously, waiting to see who it was; Caroline was usually unflappable, and it must be someone really important to have her so on edge.

Her brows rose when George and Olivia Warren came into the room; the Warrens were part of the social hierarchy, but Caroline had been friends with them for years. Cheryl Warren followed them, her ash blond hair a mass of carefully disarranged curls, her svelte body outlined in a form-fitting black dress . . . and behind her, towering over her, his bearded face sardonic, was Cord Blackstone.

So that was why Caroline was nervous! She'd known that Cord would be with Cheryl Warren, and she was on pins and needles at having Cord and Preston in the same room.

She needn't have worried, Susan thought, glancing at Preston. He wouldn't like it, but neither would he make a scene in someone else's home. If Cord just behaved himself, the evening would go smoothly, though she was acutely aware that Cord would behave himself only if it suited his own purposes.

But, surprisingly, he was a perfect gentleman throughout

the long dinner. He was politely attentive to Cheryl, a fact
which made Susan's stomach knot. She tried not to look at
him, and told herself wryly that she shouldn't have been
surprised to see him with another woman . . . any other
woman. He was a man who would always have a female
companion. She *was* surprised, however, by the jealousy
that jolted her whenever she heard Cheryl's clear laughter,
or caught the dark murmur of Cord's voice under the noise
of the general chatter.

Caroline had cleared the large living room for dancing,
and after dinner she put a stack of easy-listening albums on
the stereo, keeping the volume low so her guests could
dance or talk as they wished. Susan danced a few dances
and talked with her friends, wishing that Preston would cut
the evening short and take her home, but he was effectively
caught in a group of men earnestly talking politics, and she
knew that it would be hours before he was free. She sighed
and absently watched the slow-moving couples swaying to
the music, then stiffened as her gaze accidentally locked
with Cord's pale, glittering eyes. Cheryl was held securely
in his strong arms, but he wasn't paying any attention to her
as he stared at Susan over Cheryl's bare shoulder. He didn't
smile; his gaze slid down her body in a leisurely journey,
then returned to her face, staring at her as if he could pierce
her thoughts. She paled and looked away. Why had he done
that? He'd made it plain by his silence these past three
weeks that their flirtation hadn't meant anything to him;
why look at her now as if he meant to drag her away to his
lair? How *could* he look at her like that, when he held
Cheryl in his arms?

Susan pushed her thoughts away by entering into a
conversation about vacation cruises, and kept her back
turned to the center of the room. It was a tactical error, but
one she didn't realize until she felt the fine hairs on the back
of her neck standing on end, the age-old warning of danger

nearby, and she knew that Cord was behind her. She tensed, waiting for the contact that she knew was coming. His hand touched her waist at the same time that his dark, husky voice said above her head, "Dance with me."

A variation of the same tune, she thought dazedly, allowing herself to be turned and taken into his arms. *Taken* . . . that was the operative word. She felt taken, as if the simple closing of his arms around her had sealed her off from the rest of the world, drawn her deeply and irrevocably under his spell. She was crazy to dance so close to the flame, knowing that she would be burned, but she felt helpless to resist the temptation of his company. As his arms brought her close to his body, the virile scent of his subtle cologne, mingled with the intoxicating smell of his male flesh, went straight to her head and she all but staggered. His hand was burning through the fabric of her dress and scorching her skin; her breasts throbbed and tightened in mindless response, completely out of her control, and she closed her eyes at the powerful surge of desire. Her heart was thumping heavily in her chest, almost painfully, sending her blood zinging through her veins like electrical charges.

There seemed to be nothing to say, so she didn't try to make conversation. She simply followed his lead, intensely aware of the fluid strength of his body, the animal grace of his movements. His warm breath was caressing her temple like the fragrant spring breezes that she loved, and without thinking she opened her eyes, lifting her misty, dreaming gaze to meet the laser intensity of his.

Something hard and frightening was in his gaze, but it was swiftly masked before she could read it. The hard planes of his face were taut, as if he were under some sort of strain. He muttered, "I've tried to stay away from you."

"You've succeeded." Confused, she wondered what he meant. *He* was the dangerous one, not she. Why should he want to stay away? She was the one who should be running for safety, and the fact that she wasn't had her almost in a panic.

"I haven't succeeded at all," he said flatly. The arm at her waist tightened until she was pressed into his body, his hard thighs sliding against her, making his desire firmly obvious. Susan pulled in a wavering breath as her fingers tightened on his shoulder. He dipped his head until his mouth was against her ear, his voice a low rumble. "I want to make love to you. You're responsible for this, sweetheart, and I'm all yours."

The words should have frightened her, but she was beyond fright, already oblivious to anything beyond this man. Her senses had narrowed, sharpened, until he was the only person in the room who was in focus. Everyone else was blurred, distant, and she danced with him in an isolated glow. She closed her eyes again at the thrill that electrified her from head to toe.

He swore softly under his breath. "You look as if I'm making love to you right now. You're driving me out of my mind, sweetheart."

He *was* making love to her, with his words, with every brush of his body against hers as they moved in time with the music. And if he was tortured, so was she. She had been utterly chaste since Vance's death, not even kissing another man, but now she felt as if Cord possessed her in the most basic sense of the word.

"Cheryl came with me, so I'll take her home," he said, placing his lips against her temple as he talked. "But we're going to have to talk. Will you be at home tomorrow afternoon?"

Dazedly, she tried to recall if she had made any plans for the next day; nothing came to mind. It didn't matter; even if she had, she would cancel them. "Yes, I'll be there." Her voice sounded odd, she noted dimly, as if she hadn't any strength.

"I have some business to take care of tomorrow, so I can't nail down an exact time when I'll be there, but I *will* be there," he promised.

"Do you know where I live?"

She could feel his lips curving in a smile. "Of course I know where you live. I made a point of finding out the day after I met you."

The song ended, and she automatically moved away from him, but his arm tightened around her waist. He grinned, his teeth flashing whitely in the darkness of his beard. "You're going to have to shield me for a few more minutes."

A delicate rise of color tinted her cheeks. "We shouldn't dance. That would only . . . prolong the situation."

"We'll find a corner to stand in." A twinkle danced in the glittering depths of his eyes. "We'll have to stand; I'm incapable of sitting down right now."

She felt her blush deepen, and he chuckled as he moved with her to the edge of the room. She was aware deep inside herself that her heightened color wasn't from embarrassment, but from a primal excitement. She wasn't shocked that he was aroused; she was proud!

He positioned himself with his back to everyone else, his broad shoulders effectively blocking her view of the room. His eyes roamed slowly, intently over her face, as if he were trying to read something in the serenity of her expression. "Did you come with Preston?" he asked abruptly.

"Yes." Suddenly she wanted to launch into an explanation of why she was there in Preston's company, but she left the words unsaid and let her simple reply stand on its own. Preston was her brother-in-law, and she was fond of him; she wouldn't apologize for being with him.

The magnetic power of Cord's eyes was frightening; tiny prisms of light seemed caught in them, holding her gaze captive. Her breath caught in her throat and hung there, swelling her lungs, as she waited for him to release her from his spell. "Am I horning in between you and Preston?" he finally asked in not much more than a whisper. "Are you involved with him?"

The breath that she'd been holding was released on her soft answer. "No."

A smile lifted one corner of his hard mouth. "Good. I just wanted to know if I have any competition. It wouldn't stop me, but I like to know what I'm up against."

No, he didn't have any competition—in any sense. He stood out like a cougar among sheep. The thought of him turning his single-minded attention on her was alarming, but at the same time, she already knew that she wouldn't say the words necessary to turn him away. She knew that she should run like crazy, but her body refused to obey the dictates of common sense.

A tiny frown flickered across his brow as he stared down at her, as if he had seen something that he hadn't expected. He couldn't be wary of her, or alarmed by her femininity; he had known far too many women for there to be any mysteries left for him. Perhaps he was surprised to find himself flirting with her, because she certainly wasn't his type. Perhaps he was looking at her quiet face, her becoming but unspectacular dress, and wondering if he'd temporarily lost his mind. Then the frown was gone, and he smiled faintly as he brushed her cheek with the tips of his fingers. "Tomorrow, sweetheart."

"Yes."

Susan both dreaded and longed for the next day to arrive, but with outward calm and practiced self-discipline, she made it through the remainder of the evening with her usual dignity, chatted normally with Preston on the drive back home, and even went through her nightly routine without missing a beat. Once she was in bed, however, lying alone in the darkened room, she couldn't keep her thoughts from swinging dizzily around Cord, picturing his saturnine face, his incredible lodestone eyes, the black beard that was as soft as a child's hair.

He had a black magic that went to her head like the finest champagne, but how could she be so foolish as to let herself be drawn into the whirlpool of his masculine charm? She'd be sucked so far under the dark waters that she'd have no control over herself or her life; she'd be his plaything, as other women had been, toys that interested him intensely for a short while before they were discarded in favor of a new and more intriguing amusement. Could she really let herself become one of his toys? She'd known real love with Vance, a love that had endowed their physical union with a deep and satisfying richness. Having known that, how could she settle for anything less?

Her mind, her heart, the very core of her being—all said no. Her body, however, lying warm and quivering, yearning for the touch of his strong, lean hands, rebelled against the common-sense strictures of her mind. She was learning now how primitive and powerful desire could be, how disobedient the flesh could be to the demands of conscience. Her soft, feminine body had instinctively recognized the touch of a master, a man who knew far too many ways to bring pleasure to her.

She lay awake for several long, tormented hours, but at last her quietly indomitable will won out over her fevered, longing body. She was not now, never had been, and never would be, the type to indulge in a shallow affair, no matter how physically attractive a man was. If he wanted her company for something other than sex, then she would be happy to be his friend, but the thought of sex without love was abhorrent to her. Making love with Vance had been spiritual and emotional, as well as physical, and her knowledge of the heights had left her dissatisfied with the lower peaks that could be scaled without love.

Not once, during the dark hours, did she have any doubts about the nature of the relationship that Cord wanted with her. He'd told her bluntly that he wanted to make love to her; she sensed that he was always that honest about his desires. His honesty wasn't the courageous openness of honor, but merely his lack of concern over what anyone else thought or had to say about him. He was already an outlaw; why worry about ruining his reputation further?

If only the forbidden weren't always so enticing! Her mind darted and leaped around his image, held so clearly in her memory. He was wickedly attractive; even talking to him gave her the sense of playing with fire. She had to admit that Cord had certainly captured her imagination, but it was nothing more than that, surely, except for his obvious physical charm. The ways of the wicked have always held a fascination for those who walk the bright and narrow path of morality.

But that bright and narrow path was where she belonged, where life had placed her, where she was happy. The shadows where Cord Blackstone stood weren't for her, no matter how intriguing the weary knowledge in his crystal-line eyes.

She slept little, but woke feeling calm and rested. Her inner surety of self often masked such physical weaknesses as tiredness or minor illness; her features might be pale, but there was always a certain calmness that overlay any signs of strain. It was Sunday, so she dressed and drove her eight-year-old blue Audi over to Blackstone House to attend church with Imogene and Preston, as she had always done. To her relief, Preston didn't mention that Cord had been at the party the night before; he was too interested in relating to Imogene the details of William Gage's infant political career. Susan commented little, entering the conversation only when she was addressed directly. She sat quietly through the church service, accepted Imogene's invitation to lunch, and maintained her mood of strong reserve all through the meal. Her in-laws didn't try to draw her out of her relative quiet; they had learned to accept her occasional silences as they accepted her smiles. Susan didn't run to a comforting shoulder to unburden herself whenever something troubled her; they might never know what made her deep blue eyes so pensive, and they didn't ask.

They had just finished lunch and were moving into the den when Mrs. Robbins, the housekeeper, appeared with a visitor at her elbow. "Someone to see you, ma'am," she told Imogene, and went about her business. Mrs. Robbins had been with the Blackstones for five years, but she had evidently not heard the rumors and wild tales that had circulated about Cord Blackstone, because there hadn't been a flicker of recognition in the woman's features as she admitted him.

Susan's eyes swept over his face, and she surprised a look of irritation that drew his level brows together in a brief frown when he saw her. Then the frown was gone, and he crossed the room with his easy grace to kiss Imogene, bending down to touch his lips to her cool, ageless cheek. Once again that astonishing color pinkened Imogene's face, though her voice was as controlled as always when she spoke. "Hello, Cord. We've just finished lunch, or I'd invite you to eat with us. Would you like something to drink?"

"Thank you. Whiskey, neat." His mobile lips quirked at the iron-clad Southern manners that demanded she offer him food and drink, even when he knew that she despised him. Watching him, Susan surprised herself by reading exactly the thoughts that were only hinted at in his expression. She would have thought that Cord would be more difficult to read.

He chose one of the big, brown leather armchairs, and accepted the short, wide glass of amber liquid that Imogene extended to him, murmuring his thanks in a low voice. Totally at ease, he stretched his long legs out before him and sipped the whiskey.

The room was totally silent, except for the rhythmic

ticking of the antique clock perched on the massive oak mantel. Cord seemed to be the only one who was comfortable with the silence. Preston was becoming increasingly red in the face, and Imogene fidgeted with her skirt before she caught herself and commanded her hands to lie calmly in her lap. Susan didn't fidget, but she felt as if her heart were going to bruise itself against the cage of her ribs. How could he have this effect on her by simply walking into the room? It was insane!

He was dressed with fine disregard for the capricious March weather, wearing only impeccable black slacks, creased to a razor's edge, and a thin blue silk shirt through which she could see his darkly tanned flesh and the curling black hair on his chest. Her eyes drank in the details of him, even as she tried not to look at him. For the first time, she noticed the small gold band that he wore on the little finger of his right hand, and she wondered if it was a woman's wedding band. The thought jolted her. What woman had been so important to him that he would wear her ring?

Behind her, Preston had evidently reached the end of his patience. "Did you have a reason for coming here?" he asked bluntly.

A level brow rose in mocking query. "Do you have a reason for being so suspicious?"

Preston didn't even notice the way his words had been turned back on him, but Susan did, and she lifted her head just a fraction of an inch, only a small movement, but one that signaled to people who knew her well that she wasn't pleased. Preston and Imogene knew, and Preston gave her a look that was abruptly apologetic. He had opened his mouth to apologize aloud, a concession that Susan knew didn't come easily to him, when Cord cut smoothly across him.

"Of course I have a reason for coming, and I'm glad that you're smart enough to know that you aren't going to like hearing it. I wouldn't enjoy knowing that I have an idiot for a cousin."

Cord was being deliberately argumentative, Susan realized, and her eyes narrowed just a tiny bit as she stared at him, but she didn't say anything.

Again silence reigned, as Preston and Imogene seemed to stiffen, waiting. After a moment's surprise, Susan realized that both of them seemed to know what Cord was getting at,' and she looked from her in-laws back to Cord's faintly amused expression. He let the quietness draw itself out until the room fairly reverberated with tension; then he negligently crossed one booted foot over the other.

With an air of idle musing, he said, "I know you've probably thought that I've spent the past few years bumming around the world, but I've been gainfully employed most of the time since I left Mississippi. I work for an oil company, as a sort of troubleshooter." His pale eyes gleamed with amusement as he watched the parade of astonishment marching across the features of his cousin and aunt. He didn't look at Susan at all.

"I . . . smooth things out for them," he continued silkily. "I don't have a title; I have contacts, and methods. I'm surprisingly good at my job, because I don't take no for an answer."

Imogene was the first to recover, and she favored Cord with a polite smile. "I appreciate that you're very well suited for your job, but why are you telling us about it?"

"I just wanted you to understand my position. Look at it as honor among thieves, if you prefer. Now, let's get down to business."

"We don't have any business with you," Preston interjected.

Cord flicked an impatient glance over him. "The Blackstones own a lot of land in Alabama, southern Mississippi, and Louisiana. I inherited my share of it, so I should know. But the land that I'm interested in isn't part of my inheritance; if it was, I wouldn't be here now. I know that several oil companies have approached you in the last ten years for permission to drill in the ridges, but you've turned them all down. Newer surveys have indicated that the reserves of oil or gas in the ridges could be much larger than originally projected. I want to lease the ridges for my company."

"No," said Preston without hesitation. "Mother and Vance and I talked it over when we were first approached years ago. We don't want any drilling on Blackstone property."

"For what reason, other than a vague idea that it's too money-grubbing for a blue-blooded old Southern family like the Blackstones?"

Susan sat very still, nothing in the room escaping her attention. A cold chill was lacing itself around her body, freezing her in place. The ridges weren't exactly ridges; they were only ripples in the earth, clothed in thick stands of pine. She liked the ridges, liked the peacefulness of them, the sweet smell of pure earth and pine. But why was Cord asking Imogene and Preston about them? Didn't he know?

"It was nothing as silly as that," Imogene explained calmly. "We simply didn't feel that the chances of a significant oil find were great enough to justify disturbing the ridges. There aren't any roads into them except for that one Jeep track; trees would have to be cut, roads made. I've seen the messes that drilling sites make."

"Things have changed in the last ten years," Cord replied, carrying the glass of whiskey to his lips. "A lot more care is taken not to disturb any area, and, as I said, it looks as if there's a lot more oil in the ridges than anyone thought at first."

Preston laughed. "Thank you for the information. We'll think about it; we might decide to allow drilling in the ridges after all. But I don't think we'll use your company."

A slow, satisfied smile began to move Cord's lips. "I think you will, cousin. Or you can face criminal charges."

Susan didn't know what he was talking about, but she knew that he had led Preston to exactly that point. He had played the scene as he had wanted it, knowing what Preston's reaction would be, and knowing all the time that he held all the aces. Cord Blackstone had a streak of ruthlessness in him, and her chill deepened.

Preston had gone pale. Of course, she thought absently. Cord wouldn't have made a statement like that without being very sure of himself. She noted that Imogene was also as white and still as a china doll, so Imogene also knew what was going on.

"What are you saying?" Preston asked hoarsely.

"My inheritance." Cord smiled lazily. "I'm a Blackstone, remember? I own stock in all the Blackstone companies. The funny thing is, I haven't been receiving my share of any of the profits. Nothing has been deposited into my accounts at any of the banks we use. I didn't have to dig very deep before I found some papers that had my signature forged on them." He took another sip of whiskey, slowly tightening the screws. He knew he had them. "I believe forgery and theft are still against the law. And we aren't talking about pin money, either, are we? You didn't think I'd ever come back, so you and Aunt Imogene have been steadily lining your own pockets with my money. Not exactly an honorable thing to do, is it?"

Imogene looked as if she would faint. Preston had been turned into stone. Cord looked at them, totally satisfied with the effect he'd had. He smiled again. "Now, about those leases."

Susan stood, her movements slow and graceful, drawing all attention to her. She felt curiously removed from them, as if she were swathed in protective layers of cotton. Somehow she wasn't surprised, or even shocked, to learn that Preston and Imogene had been taking profits that were legally Cord's. It was a stupid thing to do, as well as illegal, but they had a different view of things. To them, what belonged to one Blackstone belonged to all of them. It was a feudal outlook, but there it was. The most trouble she'd ever had with Imogene had been when Vance died and it became known that he'd left everything to Susan, instead of returning it to the family coffers. That was the one mistake Cord had made, in assuming that Vance had left his mother and brother in control of his share. It was an uncharacteristic mistake, and one that he had made because he was a Blackstone himself, with all of their inborn arrogance.

"You're bullying the wrong people," she told Cord remotely, her low voice cutting through the layers of tension and hostility. She felt the lash of his suddenly narrowed gaze, but she didn't flinch under it. "If Preston and Imogene are guilty, then so am I, by association if not actual knowledge. But they can't get you the leases to the ridges. The ridges belong to me."

Chapter 3

SHE DIDN'T REMEMBER DRIVING HOME. SHE'D WALKED out, not even pausing to get her coat, but hadn't felt the cold in her detachment. The house was empty, when she got home, without any welcoming smells emanating from the kitchen, because Sunday was Emily's day off. Susan knew that she'd find something in the refrigerator already prepared, if she was hungry, but she didn't think she'd be able to eat again that day.

She changed clothes, carefully hanging the garments in the closet, then immediately took off the casual clothing she'd just put on. She needed a hot bath, something to take away the coldness that had nothing to do with her skin, but was rather a great lump inside her chest. She threw some sweet herbs into the hot water and eased into the tub, feeling the heat begin to soothe away her stress.

Why did she feel so stunned? Preston had warned her that Cord was ruthless; why hadn't she believed him? It wasn't even what he had done, as much as the way he had done it.

He had a right to punish Preston and Imogene for taking what was, essentially, his birthright. If he had wanted to trade that for the leases to the ridges, that was also his right. But he had played with them, leading them step by step to the point where they would feel the shock the worst, and he had enjoyed the effect his words had had on them. There was obviously no love lost between them, but Susan didn't believe in inflicting unnecessary pain. Cord had wanted them to squirm.

When the water had cooled, she let it out and dried herself, sighing as she dressed again in the dark brown slacks and white shirt she'd chosen. The bath had helped, but she still felt that inner chill. She checked the thermostat and found that it was set at a comfortable level, but she didn't feel comfortable. She lit a fire under the logs that had already been placed in the fireplace in the den, then wandered into the kitchen to put on a pot of coffee.

The fire was catching when she went back into the den, and she sat for long, increasingly peaceful moments, staring at the licking blue and orange flames. There was nothing as calming as a fire on a cold day. She thought about the needlepoint she was doing, but discarded the idea of working on it. She didn't want to sew; sewing left her mind free to wander, and she wanted to wipe the day from her mind, occupy her thoughts with something else. She got up and went over to the bookshelves, then began to run her finger across the spines of the books, considering and rejecting as she read the titles. Before she could choose a book, the doorbell chimed, then was followed promptly by a hard knock that rattled the door.

She knew instinctively who it was, but her steps didn't falter as she went to the door and opened it.

He was leaning against the door frame, his breath misting in the cold air. His blue eyes were leaping with a strange anger. "I didn't want you involved in this," he snapped.

Susan stepped back and waved him into the house. He

had made some concession to the weather, after all, she noted, as he shrugged out of the lightweight jacket he wore. She took it from him and hung it neatly in the coat closet. She was calm, as if the shock of seeing his cruelty had freed her from the dizzying spell of his sensuality. Her heartbeat was slow and steady, her breathing regular.

"I've just put on a pot of coffee. Would you like some?"

His mouth thinned into a hard line. "Aren't you going to offer me whiskey, try to get me drunk so it'll be easier to handle me?"

Did he think that was why Imogene had offered him something to drink? She started to ask him, then shut her mouth, because it was possible that he was right. Imogene could have offered coffee, because there was always a fresh pot made after every meal. And neither Imogene nor Preston drank very much, beyond what was required socially.

Instead she treated his question literally. "I don't have any whiskey in the house, because I don't drink it. If you want something alcoholic, you'll have to settle for wine. Not only that, I think it would be difficult to get you drunk, and that being drunk would make you harder to handle, rather than easier."

"You're right about that; I make a mean drunk. Coffee will do fine," he said tersely, and followed her as she went into the kitchen. Without looking, she knew that he was examining her home, seeing the warmth and comfort of it, so different from the formal perfection of Blackstone House. Her rooms were large and airy, with a lot of windows; the floors were natural wood, polished to a high gloss. A profusion of plants, happy in the warmth and light, gave the rooms both color and coziness.

He watched as she took two brown earthenware mugs from the cabinet and poured the strong, hot coffee into them. "Cream or sugar?" she asked, and he shook his head, taking the cup from her.

"There's a fire lit in the den; let's go in there. I was cold when I got home," she said by way of explanation, leading the way into the other room.

She curled up in her favorite position, in a corner of the loveseat that sat directly before the fire, but he propped himself against the mantel as he drank his coffee. Again he looked at his surroundings, taking in her books, the needlepoint she'd been working on, the television and stereo system perched in place on the built-in shelves. He didn't say anything, and she wondered if he used silence as a weapon, forcing others to make the first move. But she wasn't uncomfortable, and she felt safe in her own home. She drank her coffee and watched the fire, content to wait.

He placed the mug on the mantel with a thud, and Susan looked up. "Would you like more coffee?" she offered.

"No."

The flat refusal, untempered by the added "thank you" that politeness demanded, signaled that he was ready for the silence to end. Susan mentally braced herself, then set her cup aside and said evenly, "I suppose you want to talk about leasing the ridges."

He uttered an explicit Anglo-Saxon phrase that brought her to her feet, her cheeks flaming, ready to show him the door. He reached out and caught her arm, swinging her around and hauling her up against his body in a single movement that stunned her with its swiftness. He wrapped his left arm around her waist, anchoring her to him, while he cupped her chin in his right hand. He turned her face up, and she saw the male intent in his eyes, making her shiver.

She wasn't afraid of him, yet the excitement that was racing along her body was very like fear. The false calm she'd been enjoying had shattered at the first move he'd made, and now her heart was shifting into double time, reacting immediately to his touch. He wouldn't hurt her; she wasn't afraid of that. It was her own unwilling but powerful attraction to him that made her uneasy, that brought her hands up to press against his chest as he bent closer to her.

"Stop," she whispered, turning her head aside just in time, making his lips graze her soft cheek. His grip on her chin tightened, and he brought her mouth back around, holding her firmly, but instead of taking her lips he let his mouth wander to her ear, where his teeth nibbled sharply on the lobe. Susan caught her breath, then forgot to let it out as the warm slide of his lips went down the column of her throat and nuzzled her open collar aside, to find and press the soft, tender hollow just below her collarbone. She felt his tongue lick out and taste her flesh, and her breath rushed from her lungs.

"Cord, no," she protested frantically, alarmed by the tingling warmth that coursed through her body, spreading like wildfire from the touch of his mouth on her. Her pushing hands couldn't budge him. All she succeeded in doing was making herself deeply aware of the powerful muscles that layered his chest and shoulders, of the wild animal strength of him.

"Susan, honey, don't tell me no," he murmured insistently into the fragrant softness of her shoulder, before licking and kissing his way up her throat. Her fingers dug into his shoulder as every tiny flick of his tongue sent her nerves into twitching ecstasy. He finally lifted his head and hovered over her, their lips barely separated, their breaths mingling. "Kiss me," he demanded, his voice harsh, his eyes narrowed and intent.

Her body was quaking in his arms, her flesh fevered and aching for greater closeness with him, but her alarm equaled her physical need. The look in his pale eyes was somehow both cold and fiery, as if his body were responding to her but his actions were deliberately planned. Horrified, she realized that he knew exactly what his touch did to her, and if she didn't stop him soon, she would be beyond stopping him. He'd actually done so little, only kissing her shoulder, but she could feel the hardened readiness of his body and the tension that coiled in his muscles. He was a fire waiting to consume her, and she was afraid that she didn't know how to fight him.

"No, I can't—" she began, and that was all the chance he needed. His mouth closed on hers, and Susan melted almost instantaneously, her body telegraphing its need for him even though her mind rebelled. Her lips and teeth parted to allow the intrusion of his tongue; her hands slid up to lock around his neck, her fingers clenching in the thickness of his hair. As a first kiss, it was devastating. She was already at such a high level of awareness of him that the growing heat of the kiss was inevitable. She gave in without protest to the increasing pressure of his arms as he gathered her even closer to the heated need of his body.

The warning voice of caution was fragmented into a thousand helpless little pieces, useless against the over-whelming maleness of him. Too many sensations were attacking a body that had been innocent of sensuality for five long years, turning her thoughts into chaos, her body into a dizzying maelstrom of need.

She'd never before been so aware of a man's kiss as a forerunner to and an imitation of the act of sexual posses-sion, but the slow penetration and withdrawal of his tongue sent shudders of pure desire reverberating through her. Mindlessly she rose on tiptoe, and he reacted to the provocation of her movement, his hands sliding down her back to curve over and cup the roundness of her buttocks, his fingers kneading her soft flesh as he lifted her still more, molding her to him so precisely that they might as well have been naked for all the protection their clothing afforded her from the secrets of his body. A moan, so low that it was almost a vibration rather than a sound, trembled in the air, and after a moment Susan realized with shock that it was coming from her throat.

No.

The denial was, at first, only a forlorn whisper in her own mind, without force, but some portion of her brain heard and understood, accepted that she couldn't allow herself to sample the lustful delights this man offered her. With the age-old wisdom of women, she knew that she couldn't offer herself casually, though he would take her casually. It would be nothing to him; a moment of pleasure, good but unimportant and swiftly forgotten. Susan, being the woman she was, would have to offer her heart before she could offer her body, and though she was dangerously attracted to him, she was still heart whole.

No! The word echoed in her mind again, stronger this time, and she tensed in his arms, oblivious now to the seduction of his mouth. The protest still hadn't been voiced aloud, she realized, and with an effort she pulled her mouth free of his. She was suspended in his arms, her toes dangling above the floor while he cupped her hips to his in a position of intimacy, but her stiffened arms held her head and shoulders slightly away from him. She met his glittering diamond eyes evenly. "No."

His lips were red and sensuously swollen from their kiss, and she knew that hers must look the same. His dark beard had been so soft that she hadn't been aware of any prickles, and a rebellious tingle of desire made her want to nuzzle her face against that softness. To deny herself, she said again, "No."

His mouth quirked, amusement shining like a ray of sunshine across his face. "If people learn through repetition, than I have that word engraved on my brain."

Under any other circumstances she would have laughed, but her nerves were too raw to permit humor. She increased the pressure of her hands against his heavy shoulders, desperately trying to ignore the heat of his flesh searing her through the thin silk of his shirt. "Put me down. Please."

He obeyed, slowly, and his obedience was almost as provocative as his sensual attack. He let her slide with excruciating slowness down the hard length of his body, turning her release into an extended caress that touched her from her knees to her shoulders. She almost faltered, almost let her hands leave his shoulders to slide up and clasp around his neck again. Alarmed, determined, she stepped back as soon as her feet touched the floor, and with a wry smile, he let her go.

"You weren't so wary of me last night," he teased, but he watched sharply as she carefully placed herself out of his reach.

That was nothing less than the truth, so she agreed. "No, I wasn't."

"Do I look more dangerous in daylight?"

Yes, infinitely so, because now she'd seen a ruthlessness in him that she hadn't realized was there. Susan regarded him seriously, not even tempted to smile. She could try to put him off with vague excuses, but they wouldn't work with this man. He was still watching her with the deceptive laziness of a cat watching a mouse, letting it go just so far before lashing out with a paw and snatching it back. She sighed, the sound gentle in the room. "I don't think I could trust anyone who did what you did today."

He straightened from his negligent stance, his eyes narrowing. "I only went as far as I had to go. If they'd agreed to lease the ridges, the threat wouldn't have been made."

She shook her head, sending her dark hair swirling in a soft, fragrant cloud around her face. "It was more than that. You set it up, deliberately antagonized both Imogene and Preston from the moment you walked in the door, pushing them so hard that you *knew* they wouldn't lease the ridges to you, *knew* you were going to hit them with your threats. You led them to it, and you gloated every inch of the way."

She stopped there, not voicing the other suspicion that was clouding her mind. Even without really knowing him, she felt as if she knew enough about him to realize that he seldom made mistakes; he was simply too smart, too cunning. But he had either made a mistake in not completely investigating the ownership of the ridges, or he had known all along that she was the owner, and hoped to use his threat against Imogene and Preston as a means of forcing her to sign the leases. It was common knowledge in the area how close she was to her in-laws; even an outsider could have discovered that. Cord might not have the means of threatening her personally, but he would see right away that she was vulnerable through her regard for her husband's family. And even worse than that, she had another suspicion: Was he bent on seducing her for some murky plan of revenge, or as a less than honorable means of securing the lease on the ridges? Either way, his attention to her was suddenly open to question, and she shrank from the thought.

He was still watching her with that unsettling stare. "Guilty as charged. I enjoyed every minute of making the slimy little bastard squirm."

Shaken by the relish in his tone, she winced. "It was cruel and unnecessary."

"Cruel, maybe," he drawled. "But it was damned necessary!"

"In what way? To feed your need for revenge?"

It had been a shot in the dark, but she saw immediately that it had been dead on target. The look he gave her was almost violent; then he turned and took the poker in his hand, bending down to rearrange the burning logs in the fireplace, expending his flare of anger on them. Straightening, he returned the poker to its place and stood with his head down, staring into the hypnotically dancing fire.

"I have my reasons," he said harshly.

She waited, but the moments stretched out and she saw that he wasn't going to explain himself. He saw no need to justify himself to her; the time had long passed when he needed anyone's approval of his actions.

The question had to be asked, so she braced herself and asked it. "What are you going to do about the money Preston owes you, now that you know he doesn't control the ridges?"

He gave her a hard, glinting look. "I haven't decided."

Chilled by the speculation in his eyes, Susan resumed her seat, an indefinable sadness overwhelming her. Had she really expected him to trust her? He probably trusted no one, keeping his thoughts locked behind iron barricades.

It had to be due to a streak of hidden perversity inside her that, even though she'd rejected the idea of having an affair with him, now she was hurt because she thought he might have an ulterior motive for pursuing her. If she had any brains at all, she'd not only keep the mental distance between them, she'd widen it. He'd made a pass at her, but she couldn't attach any importance to it; he probably made passes at a lot of women. If his kisses were anything, they were a subtle means of revenge. She was a Blackstone by name, and automatically included in his target area. Besmirching the reputation of Vance Blackstone's widow would be a scheme likely to appeal to Cord, if he wanted the Blackstones to squirm.

Because she couldn't stand the horror of the thought, her tone was abrupt when she spoke again. "I can't give you an answer about the ridges. I won't say no, but I can't say yes, either. I'll have an independent geological survey made, as well as gather several opinions about the ecological damage to the area, before I can reach a decision. And the decision I make will be based on the results of the surveys, not on any blackmail you may try to use."

"I don't remember asking you about the ridges," he murmured, smiling coldly.

"That's why you're here, isn't it?"

"Is it?"

"Oh, please." She waved her hand tiredly. "I don't feel

up to playing word games. I know the ridges are what you're after."

His eyes sharpened, and a certain tension invaded him, giving him a stillness that reminded her of an animal poised to attack. "I've never prostituted myself for an oil lease yet," he drawled, yet anger lay beneath his lazy tone like a dark shadow.

Susan darted a glance up at him. "We both know I'm not your usual type."

"Hell, no, you're not! I'll agree to that!" He glared at her, his lips compressed into a grim white line. "You sit there as cool as a cucumber and accuse me of something pretty low, but you never even raise your voice, do you? Tell me, lady, is there anything that gets a rise out of you? Do you have feelings, or are you just a china doll, useless but nice to look at?"

She almost recoiled in shock, feeling the force and heat of his anger. "Yes, I feel," she whispered. "I don't want to be hurt. I don't want you to use me."

Suddenly he crouched down until his eyes were on a level with hers, and he leaned forward, so close that she pressed herself back into the cushions to relieve the sensation of being swamped by him. "I don't think you feel anything at all," he rasped. "Or rather, you're afraid of what feelings you do have. You want me, but you're too afraid of what people will say to reach out and take me, aren't you? You're too tied to the security of your network of leeches, all of you pretty, useless people who live off the work of others. You're pretty, sweetheart, but you're nothing but a blood-sucker."

His words hit her like blows, but she lifted her chin proudly. "You don't know anything about me," was all she said.

"I know enough to know that trying to get passion from you is a hopeless cause," he returned caustically. "Look,

I'll be in touch about the leases, but don't save any dances for me.''

She sat there for a long time after he left, wishing he would come back so she could spill out her fears and uncertainties to him, but knowing that it was for the best that he'd gone. He was right; she did want him, and she was afraid that if he knew just how weak she was, he'd play on those weaknessess and use her in any way he wanted, even as a means of revenge. If nothing else, she couldn't let that happen.

How quickly he had destroyed the peace, the even tenor of her days! She spent another night lying awake, twisting under a mantle of unhappiness. When dawn finally came, revealing a low gray sky, she wanted to do nothing more than lie in bed all day as a refuge from the thoughts that whirled around in her tired mind. But with her usual determination she forced herself out of bed; she would maintain her regular schedule if it killed her! She wasn't going to let Cord Blackstone tear her life to pieces.

She went to the offices in Biloxi every day; Preston ran everything, but since Vance's death she had become more immersed in the daily details of running a corporation with a myriad of interests, and Preston had long ago gotten in the habit of talking everything over with her. He had the training, but she was quick and knowledgeable, and had good instincts about business. After Vance's death, taking over his office had been a means of keeping her sanity, but before long she'd found herself enjoying the work, enjoying the flood of information on which decisions were based.

She arrived early, but Preston was even earlier. Having seen his car in the parking lot, she went straight to his office, knocking softly on his door. Their mutual secretary hadn't arrived yet, and the building echoed with sounds not usually heard during the busy days.

He looked up at the interruption, and a welcoming smile

eased the shadow of worry that had darkened his face. "Come on in. I've already put the coffee on."

"I could do with an extra jolt of caffeine," Susan sighed, heading straight for the coffeepot.

They sipped the hot brew in companionable silence for several minutes, then Susan put her cup down. "What are we going to do?"

He made no pretense of misunderstanding. "I went over the old books last night, trying to nail down exactly how much we owe him. It's a lot, Susan." He rubbed his forehead wearily.

"You're going to try to replace the money, aren't you?"

He nodded. "What else can I do? The hell of it is, we don't have that much ready cash right now. We've invested heavily in research that won't pay off for another couple of years, but you know that as well as I do. I'm not going to touch anything that you have an interest in; Mother and I agreed on that last night. We're going to liquidate some of our personal assets—"

"Preston Blackstone!" she scolded gently. "Did you think I wouldn't be willing to help you?"

"Of course not, honey, but it wouldn't be fair to you. Mother and I did this, and we knew that we were taking a chance. We gambled that Cord wouldn't come back until we'd been able to replace the money, and we lost." He shrugged, his blue eyes full of wry acceptance of his own mistake. "It didn't seem so wrong at the time. We didn't use the money for anything personal; every cent of it was invested back into the corporation, but I don't suppose that would make any difference in a court of law. I still forged his signature on some papers."

"Will you be able to raise enough?" He might protest, but if they couldn't cover the amount they owed Cord, then she would insist on helping them. She didn't want to do anything to jeopardize the corporation, so she agreed that its assets shouldn't be touched, but Vance had left her a lot of personal assets that could easily be liquidated, including some highly valuable property. She also had the ridges, she realized with a sudden start. How badly did Cord want them? Badly enough to take the land in exchange for not pressing charges against Imogene and Preston? Two could play his game!

"I have an idea," she said slowly, not giving Preston time enough to answer her question. "I have something he wants; perhaps we could make a trade."

Preston was a smart man, and he knew her well; he leaned back in his chair, his blue eyes narrowing as he stared at her and sorted out the options and details in his mind. He didn't waste time on unnecessary questions. "You're talking about the ridges. You know that even if you lease the ridges to him, he can still file charges, don't you? He might swear that he wouldn't, but I don't think his word of honor is worth much. Not only that, you'd be giving in to his blackmail."

"Not quite," she said, thinking her way through the situation. "I'll have to have those surveys made, and estimate the worth of an oil lease on the ridges, but if he accepts the leases as restitution for the amount you owe him, then he doesn't have a case any longer, does he?"

Preston looked thunderstruck. "My God, you're talking about letting him have the oil leases for free? Do you have any idea what a rich field could be worth?"

"Millions, I'd imagine, or he wouldn't be so determined to have it."

"A lot more than what we owe him! He'd jump at the deal, but you'd be losing a fortune. No, there's no way I can let you do that."

"There's no way you can stop me," she reminded him, giving him a tender smile. She'd gladly give up a fortune to keep her family intact and safe. Preston had his faults, as did Imogene, but she knew that they'd never turn their backs on her, no matter what happened. They weren't easy people to know—the stiff-necked Blackstone pride and arrogance was present in abundance in both of them—but they also had a loyalty that went all the way to the bone. When she married Vance Blackstone, she had been taken into the family and guaranteed its protection. Preston had been a lifesaver for her when Vance died, pushing his own grief for his brother aside to comfort her and protect her to the best of his ability. Even Imogene, whose proud head had never lowered even on the day of Vance's funeral, had helped Susan by showing her a gritty courage and determination that wouldn't falter.

Preston's frustration was evident in his eyes as he glared at her. "I don't like it when you use that soft, sweet tone of voice. That means you've dug in your heels and won't budge, doesn't it?"

A sound in the outer office alerted them to the arrival of their secretary, Beryl Murphy. Knowing that they both had a lot of paperwork to handle, Susan got to her feet and used that excuse to escape to her own office, even though she knew Preston wanted to try to talk her out of letting Cord have the ridges. Blue fire was in his gaze as he watched her leave the office, but Beryl was already approaching with the first of the day's crises, and he groaned in momentary surrender.

Susan had a stack of reports left on her desk from the Friday before, and she dutifully began reading them, but before long she'd lost the thread of meaning as her mind worried at every angle of the deal she'd be offering Cord.

She really needed to know the monetary value of the oil leases on the ridges before making a deal, but on the other hand, she didn't want to wait before approaching Cord about it. Though he could file charges immediately, she didn't think he would; he would wait, as much to worry everyone as to make up his mind. He probably had already made up his mind, she realized with a burst of panic.

Should she wait, or should she tell him right away about the deal? Finally she decided to approach him immediately, before he could take any legal action. If any formal charges were ever made, there would be no way of keeping them from becoming public knowledge, and that would hurt her in-laws enormously.

The realization that she would have to see him, that day if possible, sent a chill down her spine. Just the thought of being close to him again made her blood tumble madly through her veins, whether in dread or anticipation she couldn't say. The way he had kissed her the day before was still seared into her mind, and she couldn't get the taste of his mouth from her lips, or rub from her skin the lingering sensation of the soft brush of his moustache and beard. He was a dangerous animal, but he appealed to her on a primitive level that she had never before suspected existed within herself. She wanted him, and her body's longing made every meeting with him hazardous, because she wasn't certain of her mind's ability to retain control.

But how silky his beard was! Not bristly at all, but soft and sensuous. Was the hair all over his body as soft as that? An image of his nude form sprang into her mind, and a wave of heat washed over her, forcing her to take off the suit jacket she was still wearing.

My God, what was she thinking?

It was useless to entertain daydreams of him. Oh, he'd willingly use her sexually, but for reasons that had nothing to do with being attracted to her personally. Her feminine spirit couldn't take that, nor could her conscience allow her to so abandon her morals.

She got through the day, and somehow avoided Preston when he tried to pin her down at lunch. He didn't want her to sacrifice anything, and Imogene would also object. She'd have to stay one step ahead of both of them, and she meant to do that by seeing Cord as soon as possible. She made the necessary phone calls to get the geological survey in progress and grimly ignored the thought that now she couldn't let any ecological damage to the area matter.

By afternoon a weak sun was trying to break through the cloud layer, and a brisk wind had sprung up. Would Cord be working on the old cabin at Jubilee Creek? If he wasn't, she had no idea where to find him. She'd deliberately tried not to listen to all the gossip about him these past few weeks, and now she wished instead that she'd absorbed every word; at least then she might have an idea of where he was. She could ask Preston, but she knew what fireworks that would set off, so she decided simply to try her luck at Jubilee Creek.

She left early, because she wasn't certain of her memory of the location of the cabin. Secondary roads wound through the region like grape runners, criss-crossing each other and meandering in no particular direction, it sometimes seemed. Vance had taken her to the Jubilee Creek area a few times, early in their marriage, but that had been years ago.

Suddenly the sun brightened, as the wind pushed the clouds away, and she squinted against the sudden glare of sun on the wet highway. Reaching above the visor, she grabbed her sunglasses and quickly slid them on. Perhaps the sun was an omen; then she made a face at herself at the frivolous thought. She didn't believe in omens.

She was nervous, her stomach queasy at the thought of dealing with him, and to take her mind off of it she tried to concentrate on the passing scenery. The weather might be chilly, but there were signs of spring after all, even discounting the stubborn jonquils. Oak trees had that fuzzy look conveyed by new leaves, and patches of green grass were shooting up. In another week, two at the most, color would be rioting over the land as shrubs and trees bloomed, and it couldn't happen soon enough for her. It was already what she counted as a late spring.

She almost missed the turn onto the narrow road that she

thought was the correct one. It was only a roughly paved secondary road, without benefit of a painted center line or graded shoulders. She slowed down, looking for the next turn, and just when she had almost decided that she'd taken the wrong road, she recognized the turn she was supposed to take. It was an unpaved lane that was really only two tracks, crowded on both sides by tall, monolithic pines and sweeping oaks that rapidly hid the secondary road from view. The lane made a long curve; then she found herself rattling across an old wooden bridge that spanned Jubilee Creek itself.

The rain had filled the broad, shallow creek, and the muddy water tumbled over the rocks and around the meandering curves as the creek snaked its way south to empty eventually into the Gulf. She could see the cabin now, a small structure dwarfed by three massive oaks behind it, capping the crest of a small rise. Even from where she was, it was evident that the porch that ran the length of the cabin was completely new, and as she drew closer she could see that the roof was also new, shingles replacing the rusted tin that had been there before.

She didn't know what kind of car he drove, but it didn't matter anyway, since there was no sign of any vehicle. Her heart sank. She slowed her own car to a stop in front of the cabin, staring at the curtainless windows in despair. Where could she find him?

She was just about to put the car in reverse when the door opened and he stepped onto the porch. Even from that distance she could see the icy glare of his eyes, and she knew that this wasn't going to be easy. She drew a deep breath to brace herself, then cut the ignition off and got out of the car.

Walking up the steps was like running a gauntlet; he leaned against the door frame and watched her in nerve-wracking silence, his arms crossed over his chest. He looked huge, she noticed; perhaps it was his clothes. He wore only a pair of faded jeans and a black T-shirt, and scuffed brown boots on his feet. The short sleeves of the T-shirt revealed his brawny forearms, sprinkled with dark hair and corded with veins that pulsed with his hot, life-giving blood. From the way the thin cotton clung to his torso, she knew that the image she'd had of his nude body had been remarkably accurate, and her mouth went dry. He was lean and hard and muscular, and his chest looked like a wall.

His glacial eyes swept her from her neat spectator pumps to her head, where her dark hair had been swept into a simple chignon. "Slumming?" he drawled sarcastically.

She controlled the quiver that wanted to weaken her legs, and ignored his opening salvo. "I want to make a deal with you," she said firmly.

Amusement, and a savage satisfaction, glinted in his eyes. He stepped away from the door and waved her inside with an exaggerated bow. "Come inside, lady, and let's hear what you have to offer."

Chapter 4

THEIR STEPS ECHOED HOLLOWLY AS SHE ENTERED THE
cabin and he followed, closing the door behind them. The
smell of newly cut wood struck her nostrils, and fine
particles of sawdust floated through the air. Through an
open door she could see a couple of sawhorses with a length
of wood lying across them, and she realized that she had
interrupted his work. She wanted to apologize, but the
words refused to leave her thickened throat. To give herself
time to recover, she looked around the empty cabin; despite
the improvements, it still had an atmosphere of being old
and still felt incredibly solid anyway. The new windows,
large and airtight, let the light in but kept the damp chill
out. An enormous fireplace, laid with logs but unlit, gave
the promise of cozy fires. The open door to the right of the
fireplace indicated the only other room, and except for it,
she could see all of the cabin from where she stood.
Beneath her feet, the floor was pine, treated and polished,
then left alone to glow with its natural golden color. In spite

of her nervousness she was charmed by the old cabin, as if she could feel at peace here.

He stepped past her and leaned down to strike a match and touch it to the old newspaper in the fireplace. It flamed with tongues of blue, which quickly caught the kindling, and soon the fire was licking at the big logs. "I don't feel the cold much while I'm working," he said by way of explanation. "But since you've interrupted me . . ."

"I'm sorry," she murmured, feeling incredibly awkward.

There was nowhere to sit, but he looked perfectly comfortable as he wedged one strong shoulder against the mantel and gave her a sardonic look. "Okay, lady, you wanted to talk turkey. Talk."

He wasn't going to give an inch. She didn't waste time pleading with him to be reasonable; she lifted her chin and plunged in. "Have you filed charges yet?"

"I haven't had time today," he responded lazily. "I've been working here."

"I . . . I want to make you an offer, if you'll agree not to file charges."

His ice blue eyes sharpened and raked down her slim, tense body. "Are you offering yourself?"

The thought jolted her, and she wondered what would happen if she said yes. Would he take her now, on the bare floor? But she said, "No, of course not," in a low voice that disguised her reaction.

"Pity." Nonchalantly, he surveyed her again. "That was the one offer you could have made that might interest me. It might have been fun to see if you get mussed up when you're having sex. I doubt it, though. You're probably starched all the way through."

Susan curled her fingers into her palms, and only then did she notice how cold her hands were. "I'm offering you the lease on the ridges."

He straightened, his hard mouth curving in amusement.
"Let me remind you that that was my original offer. But
I've thought about it since then, and I've changed my mind.
And didn't you tell me yesterday that you couldn't be
blackmailed into selling me the lease?"

She stepped closer, to get nearer the fire as much as to
read his eyes better. "I'm not offering to sell you the lease;
I'll *give* you the lease, as restitution for the amount owed to
you by Preston and Imogene."

He laughed, throwing back his dark head on the rich
sound. "Do you have any idea how much money you're
talking about?"

Preston had asked her the same thing, and her answer
was still the same. "More than what they owe you. I realize
that; I'm asking you to accept the lease as restitution."

He stopped laughing, and his eyes narrowed on her.
"Why should you pay their debts? Why should I let them
off scot-free?"

"They're my family," was all she could offer by way of
explanation.

"Family, hell! They're pit vipers, sugar, and I should
know better than anyone else. I don't want *you* to pay; I
want *them* to pay."

"Like you said last night, you want them to squirm."

"Exactly."

"You're turning down an oil lease worth a fortune just
for your petty sense of revenge?" she cried.

Anger darkened his face. "Easy there, lady," he said
softly. "You're pushing me."

Susan swept an agitated hand across her brow. "You
need pushing! How can you be so stubborn?" He wasn't
going to agree, and desperation clawed through her stomach. "Why won't you take the lease as payment?"

He grinned, but it wasn't from amusement; his grin was
one of grinding rage and grim anticipation. "Because if I
accept the lease under those conditions, then I no longer

have a case against them, as you well know. Did Preston talk you into this? Well, it won't work. I'll pay you for the lease, and I'll pay you well, but I won't let Preston hide behind your skirt. It's no deal.''

Tears stung her eyes as he turned away from her to kick the burning logs into better position. She clutched at his arm, feeling his warm flesh, the steeliness of the muscles underneath. "Please!" she begged.

He swung around, looming over her, the red flames of the fire reflected in his pale eyes and making them glow like a devil's. "Damn you!" he spat from between his clenched teeth. "Don't you dare beg for them!"

Wildly she reached out with her other hand and grasped the fabric of his T-shirt, trying to shake him, but unable to budge him. She had to make him understand! How could he destroy his own family, his own blood? The thought was so horrible that she couldn't stand it. She had to do something, anything, to convince him how wrong and futile revenge was. "Don't do this, please!" she cried frantically. "I *am* begging you—"

"Stop it!" he ordered, his deeper, darker voice completely overriding hers. He jerked her hands off him and held her, his long fingers wrapped around her upper arms. Anger made his fingers bite into her soft flesh, and she gasped, twisting in an effort to free herself. Immediately his grip relaxed, and she jerked away. In the silence that fell between them, her breathing was swift and audible as she gulped in air, her breasts rising and falling. His eyes dropped to the soft mounds as they moved, lingered for a long, heart-stopping moment, and when he finally looked back up to her face, black fury had filled his gaze. "You begged . . . for *him*. Get out of here. You can tell him that his little scheme didn't work. Go on, go back to him, and to his bed.''

Susan came apart under the tension and the lash of his words. She, who never lost control, whose nature was

serene and peaceful, suddenly found herself flying at him,
thrusting her face up close to his and yelling, "It was *my*
scheme, not his! He tried to talk me out of it! You fool!
You're so wrapped up in the past, in your sick need for
revenge, that you can't even see how self-destructive you
are! If this is how you were fourteen years ago, no wonder
you were run out of town—mmmmph!''

He had reached out, his hard hands closing on her waist,
and had jerked her against him with enough force to knock
the breath out of her. She threw her head back, gasping, and
his mouth came down, attacking, fastening on hers, forcing
her lips to part and mold themselves to his. There was
nothing gentle or seductive in his kiss this time; he forced
her response, his arms locking around her and holding her
to him, one hand going up her back to fasten in her hair and
hold her head back for him to drink as he willed from her
mouth. Dazed, dizzied by his sudden sensual attack, she
made no effort to wrench away from him.

He kissed her again and again, his tongue making forays
that brought her onto her tiptoes, straining against him,
forgetting the anger between them, forgetting the reason
she was there. The feel of him, so hard and warm, so
strong, was all she wanted in the world, the source of every
comfort she could imagine. His kisses became deeper,
longer, sweet-tart with the passion that turned their embrace
into pure fire. His hand went under her jacket, sweeping up
to close over her breast with a sure touch that didn't allow
her to deny him the right to touch her so intimately. Her
blouse was opened so roughly that she was dimly surprised
when the buttons didn't fly off; then his hand was inside,
sliding between her bra and the soft, satiny flesh beneath it,
her nipple stabbing into his rough palm.

She whimpered into his mouth as his hand stroked and
kneaded, his demanding man's touch swamping her with a
sensual delight that turned her body into pure molten need.
Her breasts were very sensitive, and his expertise made

them harden with desire, turned the velvet nipple into a taut, throbbing point. She was throbbing everywhere, her entire body pulsating, her own hands digging into the deep valley along his spine, then pulling frantically at his T-shirt until it came free of his pants and she could slide her hands under it, running her palms up the damp, muscled expanse of his back. He quivered under her touch, telling her without words that he was as aroused as she. He had the raw, musky smell of sweat mingled with his own potent masculinity; and she wanted to spend the rest of her life locked in his hard arms, breathing in that scent. It was mad, but oh, it was sweet.

When he released her and stepped back, she was as shocked as if a bucket of icy water had been hurled in her face. Disoriented, lost without the heat of his body, the hard security of his arms, she stared up at him with bewildered blue eyes grown so huge that they dominated her face.

He wasn't unaffected; he was breathing hard, and color was high in his face. When he looked at her open blouse and his pupils dilated, she swayed on her feet, thinking for a moment that he was going to return to her. Then he thrust a rough hand through his hair, ruffling the silky strands. "Is this Plan Two to get me to agree to your deal?"

Susan stepped back, her face losing its color. "Do you really believe that?" she choked, anguish twisting her insides.

"It seems possible enough. You don't have the guts to admit that you want me; you have to cling to your spotless, genteel reputation. But if you sacrifice yourself to me to save your family, why, then you're a noble martyr, and you get to enjoy the sin without sinning. I admit, it sounds like something out of a Victorian novel, but that's what you make me think of."

"A coward," she said painfully.

A hard smile twisted his mouth. "Exactly."

She stood poised, uncertain if she should go or try again

to convince him not to press charges against her family. She badly wanted to leave; she was afraid that if he threw any more harsh words against her, her dignity and self-control would be totally destroyed and she'd begin crying, and she didn't want that. She swallowed to force control on her voice, and said quietly, "Please reconsider. How can you turn down a fortune? You know what those ridges are worth if the geologists are right, and what the lease would normally cost you."

"You're offering to save my company a fortune," he pointed out coolly. "I wouldn't get any of the money personally. What's in it for me?"

Confused, she stared at him. How stupid of her! Her great plan had been to offer him personal gain, and he had let her make a complete fool of herself before reminding her that giving the lease to him would benefit the company he worked for, not him personally. Mortified, she turned and walked quickly to the door, wanting nothing more than to leave. A deep chuckle followed her, and as she opened the door and stepped onto the porch, he called, "But it was a good try!"

Susan kept her pace steady as she went to the car, trying not to run even though she wanted to get away from him as fast as she could. What a colossal blunder she'd made! And how he must be laughing at her! When she thought of the way she'd returned his kisses, she blushed, then turned pale. Good Lord, how could he think she was anything but cheap, after she'd virtually offered herself to him? He'd thought that she was just part of the deal, and she couldn't blame him for that; what else could he think, when she'd kissed him back so hungrily?

When she pulled into her own driveway and saw Imogene's Cadillac in front of the house, she groaned aloud. The last thing she felt like right then was facing Imogene's drilling; she wanted to take a long bath and pamper herself in an effort to soothe her ragged nerves. She knew that

Preston would have called Imogene and talked to her about Susan's ploy, and now Imogene was here to discover how things had gone. Why couldn't she have waited just a few hours more?

There would be no easy way to dash Imogene's hopes, and the strain was evident in Susan's face as she entered the house and walked to the den, where she knew her mother-in-law would be waiting. The older woman rose to her feet when Susan entered, and her shrewd gray eyes examined every nuance of expression in Susan's face. "He turned you down, didn't he?" It wasn't like Imogene to give in to defeat, but now her discouragement gave a leaden cast to her eyes, dulled her voice.

He'd turned her down in more ways than one, Susan thought wearily. Her mental and physical fatigue muted her voice as she sank down in one of the chairs. "Yes."

"I knew he would." Imogene sighed and resumed her seat, her patrician face stiff with effort. "It would be too easy to let you pay; it's Preston and me that he's after."

Remembering the cold contempt in his eyes when he had looked at her, Susan couldn't agree fully with Imogene. A hard knot of pain formed in her chest; why did it have to be like that? When she remembered the intense magic of their first two meetings, she wanted to weep at the harsh words that had passed between them since then. She felt as if she had lost something precious, without ever having held it in her hands. He was a hard man, yet inexplicably she wanted to get closer to him, to get to know him, learn his moods and his laughter as well as his anger, delve into his protected personality until she found some inner core of tenderness. When he had kissed her the first time, it had been with a tender consideration for her soft flesh. But today . . . Susan raised her fingers and touched her lips, still a little swollen and sensitive from his hard kisses. He hadn't been gentle today; he had been angry, and he had punished her for daring to try to protect Preston.

Suddenly she realized that Imogene had followed the tell-tale gesture with knowing eyes, and she blushed.

Imogene sat upright. "Susan! He's interested in you, isn't he? How perfect! Thank God," she said fervently.

Susan had expected a subtle scolding, not Imogene's almost rapturous joy. "What's perfect?" she asked in confusion.

"Don't you see? You're in a marvelous position to find out what he's planning and keep us informed; that way we can take steps to counteract anything he does. Why, you might even be able to talk him out of staying here!"

Stunned, she stared at Imogene, not quite able to believe what was being asked of her, what Imogene automatically assumed she would do, without protest. After all, she was family, and her first allegiance was to that family. It was the same sort of thinking that had allowed Imogene and Preston to use Cord's money illegally in the first place; it wasn't as much Cord's money as it was Blackstone money, and therefore available for their use.

She strove for an even tone. "He's not interested in me. If anything, I'm tarred with the same brush he's used to paint you and Preston."

Imogene waved that thought aside with a brisk movement of her hand. "Nonsense." She examined Susan critically, her gray eyes narrowed. "You're a lovely woman, though of course not his usual sort. It shouldn't be difficult for you to get around him."

"But I don't want to get around him!"

"Dear, you *must!* Don't you see that the only way we can protect ourselves is to know in advance what he's planning?"

Agitation tumbled Susan's insides with a restless hand, and she got to her feet, unable to sit still. "It's impossible," she blurted. "I'm not a . . . a slut. I can't sleep with him just to *spy* on him!"

Imogene looked affronted. "Of course you wouldn't, but

I'm not asking that of you, Susan. All I'm asking is that you see him, talk to him, try to find out what he's planning. I realize that it may cost you a few kisses, but surely you're willing to give that in exchange for our protection.''

A few kisses! Did Imogene really know so little about her own nephew? Susan shook her head slowly, denying the idea to herself, as well as to Imogene. ''A few kisses isn't what he wants,'' she said, her voice muffled. And even if she went to bed with him, he still wouldn't divulge any secrets to her. All he wanted from her was a good time in bed, physical release, a momentary pleasure.

Imogene didn't give up easily; there was steel in her spine, in her character. Sitting very upright, her chin lifted proudly, she said firmly, ''Then it's up to you to keep him under control. You're not a teenager, to be seduced in the back seat of a car to the theme of 'but everyone does it.' You can string him along.''

If Susan had been less shocked, she would have laughed aloud, but as it was she stood frozen, staring at Imogene as if she were a stranger. What her mother-in-law was telling her to do struck her as little less than prostitution, and she felt chilled by the realization that Imogene had so little regard for her feelings, her morals. She was simply supposed to do whatever was asked of her.

''No,'' she refused in a low voice. ''I can't . . . I *won't* do it.''

A cold fire began snapping in Imogene's eyes. ''Really? Do you care so little for me, for Preston, that you'll simply stand and watch while that wretch destroys us? We won't be in it by ourselves, you know. You'll suffer, too. If he decides to sue us for damages, he could bankrupt the company, and there would go the standard of living that you currently enjoy. People will talk about you just as they would about us; everyone will believe that you knew about the money from the beginning. You've made a big show of 'working' at the company since Vance died, so people will assume that not only did you know about it, you approved.''

Susan had seen Imogene in action before, and knew that few people could stand up to her when she lashed out with her lethal tongue, when she stared at someone with those cool, hard eyes. Most people gave in to her without even a hint of resistance. Vance had had the strength to soothe her, agree with her, and calmly go about his own business in his own way, smiling at her and charming her whenever she realized that he'd ignored her directions. Preston wasn't that often at variance with her, though he was a lot warmer, a lot more human. Because she had been challenged so seldom in her life, she didn't expect anyone to disobey her openly. The quiet determination Susan had shown in becoming Vance's wife, then in taking up the reins of his business interests at his death, should have told her that Susan wasn't like most people, but still she wasn't prepared for a refusal.

Susan stood very straight, very still, her expression calm, her dark blue eyes quiet and level. ''Regardless of what anyone says, I'll know that I haven't done anything wrong, and that's what's important to me. I'll help you any way I can, except for that way. I'll sell everything I own, but I won't play the whore for you, and that's what you're asking me to do. You know as well as I do that Cord isn't a man who can be controlled by any woman.''

Imogene got to her feet, her mouth tight. ''I expected more loyalty from you than this. If you want to turn your back on us when we're in trouble, I can't stop you, but think very carefully about what you stand to lose.''

''My self-respect,'' Susan said dryly.

Imogene didn't storm out of the house; she swept out, regally, in a cold rage. Susan stood at the window and watched her drive away, her chest tight with hurt and sadness because she hadn't wanted to damage the relationship she had with Imogene. Since she'd first met Vance's mother, she had carefully cultivated a closeness with the older woman, knowing how important the ties of family were to a marriage, and how much Vance had loved his mother despite her reserve. Imogene wasn't a villain, even though she was autocratic. When she loved, she loved deeply, and she'd fight to the death for those she cared about. Her blindness was her family; anything was acceptable to her if it protected her family. Until now Susan had been wrapped in that fierce blanket of protection, but now she felt that she'd been cast out as Cord had been cast out. Dues had to be paid if someone expected to benefit from that protection; conformity was expected, and a willingness to sacrifice oneself for the well-being of the whole. Cord had been cast out because he hadn't conformed, because he'd left the family open to gossip. His reputation hadn't been up to par, and he'd been forced out of the closed circle.

Had he felt like this? Susan wondered, running her hands up her chilled arms. Had he felt lost, betrayed? Had he been alarmed to be without the support that he'd known since birth? No, he hadn't been alarmed, not that man; instead he would have thought with grim delight of punishing them for turning their backs on him. Wasn't that what he was doing now?

Cord. Somehow all her thoughts these days returned to him, as if he had become the center of her world. She hadn't wanted him to, but since the moment he'd walked in from the night, he had eclipsed everyone else in her every waking thought, in her dreams, had invaded even her memory, so that she constantly had the taste of his mouth on her tongue, felt the hard warmth of his hands on her flesh. *I could love him!* she thought wildly, and shuddered in half-fear, half-excitement. Loving him would be the most dangerous thing she'd ever done in her life, yet she felt helpless to deny the effect he had on her. If it wasn't love yet, it had nevertheless gone beyond mere desire, and she was teetering on the edge of an emotional chasm. If she fell into it, she'd be forever lost.

The emotional strain that she was under was visible on her face the next morning when she walked into the office, later than usual for her because she'd spent a restless night, then overslept when she finally did manage to fall asleep. Because she felt so frazzled, she'd attempted to disguise her emotional state by hiding behind an image that was sterner than the one she usually projected. She'd pulled her soft dark hair back into a tight knot and applied makeup carefully, hoping to divert attention from the lost expression in her eyes. The dress she had chosen was sleekly sophisticated, a black silk tunic with narrow white vertical stripes, cinched about her slender waist with a thin black belt. It wasn't a dress that she wore often, because it had always seemed too stark for her, but today it suited her mood perfectly.

She told Beryl good morning, then went straight through to her office and closed the door, hoping to submerge herself in the reports that she hadn't finished the day before, because she'd been in such a hurry to see Cord. A wasted effort, she thought with a painful catch in her breath. Resolutely she pushed away the thought of her failure and picked up the first report, only to replace it when someone knocked firmly on her door.

Without waiting for an answer, Preston let himself in and sauntered over to ease himself into the chair opposite her desk. He sprawled in it and pressed his fingers together to form a steeple, over which he peered with blue eyes alive with curiosity. "What did you say to Mother?" he asked with relish. "I haven't seen her so angry in years."

Susan caught the grin that twitched at his mouth, and against her will she found herself smiling at him. Preston had a little bit of the devil in him at times, a puckish sense of humor that he seldom allowed to surface. Whenever he did, it made his eyes sparkle in a manner that reminded her strongly of Vance. Now was one of those times. Despite the pressure he was under, he was being eaten alive with curiosity, wondering what Susan could possibly have said to his mother to put her in such a snit.

She wasn't certain just how much to tell him, if anything. She decided to stall. "Did Imogene tell you that Cord turned down my offer of the ridges?"

He nodded. "I'm glad, too. I know it would've been the easy way, but I don't want you to pay for something that was our fault. You know that." He gave a graceful shrug. "Mother didn't agree; she thought that it would be worth it if we stopped any trouble before it began."

Yes, head off scandal, at any cost. Deciding to tell him the truth in the hope that he would support her, she took a deep breath and braced herself. "She wanted me to see Cord—play up to him—and try to find out what he was planning so you could counteract it. I refused."

Preston's eyes had widened, then narrowed as he realized the scope of her simplified explanation. He swore softly. "Thank God for that! I don't want you around him. Mother shouldn't have suggested anything like that."

"She'd do anything to protect her family," Susan offered in Imogene's defense.

"Telling you to play up to Cord is like throwing a lamb to the wolves," he snapped. "You wouldn't have a chance. What in hell ever gave her the idea?"

A faint blush crept into Susan's cheeks, and she looked away from him. "She knows that he kissed me. . . ."

Preston bolted upright in his chair. "He what?"

"He kissed me," she repeated steadily. Did Preston think that was something to be ashamed of?

He'd turned pale, and abruptly he surged to his feet, running his fingers through his neat hair in an uncharacteristic gesture. "I thought, the night he first showed up, that he was just playing up to you to get back at me. Is that all it is?"

Susan bit her lip; she honestly didn't know. Her body told her that Cord Blackstone's interest wasn't limited to her name, but her mind worried over the issue. A man's sexual instincts could be aroused even when he had another motive for seducing a woman, so she couldn't let herself be confused by the physical responses he'd shown. Yet, he'd responded to her from the very beginning. . . . Just when her heart was beginning to beat faster in faint hope, she saw herself stretching out her hand to him, and heard herself saying, "I'm Susan Blackstone. . . ." No, he'd known from the first that she was a Blackstone, married to either Vance or Preston. Unhappily, she looked up at Preston. "I don't know," she said miserably.

He began to pace around the room. "Susan, please, don't have anything else to do with him. Don't see him at all, unless you have to. You don't have any idea of the type of man he is."

"Yes, I do," she interrupted. "He's a hard, lonely man." How could he not be lonely? He might have built an emotional wall to guard him, but he was all alone behind it.

Preston gave her a derisive, unbelieving look. "My God, how can you be so naive? You've got to stop seeing good in everyone! Some people are bad all the way through. Will you promise me not to see him again, and protect yourself before he has a chance to really hurt you?"

There was a very real chance that *he* wouldn't want to see *her*, but suddenly she knew that if by some miracle he gave her another opportunity, she'd seize it with both hands. She wanted to be with him. She wanted to kiss him, to try to discover if what she felt for him was a fleeting sexual magic, or if the seeds of real love had been sown. For five years she'd grieved for Vance, and though her love for him would never die, neither would it grow. Vance was frozen in place in her heart, but he didn't occupy all of it. There was still so much love in her to give! She wanted to love again; she wanted to marry again, and bear children.

Perhaps Cord wasn't the man who would be able to touch her heart, but she already knew that she had to take the chance. If she let the opportunity pass, she'd always wonder about it, and mourn for lost chances for the rest of her days.

She looked Preston in the eye. "I can't promise that."

He swore softly, and suddenly his shoulders hunched. "All of these years," he muttered. "First you were Vance's wife, then his widow. I've waited, knowing you weren't over Vance, that you weren't ready to become involved with anyone else. Damn it, why does it have to be Cord?" The last sentence was a harsh cry, and his chest swelled with the fury inside him. He gave Susan a look so tortured that tears welled in her eyes.

She found herself on her feet, unable to calmly sit there while he bared his deepest secret to her. "Preston . . . I didn't know," she whispered.

His clear blue eyes were a little shiny, too. "I know," he said, taking a shuddering breath. "I made sure I kept it from you. What else could I do? Try to steal my brother's wife?"

"I'm sorry. I'm so sorry!" What else was there to say? Events couldn't be altered. Perhaps, if their lives had been allowed to go on undisturbed, she might one day have come to love Preston in the way he wanted, though she rather thought that instead she would always have seen him as Vance's brother, and looking at him would always have been like looking at a slightly altered photo of Vance. But the even tenor of her life had been disrupted from the moment she'd seen Cord, and crossing that dance floor to take his hand and shield him from the scene that had been brewing had forever altered her, in ways that she hadn't yet discovered.

"I know." He turned his head away, not wanting her to see the depth of his pain. He was a man of pride and patience, and his patience had gained him nothing. All he could do now was cling to his pride. He walked to the door and left, his shoulders square, his gait steady, but still Susan knew what the effort cost him, and her vision blurred as she watched him.

Would Cord be glad that, even involuntarily, he'd managed to hurt Preston? She winced at the thought. She'd certainly never tell him that Preston had hoped for a deeper relationship. What he'd told her today would go no further; it was the least she could do for someone she loved as much as she could, even though, for him, that wasn't enough.

Chapter 5

By Friday her emotional turmoil had taken its toll on her, and the price she'd paid was evident in an even more slender waistline, and a fragility in her face that was startling. She and Imogene had made up, in a way. They had spoken to each other on the phone, never making reference to their difference of opinion, but their conversation had been stilted and brief. Imogene had simply asked her if she would be attending Audrey Gregg's Friday night fund-raising dinner for a local charity. Imogene had a prior commitment, and she wanted Susan to go, since Audrey was a very good friend. Susan had agreed, reluctant to face an evening of having to smile and pretend that everything was all right, but acknowledging her family duty. At least it wasn't formal, thank God. Audrey Gregg believed in keeping her guests entertained; there would be dancing, a generous buffet instead of a sit-down dinner, and probably a night club act brought in from New Orleans.

Spring was tantalizing them again with marvelous weather, though only the day before it had been cold and

overcast. Today the temperature had soared to eighty, and
the forecasters had promised a mild night. With that in
mind, Susan dressed in a floaty dress in varying shades of
lavender and blue, with a wrap bodice that hugged and
outlined her breasts. She was too tired and depressed to fool
much with her hair, and simply brushed it back, securing it
behind each ear with filagree combs. The sun was setting in
a marvelous skyscape of reds and gold and purples when
she drove over to Audrey's house, and the natural beauty
lifted her spirits somewhat. How could she keep frowning
in the face of that magnificent sunset?

The brief lifting of her spirits lasted only until she
glanced over the crowd at Audrey's and saw Cord, casually
sophisticated in gray flannel slacks and a blue blazer,
dancing with Cheryl Warren. Cheryl again! Though Cheryl
was a likable person, unexpectedly kind despite her chorus-
girl looks, Susan felt an unwelcome sting of jealousy. It was
just that Cheryl was so . . . so sexy, and so *together*. Her
tall, leggy body was svelte, with a dancer's grace; her
makeup was always a little dramatic, but always perfectly
applied, and somehow right for her. Her ash blond hair
looked wonderful—loose and sexy, tousled.

Compared to Cheryl, Susan felt nondescript. Her simple
hairstyle suddenly seemed childish, her makeup humdrum,
her dress the common garden variety. She scolded herself
for feeling that way, because she knew the dress was
becoming to her and was perfectly stylish. It was just that
Cord made her feel so insecure, so unsure of herself and
what she wanted. Then she had to admit to herself that she
did know what she wanted: She wanted Cord. But she
couldn't have him; he was all wrong for her, and he didn't
want her anyway.

Suddenly Preston was at her elbow, his strong hand
guiding her to the buffet. With a pang, Susan realized that
normally she would have been here with Preston, but this

time he hadn't even asked her. Cord had managed to drive a wedge between her and Preston, whose friendship she had depended on for so long. How pleased he would be if he only knew what he'd done!

Preston's blue eyes were worried as he looked down at her. "Relax for a minute," he advised. "You're wound up like a two-dollar watch."

"I know," she sighed, watching as he automatically filled a plate for her. He knew all her favorite foods, and he chose them without asking. When he had two laden plates in his hand, he nodded over to a group of empty chairs and they made their way across the room to claim them, with Susan stopping enroute to fetch two glasses of champagne punch.

He watched as she nibbled on a fresh, succulent Gulf shrimp. "You're lovely," he said with the blunt honesty of people who know each other well. "But you look as if you're going to fly into a million pieces, and that isn't like you."

She managed a wry smile. "I know. You don't know how I wish I could do more than catnap. At least Imogene's speaking to me again."

He grinned. "I knew she wouldn't last long. She's been so restless, it was almost funny. Honey, if it's such a strain on you, why don't you take a vacation? Forget about all of this and get away from all of us for a while."

"I can't do that now." The look she gave him was worried. "I can't leave you not knowing if . . . if . . ."

"I know." He covered her hand with his, briefly applying pressure before removing his touch. "I'm handling it, so don't worry so much. In another week to ten days, I'll have the money repaid into Cord's account."

She bit her lip. She knew that he would have had to liquidate a lot of assets to raise that much money so quickly, and she felt guilty that he hadn't allowed her to help.

Perhaps she hadn't known anything about it, but she had profited by the use of the money because it had made the company stronger.

By sheer willpower, she kept her gaze from straying too often to Cord as the minutes crawled past, but still she somehow always knew where he was. He'd stopped dancing with Cheryl, and she was surprised by the number of people who engaged him in conversation, despite how wary most of them still were of him. Why was he here? She couldn't imagine that Audrey Gregg had invited him, so he had to have come with someone else, probably Cheryl. Was he seeing Cheryl often?

For a while he stood alone, off to one side, slowly sipping a glass of amber liquid, his dark face blank of any expression, his eyes hooded. He was always alone, she thought painfully. Even when someone was talking with him, he had a quality about him that set him apart, as if he were surrounded by an invisible barrier. He'd probably had to become hard and aloof to survive, but now that very protection kept him from being close to another human being.

It was too stressful to watch him. To divert herself, she began talking to Preston, and resolutely kept her gaze away from Cord. Good friend that Preston was, he talked easily of many things, keeping her occupied. She knew that he had to be under a strain himself, even more so than she was, but he was handling it well, and his concern was all for her.

Suddenly Preston looked past her, his blue gaze sharpened and alert. "It's in the fan now," he muttered. "Grant Keller is about to tie into Cord."

Susan whirled, and gasped at the hostility of the scene. Grant Keller was a picture of aggressive, bitter hatred, standing directly in front of Cord, his fists knotted and his jaw thrust out as he spat some indistinguishable words at the younger man. His handsome, aristocratic face was twisted with hate and fury. Cord, on the other hand, looked cool and bored, but there was an iciness in his eyes that warned Susan that he was on the verge of losing his temper. His stance was relaxed, and that too was a signal. He was perfectly balanced, ready to move in any direction.

Her breath caught in her chest. He'd never before seemed so aloof, so unutterably alone, with only his natural pride and arrogance to stand with him. Her heart was stabbed with pain, and she felt as if she were choking. He was a warrior who would die rather than run, standing by his own code, loyal to his own ideals. Oh, God, couldn't they see that only pain could force a man into such isolation? He'd been hurt enough! Then, out of the corner of her eye, Susan saw Mary Keller watching her husband, with distress and a wounded look evident on her quiet face.

Suddenly Susan was angry, with a fierce swell of emotion that drove away her depression, her tiredness. That old scandal had already caused enough trouble and pain, and now another woman was about to be hurt by it. Mary Keller had to sit there and watch her husband try to start a fight over another woman, something that couldn't be pleasant. And Cord . . . what about Cord? His youthful love affair had caused him to be driven away from his family, and the hard life that he'd lived since then had only isolated him more. Grant Keller was the wronged husband, true, but he wasn't the only one who had suffered. It was time for it to end, and she was going to see that it did!

People who had never seen Susan Blackstone angry were startled by the look on her face as she headed across the room, and a path was cleared for her. Her eyes were a stormy indigo, her cheeks hot with color, as she marched up to the two men and put her slender body gracefully between them. She was dwarfed by their size, but no one had any doubt that the situation had been swiftly defused. She was practically sparking with heat.

"Grant," she said with a sweetness that couldn't begin to disguise the fire in her eyes, "I'd like to talk to you, please. Alone. Now."

Surprised, he looked down at her. "What?" His tone indicated that he hadn't quite registered her presence.

Cord's hard hands clamped about her waist, and he started to move her to one side. She looked up, smiling at him over her shoulder. *"Don't . . . you . . . dare,"* she said, still sweetly. She looked back at Grant. "Grant. Outside." To make certain that he obeyed her, she took his arm and forcefully led him out of the room, hearing the buzz of gossip begin behind her like angry bees swarming.

"Are you crazy?" she demanded in a fierce whisper when they were out of earshot, dropping the older man's arm and whirling on him in a fury. "Haven't enough people already been hurt by that old scandal? It's *over!* It can't be undone, and everyone has paid for it. Let it die!"

"I can't," he returned just as fiercely. "It's burned into my head! I walked into my own home and found my wife in bed with *him*. Do you think he was ashamed? He just glared at me, as if she were *his* wife, as if I had no right to be there!"

Yes, that sounded like Cord, able to stare down the devil himself. But she brushed all of that aside. "Maybe you have bad memories, but you're just going to have to handle them. Are you still in love with your first wife? Is that it? Do you want her back? You have Mary now, remember! Have you given her a thought? Have you thought of how she must feel right now, watching you start a fight over another woman? Why don't you just walk up and slap her in the face? I'm sure it wouldn't hurt her any worse than she's hurting right now."

He blanched, staring down at her. Perspiration broke out on his face, and he wiped his brow with a nervous hand. "My God, I hadn't thought," he stammered.

Susan poked him in the chest with her forefinger. "It's a

dead issue," she said flatly. "I don't want to hear about it
again. If anyone . . . *anyone* . . . wants to fight Cord over
something that happened fourteen years ago, they're going
to have to go over me first. Now, go back in there to your
wife and try to make it up to her for what you've done!"

"Susan—" He broke off, staring at her pale, furious face
as if he'd never seen her before. "I didn't mean—"

"I know," she said, relenting. "Go on now." She gave
him a gentle push, and he sucked in a deep breath,
obviously preparing himself to face a wife who had every
right to be hurt, humiliated and angry. Susan stood where
she was for a moment after he'd gone, drawing in her own
deep breaths until she felt calm seep back into her body,
replacing the furious rush of adrenalin that had sent her
storming across the room to step between two angry men.

"That's a bad habit you've got." The deep drawl came
from behind her, and she whirled, her breath catching, as
Cord sauntered out of the shadows. Abruptly she shivered,
no longer protected by her anger, as the cooling night air
finally penetrated her consciousness. Quickly she cast a
glance at the crowd of people visible through the patio
doors, some of them dancing again, going about their own
concerns. She had stepped in too soon for anything exciting
to happen, so there wouldn't even be much gossip.

"They all know we're out here, but no one is going to
intrude," he said cynically. "Not even Preston, the Boy
Wonder." He touched the soft curve of her cheek with one
finger, trailing it down to the graceful length of her throat.
"Didn't your mother ever teach you that it's dangerous to
get between two fighting animals?"

She shivered again, and when she tried to speak she
found that her voice wouldn't work right; it was husky,
strained. "I knew you wouldn't hurt me."

Again his finger moved, sliding with excruciating slowness over her collarbone, then stroking lightly over the
sensitive hollow of her shoulder. Susan found that the touch

of his finger, the hypnotic motion of it, somehow interfered with her breathing; the rhythm of her lungs was thrown off, and she was almost hyperventilating one moment, then holding her breath the next. She stared up at him, seeing his lips move as he spoke, but her attention was focused on his touch, and the words didn't make sense. She swallowed, licked her suddenly dry lips, and croaked, "I'm sorry. What—"

One corner of his mouth lifted in a strange almost-smile. "I said, you'd be a lot safer if you didn't trust me. Then you'd stay away from me, and you wouldn't get burned. I can't decide about you, honey."

"What do you mean?" Why couldn't her voice be stronger? Why couldn't she manage more than that husky whisper?

His finger moved again, making a slow trek over to her other shoulder, touching her in a way that made her heart slam excitedly. She'd never noticed her shoulders being so sensitive, but he was doing things to her that were rocketing her into desire. "I can't decide whose side you're on," he murmured, watching both his finger and the way her breasts were heaving as she struggled to regulate her breathing. "You're either the best actress I've ever seen, or you're so innocent you should be locked up to keep you safe." Suddenly his pale eyes slashed upward, his gaze colliding with hers with a force that stunned her. "Don't step in front of me again. If Grant had accidentally hit you, I'd have killed him."

She opened her mouth to say something, but whatever was in her mind was forever lost when he trailed his finger downward to her breasts, stroking her cleavage, then exploring beneath the cloth of her bodice to flick over a velvet nipple. She caught a moan before it surfaced, gasping in air. With a slow, sure touch he put his hand inside her dress, cupping her in his palm with a bold caress, as sure of himself as if they weren't standing on the patio where any of fifty people could interrupt them at any time. He looked at her face, soft, drowning in sensuality, and suddenly he wondered if she looked the same whenever Preston touched her. She was either the most sensual woman he'd ever seen, or she was fantastic at faking it. At the thought of Preston, he removed his hand, leaving her dazed and floundering. "You'd better get back inside," he muttered; then he turned and walked away, disappearing into the night shadows, leaving her more alone than she'd felt since Vance's death.

Her body burned from his touch, yet she was shaking with something like a chill. It was like a fever, she thought dimly, burning hot and cold at the same time. He *was* a fever, consuming her, and she reached the horrified realization that the way she felt about him was no longer under her control. Without wanting to, she cared too much about him. She was playing Russian roulette with her emotions, but it was far too late to stop.

She stood there in the cool night for several minutes longer, then slipped quietly inside to rejoin the party. Preston came over and touched her arm gently. "Are you all right?" he asked with tender concern, and in his eyes she saw the love that he couldn't quite hide.

She was calm enough now to give him her most reassuring smile, one that made most people feel that everything was right with the world. "Yes, I'm fine."

"Grant and Mary have gone home. What'd you say to him? He looked like he was in shock when he came in, and he went straight to Mary."

She shook her head, still smiling. "Nothing, really. I just calmed him down."

His look said he didn't quite believe her, but he kissed her forehead lightly in tribute. It was inevitable that when Susan glanced around she saw Cord standing across the room, staring at her with cold, unreadable eyes, and a sad pain bloomed in her heart. He'd never trust her, she thought, and wished that it didn't mean so much to her.

Audrey Gregg found the opportunity to thank her for averting a scene, and after that Susan made her excuses and drove herself home where she fell into bed in mental exhaustion, then got up ten minutes later to restlessly pace the house. Finally she turned on the television to watch an old Jerry Lewis and Dean Martin comedy, letting their antics clear her mind. She was engrossed in the movie, chuckling to herself, when the doorbell rang. Frowning, she glanced at the clock. It was almost midnight, the witching hour.

"Who is it?" she called through the door, tying the sash of her robe tighter.

"Cord."

She unlocked the dead-bolt and opened the door to him. He straightened from his slouch against the door frame and walked inside. Her eyes dropped to the whiskey bottle he carried in his hand. A half-empty whiskey bottle.

"Are you drunk?" she asked warily.

"On my way." He smiled at her and took a drink from the bottle. "It's hard for me to get drunk, but champagne does it to me every time. Something about my chemistry. I'm just trying to finish it off with this."

"Why do you want to get drunk?" He was walking toward the den, and she followed him automatically. If he was drunk, or even high, he was certainly handling it well. His walk was steady, his speech clear. He sat down on the couch and stretched his long legs out before him, sighing as his muscles relaxed. Susan went over to the television and switched it off in the middle of a Jerry Lewis pratfall.

She repeated her question. "Why do you want to get drunk?"

"It just seems like the thing to do. A sort of tribute to the past."

"So you lift a glass . . . excuse me, a bottle . . . to auld lang syne."

"That's right." He drank again, then set the bottle down with a thud and pinned her with his glittering eyes. "Why did you have to get between us? I wanted to hit him. My God, how I wanted to hit him!"

"Another tribute to the past?" she asked sharply.

"To Judith," he corrected, smiling a little. "Do you know what he said? He came up to me and said, 'So the little whore didn't stay with you, either.' I should've broken his neck on the spot."

Susan hadn't heard the name before, but she knew that Judith had been Grant's first wife, the woman caught in bed with Cord. She sat down beside him and folded her robe around her legs, waiting. Her attitude was calm, her entire attention focused on him. People often talked to her, telling her things that they'd never tell anyone else, without really understanding what it was about her that inspired such trust. Susan didn't understand it herself, unless it was that she truly listened.

He leaned his head back, and his eyelids drooped to half-mast. "She was pure fire," he said softly. "A total mismatch for Grant Keller. She had red hair and slanted green eyes, just like a cat's. She sparkled. She liked to laugh and dance and have a good time, do all of the things that Grant was too stodgy to enjoy. He wasn't the type to go skinny-dipping at night, or dance in the streets during Mardi Gras. But, as far as I know, she was entirely faithful to him." He fell silent, staring into the past.

When several moments had passed, Susan prompted him. "Until you."

He glanced up and gave her a wry look that held a curious overtone of pain and guilt. "Until she met me," he agreed harshly. With a deft movement he seized the bottle and tipped it to his mouth. She watched in amazed fascination as his strong throat worked, and when he set the bottle down it was empty. He looked at it savagely. "There wasn't enough."

Warily, she wondered if he would still be able to say that when his body began to absorb the alcohol he'd just consumed, if he would be able to say anything at all.

A fine sheen of perspiration had broken out on his face, and he wiped it away with the back of his hand. "We'd been having an affair for almost a year before we were caught." His voice was gruff, strained. "I'd asked her over and over to divorce Grant, leave with me, but beneath all of that flash, Judith was strongly conventional. Her reputation meant a lot to her, and she adored her kids. She just couldn't break all her ties. She didn't have any choice after Grant found us together."

Susan swallowed, trying not to imagine the scene. What would it do to any of the three people involved in a triangle for a husband to walk in while his wife was in bed with her lover?

"She was crucified." He heaved himself off the couch and walked restlessly around the room, and what she saw on his face frightened her. "She didn't have a friend left; her own children wouldn't speak to her after Grant threw her out of the house. My dear Aunt Imogene was the leader in ostracizing her. Preston doesn't know that I know what *he* did, because he made certain he wasn't in the group, but he organized a sort of mob scene; a group of teenage toughs danced around Judith one afternoon in the parking lot of a grocery store and called her 'Blackstone's Whore.' It sounds almost Victorian, doesn't it? I caught one of the kids that night and . . . ah, *persuaded* him to tell me who'd set it up. I hunted for Preston, but he flew the coop, and I couldn't find where he'd gone."

So that was why he hated Preston so fiercely! She could understand his bitterness, but still she stared at him, troubled. Couldn't he see that revenge so often has a backlash, punishing the avenger as cruelly as his victim?

His fists were knotted whitely at his sides, his lips drawn back over his teeth. Alarmed, Susan got up and went to him, putting her soft hands over his fists. He'd removed his tie, and his shirt was open at the throat, revealing the beginning curls of hair on his chest; her eyes were on a level with those curls, and for a moment she stared at them, entranced, before she jerked her thoughts away from the dangerous direction they were taking and looked upward.

"Where is she now?" she asked, having a vision of Judith in some sleazy bar somewhere, middle-aged and despairing.

"She's dead." His voice was soft now, almost gentle, as if he had to put some distance between himself and his memories. "My wife is dead, and that bastard called her a whore!"

Susan sucked in a quiet breath, shocked at what he'd just told her. His wife! "What happened?"

"They broke her spirit." He was breathing deeply, almost desperately, but his hands had unknotted, and now his fingers were twined with hers, holding her so tightly that he hurt her. His face was pulled into a grimace of pain. "We were married as soon as her divorce was final. But she was never Judith again, never the laughing, dancing woman I'd wanted so much. I wasn't enough to replace her children, her friends, and she just faded away from me."

"She had to love you, to risk all that she did," Susan said painfully.

"Yes, she loved me. She just wasn't strong enough not to have any regrets, not to let the hurt eat away at her. She came down with pneumonia, and she didn't want to fight it. She gave up, let go. And do you want to know the hell of it?" he ground out. "I didn't love her. I couldn't love her. She'd changed, and she wasn't anything like the woman I'd loved, but I stayed with her because she'd given up so much for me. Damn it, she deserved more than that! I did my best to make sure she never knew, and I hope she died thinking that I still loved her, but the feeling was long gone by then. I'm guilty, too, in what happened to Judith. As guilty as hell!"

His eyes were dry, burning like wildfire, and Susan realized that though he wasn't able to weep for his dead wife, he was about to fly apart before her. She forcibly tugged her hands away from his death grip and cupped his face in her palms, her cool, tender hands lying along his hot flesh like a benediction. His soft beard tickled her palms, and she stroked it gently. His eyes closed at her touch.

"She was a grown woman, and she made her choice when she decided to have an affair with you," she pointed out softly. "The stress was too much for her, but I can't see that it's any more your fault than it was hers." She wanted to ease his pain, do anything to take that look of suffering off his face. My God, he'd been little more than a boy, to bear so much!

He put his hands over hers and turned his face to nuzzle his lips into her left palm, then rubbed his cheek against her hand. His pent-up breath gusted out of him on a long, soft sigh, and his eyes opened.

"You're a dangerous woman," he murmured sleepily. "I didn't intend to tell you all of that."

Looking at him, Susan saw that the whiskey was hitting him hard and fast. Cautiously, she eased him back over to the couch, and he dropped heavily onto it, sighing as he relaxed. For a moment she stood indecisively, then made up her mind; he was in no condition to drive, so he would have to spend the night there. She knelt down and began removing his shoes.

"What're you doing?" he mumbled, his eyelids drooping even more.

"Taking off your shoes. I think you'd better stay here tonight, rather than risk driving home."

A faint smile quirked his lips. "What will people say?"

he mocked; then his eyes closed and he sighed again, a peculiarly peaceful sound.

Susan shrugged at his question; what people would say if anyone knew he'd spent the night here was almost beyond her imagination, yet she really couldn't see that she had a choice. He was mentally and emotionally exhausted, as well as drunk, and if anyone chose to gossip about that, she couldn't stop them. She wouldn't risk his life for that. She completed her task and set his shoes neatly to one side, then swung his long legs up on the couch.

He grunted and adjusted his length to the supporting cushions, dangling one leg off the side and swinging the other one over the back of the couch. Sprawled in that boneless position, he went to sleep as quietly and easily as a child.

Susan shook her head, unable to repress a smile. He'd told her that he was a mean drunk. Looking at him as he slept so peacefully made her doubt that. She went upstairs to get a pillow and blanket, returning to drape the blanket over him and place the pillow under his head. He didn't rouse at all, even when she lifted his head.

Lying alone in her own bed, she was aware of a deep feeling of contentment at just knowing he was under the same roof. The warm aching of her body told her that she wanted more from him than just his presence; she wanted the completion of his lovemaking. She wanted to be everything to him, every dream he'd ever had, every wish he'd ever made. She wanted to ease him and comfort him, and make him forget his black past. Knowing that he stood too much alone to allow anyone to mean that much to him didn't lessen the way she felt. How odd it was that, when she loved again, she loved someone so different from herself!

Yet Vance had been different. Unlike Cord, Vance had conformed, at least on the surface, but she had always known that Vance could have been a hard, dangerous man if anything or anyone had threatened those he loved. Circumstances had been different for Vance than they had for Cord, and that part of his personality had never developed, but the potential had been there. With Vance she had felt utterly protected, utterly loved, because she had sensed that he would have put himself between her and anything that threatened her, without counting the cost to himself.

The way I love Cord! she thought, shocked, her eyes wide in the darkness. It stunned her to think that she could be stirred to violence, but when she thought of the anger that had surged through her that night, she knew that she'd have done anything she could have to keep Grant Keller from punching Cord. She didn't fear for Cord; he was far too capable of taking care of himself. It was simply that she couldn't bear the idea of him suffering the least hurt. She would gladly have taken a punch on the jaw herself rather than let it land on Cord.

She fell asleep quickly and woke before her alarm clock went off. The sun coming in her window, bright and warm, told her that it was going to be another gorgeous spring day. Humming, she took a shower and put on fresh lacy underwear and chose a bright summer dress that reflected her rise in spirits. The pure white fabric, with its fragile lace trim and scattering of brightly colored spring flowers, made her feel as fresh as the new day, as full of hope. Still humming, she went downstairs and peeked into the den, where Cord still lay sprawled on the couch, sleeping heavily. He'd rolled over on his stomach, and his head was turned to the back of the couch, revealing only his tousled dark hair. Quietly she closed the door and went to the kitchen.

Emily was already there, quietly and efficiently making breakfast. When Susan entered, the older woman looked up with a smile. "Who's your guest?"

"Cord Blackstone," Susan replied, returning the smile

and pouring herself a cup of fresh coffee. While the coffee cooled, she got the plates and silverware for setting the table.

"Cord Blackstone," Emily mused, her eyes softening. "My, my, it's been a long time since I've seen that boy. He even spent a few nights under my roof, when he was younger."

"He was drunk last night," Susan explained as she arranged the plates on the table, absently placing the napkins and silverware just so, moving them around by fractions of an inch until she was satisfied.

"I don't remember him as being much of a drinker, though of course that was a long time ago. I'm not saying that he couldn't put it away, but it just never seemed to affect him. My boy would be passed out, and Cord would be as steady on his feet as ever."

After pouring another cup of coffee, Susan carried it into the den and carefully placed it on the coffee table, then knelt in front of the couch. She put her hand on his blanket-covered shoulder, feeling the warmth of his flesh even through the fabric. "Cord, wake up."

She didn't have to shake him. At her touch, her voice, he rolled over, tangling himself in the blanket, and his eyelids lifted to reveal pale, glittering irises. He smiled, then yawned, stretching his arms over his head. "Good morning."

"Good morning," she replied, watching him with veiled concern. "Do you feel like having a cup of coffee?"

"H'mmmm," he said in a rumbling, early-morning voice, a noise that could have meant anything. He heaved himself into a sitting position, raking his fingers through his hair. He yawned again, then reached around her for the coffee, holding the cup to his mouth and cautiously sipping the steaming liquid. He closed his eyes as the caffeine seared its way to his stomach. "God, that's good! Do I smell bacon cooking?"

"If you think you can eat—"

He grinned, opening his eyes. "I told you, I don't have hangovers."

Susan couldn't help the laughter that bubbled out. "Yes, but you also told me that you're a mean drunk, and you weren't anything but a big pussycat! A big, *sleepy* pussycat!"

He reached out and caught her hand, his gaze on her radiant, laughing face. "It depends on my company when I'm drunk. I can be mean if I have to." He finished the coffee and set the cup down, then slid back into a reclining position, closing his eyes, her hand still held loosely in his.

She shook his shoulder with her free hand. "Don't go back to sleep! It's time for breakfast—"

Without opening his eyes he tugged on her hand, and Susan found herself on the couch with him, sprawled over him in a very undignified position. Her eyes widened to huge blue pools, and she began squirming in an effort to push her skirt down, but her efforts were hampered because her feet had somehow become tangled in the blanket and she couldn't get her legs straight.

He sucked in his breath sharply, and his hand caught in her hair, holding her still. "I'd rather have you for breakfast," he muttered huskily, his fingers exerting just enough pressure to ease her head forward slowly, an inch at a time, until he could put his mouth to hers. Susan quivered, her lips opening to his like a soft spring blossom, her mouth being filled with the coffee taste of his. Like a welcome, familiar friend, his tongue entered lazily and explored the tiny serrated edges of her teeth, the softness of her lips, the sensual curling of her tongue as it met his. His hand left her hair and moved down her back, searching out the slender curve of her spine, as slow and inexorable as the seasons.

Susan forgot about breakfast. She wound her arms around his neck, her hands clenching in his hair, meeting the open hunger of his kiss with her own. It was so sweet and good, and it was all she could ask of life, to be in his arms. She felt his hands on her body, experienced, calm hands, as they sleeked down her sides to the graceful curve of her waist, then down to the roundness of her hips. He cupped her buttocks, grasping, filling his hands with the smooth mounds and pressing her to him. The raw sexuality of his gesture left her reeling with pleasure, unable to rein in the hot sparks of desire that were shooting through her body. She was a woman, and he knew exactly what to do with her woman's body. With a few swift movements he had her skirt up, and his hands were under the material, burrowing under the elastic waistband of her panties to brand the coolness of her buttocks with the heat of his palms.

Susan moaned aloud, and the sound was taken into his mouth. He began nibbling at her flesh, his teeth catching her lower lip, the tender curve of her jaw, the delicate lobe of her ear. Her breath was rushing in and out of her lungs, her heart racing out of control. The feel of him was driving her mad, and she wanted to sink down on him in boneless need. Now he was biting at her neck, his teeth stinging her skin; then he soothed it with tiny licks of his tongue. Her hands had made fists in his hair, pulling at the thick, vital mane mindlessly. She wanted to give him everything, every part of her, blend the softness of her body with the hardness of his.

"Two minutes!" Emily sang out from the kitchen.

Susan heard the words, but they didn't make any sense to her. Cord groaned, and his hands tightened on her buttocks in momentary denial; then he reluctantly withdrew his touch from her enticing curves. "I thought a two-minute warning was only in football," he grumbled, easing her to one side.

She sat up, dazed and aching with frustration, wondering why the narcotic of his touch had been so suddenly withdrawn from her feverish, addicted flesh. He looked at her face, so soft and vulnerable in her passion, and his jaw went rigid with the effort he had to make not to reach for her again. She was too much woman to be so prim and proper, and he was becoming increasingly fascinated by just how prim and proper she wasn't. She was forbidden fruit, and probably deceitful into the bargain, but logic had nothing to do with the way he wanted her.

Susan willed herself to be calm, forcing her shaky legs to support her when she stood, forcing her voice to a deceptive evenness. "You'll probably want to wash before eating," she murmured, and showed him the way to the downstairs bathroom. "Come through to the kitchen when you're finished."

But for all her surface serenity, it was several moments after she entered the kitchen before she had collected her thoughts. After staring blankly at the small table in the breakfast alcove, set with three places, a vase of cheerful shasta daisies in the center, she was overcome by the thought that for the first time in five years she would be sharing her breakfast with a man. And not just any man! She would be eating the first meal of the day with a man who made every other man of her acquaintance pale in comparison. A quiver of desire ran through her body again, and she blushed hotly at the thought that she would have let him take her a few moments ago, sprawled on the couch like a wanton, with Emily in the kitchen. Muttering an excuse about collecting his coffee cup, which she'd left in the den, she escaped for a few minutes of necessary solitude.

She had returned with the cup and had a refill of fresh, steaming coffee sitting by his plate when Cord paused in the doorway, assaulting her senses with his size, overpowering everything in her feminine house. He had an aura of hard vitality about him, and for a moment she could only stand and stare at him helplessly. It didn't make it any better to know that he affected every woman that way; not even Imogene was immune to him, and now Emily turned to greet him, a flush of pleasure pinkening her features. "Cord Blackstone, I swear, you're even handsomer than ever!"

He searched her face for only a second, his ice blue eyes sharp; then he grinned and his white teeth flashed. "Mrs. Ferris!" Without pause, he moved across the kitchen to take her firmly in his arms and press a kiss on her flustered mouth, a warm and friendly kiss that had Susan envying Emily for even that small moment.

Emily was laughing and patting his cheek. "That beard! You look like an outlaw for sure! Sit down, sit down. I hope you still like your eggs over easy?"

"Yes, ma'am," he replied, his inbred Southern courtesy not allowing him to address her in any other manner. He seated Susan and Emily before taking his own chair, his long legs fitting under the table with difficulty, but Susan didn't mind the way their knees bumped. His presence at her breakfast table was as natural as if it were an ordinary occurrence, and the sun was shining for her after an absence of five years. She could feel Emily's glance on her, but she couldn't control the radiance of her smile.

She wasn't the only one who was smiling; Emily was clucking around Cord, chattering at him and fussing over him, and he was eating it up with a look of pleasure that told Susan it had been a long time since he'd known the subtle delight of being cherished in the small, all-important ways. Susan didn't talk much, just listened to their conversation. She learned that Cord and Emily's eldest son had been inseparable companions during their teen years, and that Cord had eaten a lot of meals that Emily had cooked. Emily brought Cord up to date on Jack's life, but Susan noticed that Cord didn't divulge any information about himself. His past was a closed book; she realized that she didn't know anything about what he'd done or where he'd been since he'd left Mississippi, not even where he'd been immediately before returning.

She hated to see the meal end, but all too soon the table

had been cleared and the kitchen cleaned, the last cup of coffee drunk. She walked with him to the door, her heart beating slowly, heavily. It was either bright sunlight or the darkest shadows, she realized painfully; there was no middle ground in loving him. She stopped in the middle of the foyer, her heart in her eyes as she looked at him.

Chapter 6

HIS EYES WERE HOODED AND UNREADABLE AS HE watched her, but his hand smoothed over her shoulder as if he couldn't prevent himself from touching her, his fingers heating the cool silk of her skin before sliding upward over her throat to cup her chin and lift her face. He hadn't said a word, but he didn't need to; the burning possession of his lips told her all she needed to know. With a silent gasp, she melted against him, her hands going up to lie along his jawline, where the silkiness of his beard tickled her palms.

He lifted his mouth and simply held her close for a moment. Susan kept her hands on his face, stroking her fingers lightly over his beard, drowning in the enjoyment of being cuddled by him. His strong, warm throat beckoned, and she stood on tiptoe to press a light kiss onto the skin above his collar. "What do you look like without a beard?" she asked dreamily, for no other reason than that her hands were on his beard and it was the first sentence that popped out.

He chuckled, a husky, male sound that rippled over her like warm water. "Like myself, I suppose. Why? Are you curious?"

"M'mmmm," she said, letting him interpret the sound as he chose. "How long have you worn a beard?"

"Just for this past winter, though I've had a moustache for several years. I was stranded for a week or so without any way of shaving, short of scraping my face with a dull knife, and I realized just how much time I wasted in scraping hair off my face when it promptly grew back, so I kept the beard."

She trailed one fingertip over his bearded chin. "Do you have a cleft chin? Or a dimple?"

Suddenly he laughed, pulling away from her. "Well, see for yourself," he teased, catching her hand and pulling her after him as he started up the stairs with a swift, leaping stride. "Where's your bathroom?"

Susan laughed too, and tried to stop him. "What're you doing? You're going too fast! I'll fall!"

He turned around and scooped her up in his arms, and kissed her so hard that her lips stung. Holding her securely against his chest, he opened doors until he found her bedroom, then walked into it and let her slide to the floor. He looked around at the completely feminine room, the lace curtains, the cream satin comforter on her bed, the delicately flowered wallpaper. His face changed, became curious, surprised. "Vance didn't sleep in here," he said. "This is a woman's room."

Susan swallowed, a little surprised at his perception. "This was our room," she admitted. "But I changed everything when he died. I couldn't sleep in here with everything the way it had been when he was alive, so I bought new furniture and had the room redone completely. Not even the carpet is the same."

"A different bed?" he asked, watching her narrowly.

Susan shivered. "Yes," she whispered. "Everything. New mattress, new sheets . . . everything."

"Good." The single word was a low growl of satisfaction, and his gaze was so heated that she rubbed her hands up her bare arms, feeling a little singed. He looked around and indicated a door, releasing her from his visual force field. "Is that the bathroom?"

"Yes, but why—"

"Because," he answered maddeningly, catching her hand and pulling her with him again, into the bathroom. He began unbuttoning his shirt, opening it down to his waist, then pulling the fabric free of his pants and finishing the job. He shrugged out of the shirt and handed it to her; she took it automatically, folding it over her arm.

"You aren't going to do that," she said in disbelief, having realized what he intended.

"Why not? Do you have a fresh blade for your razor? And I'll need a pair of scissors to start off."

"There's a small pair in the drawer there," she said, pointing. "Cord, wait. I wasn't hinting for you to shave off your beard."

"It'll grow back, if you don't like my naked face," he drawled, opening the drawer and taking out the scissors. "Why don't you just sit down and enjoy the show?"

Because there was nothing else to do, she closed the lid on the toilet and sat down, her eyes wide with fascination as she watched him snip the beard as short as he could get it with the scissors. He asked again for her razor, and she indicated the left-hand side of the built-in medicine cabinet. He extracted the razor, new blades, and shaving gel from the cabinet, then deftly changed blades.

He wet his face with warm water and worked the gel into a lather, covering his face with enough foamy white soap to make him look like a wicked Santa Claus. Susan almost winced when the razor sliced into his beard and left a smooth streak of skin in its path. Half of her was trembling with anticipation at seeing his face, but the other half of her hated to see the beard go; it had been so soft and silky, and made her skin tingle wherever it touched.

He went through the contortions that men put themselves through when shaving, arching his neck, tilting his head, and Susan sat spellbound. It was the first time she'd seen him without his shirt, and her eyes drifted down over his muscled torso. She'd known he was strong, but now she saw the layered muscles that covered him, and her mouth went dry. His broad shoulders gleamed under the light, the skin as taut and supple as a young boy's. With every movement he made the muscles in his back bunched and rippled, then relaxed, flexing in an endless ballet that riveted her attention. His spine ran in a deep hollow down the center of his back, inviting inquisitive fingers to stroke and probe.

Susan noticed that the rhythm of her breathing had been broken, and she wrenched her gaze away from his back. Determinedly she again looked in the mirror at the reflection of his face, and the complete concentration she saw there started an ache deep inside her. That frown was so completely male, and it had been so long since she'd seen it. Vance had frowned just like that. For five years her life had lacked something because she hadn't been able to sit in the bathroom and watch her man shave; a simple pleasure, but one of the lasting ones. Cord was giving her that pleasure again, as he had given her his presence at breakfast, and somehow the simple act of watching him shave was seducing her more completely than his heated kisses could have done.

Slowly her gaze dipped, and she inspected his mirrored image. His chest was covered by a tangle of black curls that looked as incredibly soft as his beard had been; she clenched her hands to prevent them from reaching out to touch him and verify the texture. His nipples were flat circles, small and dark, with tiny points in the center of them, and she wanted to put her mouth to them. The curve of his rib cage was laced by bands of muscle, and the solid wall of his abdomen rippled with power. The tiny ringlets of hair on his chest became a straight and silky line that ran down the middle of his stomach and disappeared into the waistband of his pants. He raised his arms and his torso stretched, giving her a glimpse of his taut, shallow navel, and the thin scar that began on the right side of it, angling down out of sight.

Susan almost strangled, and this time she couldn't stop her hands; they flew out, touching the scar, tracing it lightly. Now her fevered gaze roamed over him again, anxiously, and she found other marks of other battles. A small, silvered, puckered scar on his right shoulder had to be from a gunshot wound, and her spine prickled with fear for him. Another line ran from under his left breast, around under his arm, and ended below his left shoulderblade. Obviously he hadn't always ducked in time.

Suddenly she noticed that he was very still under her hands, and she let them fall to her side, swiftly looking away from him. She was aware of his slow movements as he splashed the remnants of lather from his face and patted it dry, but she couldn't look directly at him.

"There's nothing wrong with touching me," he growled harshly, dropping his words into the sudden canyon of silence. "Why did you stop?"

She swallowed. "I was afraid you'd think I was prying. My God!" she burst out rawly. "What happened to you? All those scars . . ."

He gave a short, mirthless laugh. "Just a lot of hard living," he answered obliquely. "I was tossed off the lap of luxury a long time ago."

She glanced up at the harshness of his tone, and for the first time since he'd finished shaving, she saw his face. Her mouth went dry again.

She'd never before seen anyone who looked as hard and cool as he did. He'd left his moustache, thank God; she couldn't imagine his face without it. His jaw was lean and clearly cut, his chin square and impossibly stubborn. His lower lip had taken on a fullness that she hadn't noticed before, a new sensuality. He lacked the classic perfection of handsomeness, but he had the face of a warrior, a man who was willing to fight for what he wanted, a man who laughed at danger. The hard recklessness of him was more apparent now, as if he'd torn aside a veil that had hidden him from view. She'd thought that his beard had made him look like more of a desperado than he really was; now she realized that the reverse had been true. The beard had disguised the ruthlessness of his face.

He was looking down at her with mockery in his eyes, as if he had known that the beard had been a camouflage. The years and the mileage were etched on that hard, slightly battered countenance, but she wasn't repelled by it; she was drawn, like an animal from the depths of a cold night to crouch by the warmth of a fire. In a fleeting moment of despair, knowing herself lost, she realized that the more attractive the lure, the higher the risk, and she would be risking her entire way of life if she allied herself with him. She was by nature cautious and reserved, yet as she stood looking at him in silence, she accepted that risk; for her heart, she would disregard the past and the future, and count the reward well worth the danger. With an inarticulate murmur, she lifted her arms to him.

An odd look of strain tightened his feature; then with a harsh, wordless sound, he picked her up and carried her into the bedroom, lying down on the bed with her still in his arms, twisting until he was half on top of her. His left hand buried itself in her hair, holding her head still, and his mouth came down to imprint his possession on hers. She parted her lips willingly to the demanding thrust of his tongue, giving a tiny sigh of bliss as she curled herself against him, twining her arms around his neck and shoulders, pressing her breasts into the hard, warm plane of his chest. She kissed him with fire and delicacy, offering herself to him with gentle simplicity. He lifted his mouth a fraction of an inch from hers, his breath coming in fast, irregular gulps. "I think . . . I think I'm going to lose my head over you," he muttered. "Why couldn't you be what I'd expected?"

Before Susan could ask what he meant, before it even occurred to her to wonder at it, his mouth was on hers again, and his arms were tightening about her with a force that would have bruised her if she hadn't been boneless with need. Everything combined to overwhelm her senses. She was aware, with every pore of her body, of the warm fragrance of the new day, the slight breeze drifting in the open window, the sweet trilling of the birds as they darted about among the huge trees; then there was nothing, nothing but the touch of his hands and mouth.

He unzipped her dress, pulling it down to bare her breasts to him, and he took them hungrily, first with his knowing hands, then with the furnace of his mouth. She cried out as the strong suckling sent shock waves of primitive pleasure crashing along her nerves, and she arched into 'his hard frame.

The phone beside the bed began ringing, and he lifted his head, muttering a violent curse under his breath, then settled himself more fully on her, his muscular legs parting hers and making a cradle for him. Her nipples were buried in the curly hair of his chest, her hands clutching urgently at him; she wanted all the layers of clothing between them gone, but she hated to release him long enough to remove them. She twisted against him, wanting more, more . . .

"Susan! Telephone!"

Emily's voice wafted up the stairs, startling them as

much as if a bucket of cold water had been dashed over them. Susan drew a sobbing breath, unable to answer. No, no! Why now?

"Susan?" Emily called, raising her voice in question.

She bit her lip, then managed to call out, "Yes, I'll get it. Thanks, Emily." Her voice didn't even sound like her own, but Emily must have been satisfied.

Cord rolled off of her with a sigh. "Go ahead, answer it," he said gruffly. "She'll be up here checking on you if you don't." He lifted the receiver and handed it to her, stretching the cord across his chest, then relaxing against the pillows.

Susan wet her lips, and took a deep breath to steady herself. "Hello."

"Hello, dear," came Imogene's brisk voice. "I wanted to congratulate you on your quick thinking last night. I knew you wouldn't let us down."

Susan frowned in puzzlement, her thoughts still too fogged by desire for her to understand what Imogene was saying. How could she think when she was lying half on Cord's chest, his heady scent rising to her nostrils like an aphrodisiac. "I'm sorry, I don't understand. What do you mean?"

"Why, playing up to Cord," Imogene replied impatiently. "Remember, you have just as much to lose in this as we do. String him along and find out all you can. Last night was a brilliant move—"

Susan darted a quick, agonized look at Cord, and her blood congealed in her veins when she saw the iciness of his eyes and realized that he'd heard every word; how could he not, when she was practically on top of him? A cold, cruel smile curved his mouth as he gently took the telephone receiver from her nerveless fingers and cradled it on his shoulder. "You jumped the gun on the congratulations, Aunt Imogene," he purred with silken menace. "That was a tactical error; you should've let Susan call you when the coast was clear.''

With a deliberate movement he dropped the receiver back onto the hook, then turned back to her. The smile on his face was deadly, and she could do nothing but wait, her breath halted, her heart stopped.

''My God, you're lovely,'' he murmured, still smiling, his eyes dropping to her bare, creamy breasts. ''And so willing to give me anything I want, aren't you? No wonder you let me talk so much last night; did you think I'd spill my guts to you, tell you everything I'd planned?''

A fine trembling invaded her limbs. ''No,'' she whispered. ''You needed to talk; I was available.''

She was so close to him that she could see his pupils dilate, the inner blackness expanding until only a thin circle of blue remained. ''Are you available?'' he drawled, deliberately covering her breast with his hand. ''Are you as available for me as you are for Preston?''

She felt as if he'd kicked her, and she tried to jerk away, but he locked his other arm around her and held her to him. His fingers kneaded her soft flesh with a slow precision that frightened her, and tears stung her eyes. ''I'm not available for Preston! Except as a . . . a friend. I'm not a sexual release valve for anyone!'' She could feel her cheeks burning with mortification, and she tried to pull away again, an attempt that was useless against his effortless strength.

''Sure you're not,'' he crooned. ''That's why you're on this bed with me. You offered yourself to me, darling, for a little fun and games. But dear Aunt Imogene, bless her nosy soul, couldn't stay off the phone, and she blew it for you. Now what are you going to do?''

''It's not like that!'' she cried desperately, pleading with him to understand. ''Imogene wanted me to sleep with you so I could try to find out what you're planning to do, but I refused—''

He laughed, a low, harsh sound of disbelief. "It really looks like you refused," he taunted, stroking her breast. He adjusted her squirming body to his in a way that branded her with his male heat. "For once, she had an idea that I like. We shouldn't let a little phone call interrupt us—"

"No!" She wedged her arms between them and braced her hands on his chest, pushing against him in a useless effort to create more of a space between them. It took a tremendous effort to prevent herself from bursting into tears, but she refused to give in to that weakness and blinked her eyes fiercely.

"Why not? You'd enjoy being—"

"Used?" she broke in bitterly.

"Now, darling, I wasn't going to be crude. I was going to say that you'd enjoy being with a man again, because I don't count Preston as a man. What do you say? I promise that when I . . . *use* . . . you, I won't leave you unsatisfied."

"Stop it!" she almost shouted, horrified at what had happened, at how swiftly something that had been so *right* had deteriorated into something so ugly. "I've never had sex with Preston. Let go of me!"

He laughed and recaptured her as she almost wriggled free, his hand going to her buttocks and cupping them, pressing her into him. "Settle down," he advised, still laughing, though how he could laugh when she felt as if someone had torn her heart out was more than she could understand. "I'm not going to attack you. Though, my God, woman, if you don't stop squirming against me like that, I may change my mind!"

She stilled. After a long moment she said rawly, "Please, let me get up."

With a mocking lift of his eyebrows, he opened his arms and released her. She sat up away from him, fumbling with her dress, trying to straighten the fabric over her breasts. He got up from the bed and sauntered into the bathroom, returning with his shirt. He pulled it on and buttoned it, then unzipped his pants to tuck the shirttail in, standing nonchalantly before her. Susan sat in frozen horror, too miserable to do anything but stare numbly at him.

"Don't look so unhappy, darling," he advised in a mockery of tenderness. "I probably wouldn't have told you anything, anyway." He strolled over to where she sat on the bed and leaned down over her, his weight braced on his arms. Briefly, firmly, he kissed her, a little rough in his anger. When he straightened, a tiny fire was burning in his eyes. "Pity she couldn't have waited another half hour before she called," he said, touching her cheek with his finger. "See you around." With that nonchalant goodbye he was gone, and she sat in paralyzed agony, listening to his sure steps going down the stairs. Then there was the sound of the door, and a moment later the throaty roar of a powerful, well-tuned engine.

After a long time she managed to slide stiffly off the bed, but that was all she could force her body to do. She leaned against the wall, her eyes closed, while she tried to come to terms with what had happened. She almost hated Imogene for coming between her and Cord, even though it had been unintentional. No, if Imogene had known that Cord had been there, she wouldn't have done anything to rock the boat! She simply couldn't believe that Susan would balk at prostituting herself for the good of the Blackstones, namely Imogene herself and Preston. To her mind, if Susan had anything to do with Cord, it was based on ulterior motives.

It was particularly painful because, for a little while, he had seemed to be lowering his formidable barriers just a bit. Their kisses had been building a frail bridge of understanding between them, until Imogene's heavy touch had shattered it. For a few hours Susan had been on the verge of an ecstasy so deep and powerful, so wide in scope, that she had difficulty in believing the richness that had hovered just beyond her fingertips.

Black despair engulfed her, a depression so deep that only Vance's death compared to it. After Vance's burial, when she had been forced to admit to herself that there was no miracle that would restore him to her, for a time it had seemed that there was nothing worthwhile left in her life. If it had been possible, she would have died quietly in her sleep during that time, so bitter and helpless had she felt at the irrevocable chasm of death. Time had healed her, time and the gentle steel of her own nature, but she hadn't regained the utter delight in being alive, capable of experiencing pleasure again, until Cord had walked into her life and touched her with his hard fingers, bringing fires that had been banked for five years back into full blaze.

It was an hour before spirit began to return to her numbed brain. She had learned at Vance's death that even the most precious life could be extinguished, and she had also learned that death was final. But she was very much alive, and so was Cord. She couldn't let him just walk away from her like that! If you truly loved someone, then you had to be willing to fight for them, and she was willing to fight the entire world if need be. Thankfully, it wasn't necessary that she take on the world, but the one stubborn, dangerous man she had to face was bad enough. If it hadn't been so necessary to her life that she make him listen, she would never have been able to summon the courage. She could face down almost anyone, but Cord could intimidate the devil himself.

Without giving herself time to think, because if she paused, she'd stop altogether, she told Emily that she'd be gone for the rest of the day, then grabbed her purse and ran to the car. She broke the speed limit getting to the cabin, not daring to rehearse what she would say to him, but knowing that she had to make him listen.

She thundered across the old bridge over Jubilee Creek, and the car fishtailed when she slung it around the long, sweeping curve of the incline going up to the gentle rise where the cabin sat. A bright red Blazer with enormous tires was parked at the front steps, and she pulled up behind it, scattering rocks and dust. Before the wheels had stopped rolling, she had the door open and was out of the car, bounding up the steps in a very unladylike manner. She had pounded on the door twice with her fist when a piercing whistle reached her ears, and she spun around. Cord was standing down at the creek, about a hundred yards away. He lifted his arm, beckoning her to come to him, and she was in too much of a hurry to use the steps; she jumped off the end of the porch and headed down the slope at a fast walk.

He went back to work, his powerful arms swinging a slingblade with easy rhythm, sending showers of rioting greenery flying into the air as he sliced through a section of heavy overgrowth. Her pace slowed as she approached, and when she reached him she stood to one side, well out of the way of the slicing blade. He stopped after a moment, leaning on the handle and giving her an unreadable glance, a little smile pulling at his lips. "The honeysuckle is out of hand," he drawled, wiping his forearm across his sweaty face. "If we ever decide to conquer the world, all we have to do is ship out some cuttings of honeysuckle and kudzu, then wait a year. Everyone else would be so worn out from fighting the vines that we could just waltz in."

She smiled at the whimsy, but to Southern farmers, it wasn't that much of an exaggeration. Now that she was standing before him, she couldn't think of anything to say; for the moment, it was enough to simply be there, staring at him, drinking in the sight of his magnificent masculinity. He was glistening with sweat, his dark hair wet and stuck to his skull, and he'd twisted a white handkerchief into a band that he'd tied around his forehead to keep the sweat out of his eyes. His shirt had been discarded and was lying on the ground; his jeans were dirty. None of that mattered. He could have been wearing a tuxedo, and he wouldn't have looked any better to her.

When she didn't say anything, he tilted his head in question, a devilish gleam entering his eyes. "Did you come here for a reason?"

She swallowed, trying to conquer her voice. "Yes. I came to make you listen to me."

"I'm listening, honey, but you're not saying much."

She searched for the perfect words to use, the ones that would make him believe her, but with a sinking heart she knew that there weren't any. He was still watching her in amusement, letting her squirm, and suddenly it was unbearable. She blurted out, "When Imogene asked me to spy on you, I refused, and she's not used to anyone telling her no. Someone must have told her what happened last night, and she assumed that I'd changed my mind. I haven't."

He laughed aloud and shook his head in amazement. "So what were you doing on that bed with me? My ego isn't so big that I'll fall for the line that you just have the hots for me. I know your reputation, lady, and it's the straight and narrow all the way, as far as anyone knows. I have my doubts about Preston—"

"Shut up!" she cried, knotting her hands into fists. "I've told you and told you—"

"I know," he interrupted wearily. "You haven't slept with Preston."

"It's the truth!"

"He's in love with you."

Startled by his perception, she admitted, "Yes. But I didn't know until a few days ago. That doesn't change anything. I'm very fond of Preston, but I'm not in love with him; there's never been anything sexual between us."

"Okay, say there's nothing between you," he attacked sharply, changing positions. "That means there's been no one in your life, romantically speaking, since Vance died, which makes it just that much more unlikely for you to suddenly take up with me. There has to be a reason."

Susan turned pale. "There is. When I met you, I realized

that I'm not dead. I've mourned Vance for five years, but he's never coming back, and I'm very much alive. You make me *feel* things again. I'm not like you; I've never been brave or adventurous, or taken a gamble on anything, but when I'm with you I feel just a little braver, a little more free. I want to be with you for *me*, not for Imogene or Preston or any amount of money."

His eyes had darkened as he listened to her, and now he stared at her for a long, taut moment, taking in the tension of her slim figure, the almost desperate earnestness in her eyes, eyes of such a dark blue that they looked like the deep Pacific. Finally he untied the handkerchief from his forehead and began using the square of cloth to wipe the rivulets of sweat from his face and arms, then rubbing it across his chest. He was silent for so long that Susan could bear it no longer, and she grabbed his arm. "It's very simple," she said desperately. "All you have to do is not tell me *anything!* Since you're forewarned, how can I possibly find out anything? How can I possibly be using you?"

He sighed, shaking his head. "Susan," he finally said, his voice so gentle that she shivered at the sound of it, "you said it yourself: We're nothing alike. I've lived a hard life, and it hasn't always been on the right side of the law. You look as if you've been carried around all of your life on a satin pillow. If you think you want pretty words and pretty flowers and hand-holding in the moonlight, you'd better find some other man. I'm not satisfied with hand-holding."

She shivered again, and her lashes drooped to veil her eyes in a sultry, passion-laden manner. "I know," she whispered.

"Do you?" He moved closer to her, so close that the heady scent of his hot, sweaty body enveloped her, tantalizing her senses. "Do you really know what you're asking for?" His hands closed on her waist, his fingers biting into her soft flesh. "I'm not much on genteel gropings in the dark, on schedule every Saturday night. I'm a lot rawer than that, and a lot hungrier. I want to take your clothes off and taste you all over," he rasped, hauling her close to him so that their bodies touched. A fire alarm of pleasure began clanging inside her, and she let herself flow up against him like a tide rushing to shore. "I want to take your nipples in my mouth and suck them until they're hard and aching for more. I want to feel your legs wrapped around my back, and I want to go so deeply into you that I can't tell where I stop and you begin. That's what I want right now, and what I've wanted every time I've seen you. And if that's not what you want, too, you'd better run, because you're about to get it."

Susan sighed in delirium. Her body was alive, aching, throbbing, wanting to do those things he'd described, and more. She wanted to give her heart to him, and with it, the soft, burning ardor of her body. She couldn't give him the words; she sensed that he didn't want love, that he'd feel burdened if she admitted that she loved him, so she would bite the words back and instead content herself with the offering of her body.

"I'm not running," she said into the damp refuge of his neck.

"Maybe you should," he said roughly, releasing her. "But it's too late for that. You had your chance, honey. My sense of honor doesn't go that deep!" He leaned down and lifted her into his arms, his brawny back and shoulders taking her slight weight easily. He began walking up the slope with a determined stride, and when Susan dared to slant a quick look up at his face, she quivered at the fierceness of his expression. The thought of the risk she was about to take in giving herself to him made her feel faint with apprehension, and she turned her face into his warm shoulder. Only one man had made love to her in her life, and that with love, with deep tenderness. Cord didn't trust her; he would take her in lust but not in love, and she didn't know if she was strong enough to handle that. On the other hand, she knew beyond doubt that she had to try to reach him, that she had to try to show him with the gentle offering of herself that she wasn't a treacherous or mercenary person. She had to show him what love was, because he'd never known it.

Her sheltered life had not prepared her for this, but neither had it prepared her for the reality of her husband dying in her arms, with his blood soaking through her clothing. Since Vance's death, she had held a small part of herself sealed off from the world, protected against hurt, allowing even those closest to her only the shallowest portion of her love. The seal had remained intact until she'd met Cord. He had awakened her to a deeper knowledge of herself, an awareness that she wasn't such a creature of convention as she'd always thought. She wasn't as wild as Cord, as free, nor had she ever been a gambler, but she was willing to take a chance that she could make him care for her. She *had* to take that chance. There were many things she didn't know about him, but that made no difference to the essence of her, the combined power of heart and soul and body, which had recognized him on sight as the mate of her lifetime, the one man who could mean more to her than anyone else could even begin to imagine. She had loved Vance, loved him deeply, and yet that emotion now seemed as mild when compared to the way she felt about Cord as a light spring shower compared to the thunder and fury of a towering electrical storm. She would gladly follow this man anywhere on earth that he wanted to go, because there was no physical discomfort that could rival the hell she would endure if deprived of his presence.

His long legs ate up the distance as he moved up the slope, showing no sign that her weight in his arms was hampering him in the slightest. He leaped up the steps and shouldered the cabin door open, then turned sideways to enter with her. His boot heel collided with the door and sent it slamming back to the frame. He carried her straight through to the bedroom and set her on her feet, his narrowed eyes on her pale, strained face. A cool, cynical smile touched his face as he dropped to the bed and sprawled on its surface, dragging a pillow over to crumple it into a ball which he placed behind his dark head. He crossed his booted feet and let his gaze rake over her. "All right," he drawled. "Strip."

Susan put out a hand to steady herself as she swayed. The room was dipping crazily, and a sudden roaring in her ears made her think that she might not have heard him correctly. "What?" she asked soundlessly, then swallowed and tried it again. The second time, her voice was a weak croak.

In an insultingly casual manner, he eyed her breasts. "Strip. Take your clothes off. Since you're so all-fired anxious to try me out in the sack, I'm giving you the chance. You may have been planning on a quick flip of your skirt, but what I have in mind will take longer than that."

He didn't think she'd do it. She suddenly realized that as she stood there trying to regulate her breathing. He hadn't believed anything she'd said. He probably thought that all he had to do was push her a little and she'd run crying back to Preston. What had made him so wary that he couldn't trust anyone?

Slowly, with trembling fingers, she reached behind herself and tried to grasp the zipper of her dress. She found the tiny tab, but couldn't manage to hold it. After it slipped out of her jerky fingers for the third time, she took a deep breath and let her arms drop, turning her back to him and sitting down on the edge of the bed beside him. "I can't manage my zipper," she said thinly. "Would you do it for me, please?" For a long, silent moment, he didn't move, and she felt his eyes boring into her back. Then the mattress shifted, and he touched the zipper. Slowly, like thickened molasses, the zipper moved down, and her dress loosened. When he released the tab, she stood up before she lost her nerve and turned to face him again.

His face was expressionless, his black lashes dropping to

shield anything his eyes might have told her. An insidious quiver began in her legs and spread upward, turning her insides to jelly. She stepped out of her sandals and caught the straps of her sundress, dropping them off her shoulders and pulling her arms out of them. The cloth dropped to her waist, baring her breasts. She hadn't worn a bra with her little-nothing dress, and a fragrant spring breeze wafted in the open window, touching the pale brown of her small nipples and puckering them into soft, succulent buds. Though Cord hadn't moved, she sensed the tension that pervaded every muscle of his body. Still his eyes were veiled, but she felt them on her, visually touching the creamy slopes that she offered to him. Her breasts were high and firm, deliciously rounded, and she was suddenly, fiercely glad that her woman's body could entice him.

Deep inside her, welling up from the bottomless reservoir of her love, was the inborn need to belong to him. She was woman, and he was man. She was *his* woman, in any way he wanted her, if only he'd take her. There was nothing else as important to her as the time she had with him; that time might be fleeting, and she would have to carefully garner every precious second of it. Circumstances might separate them, or he might leave without notice, his restless spirit leading him on. He'd spent too many years wandering the dark corners of the earth to ever completely settle in one place. For whatever time she had with him, she would take each day as it came, enjoy it totally, as if that were all there was, all there would ever be. She couldn't set a limit on how much of herself she would give to him. She had to give him everything, every ounce of her love.

With precise, graceful movements she pushed the dress down over her hips and dropped it into a billowy puddle around her feet. She stepped out of it, her body completely bare to him now except for her lacy panties, letting him see her sleek, shapely legs, her flat tummy and rounded hips, the graceful curve of her waist. She stood motionless before him, letting him look all he wanted, sensing the coiling need that was beginning to throb through his body.

If time still existed, she wasn't aware of it. It could have been seconds or minutes that she stood there, waiting, hearing nothing but the cheerful songs of the birds in the trees outside the window, the drone of insects. When he didn't move, she slid her fingers inside the waistband of her panties and began sliding them down over her hips, baring the final mystery of her womanhood. Her heart was slamming so wildly in her chest that her ribs hurt. What if he didn't do anything? What if he just lay there and looked, then got up and walked out? She thought she'd die on the spot if that happened. Taking a deep, wavering breath, she pushed the panties down her thighs and dropped them to the floor.

Perhaps he hadn't meant for her to realize his reaction, but she heard the audible intake of his breath, and that gave her the courage to continue standing there before him, vulnerable in a way only another woman could understand. By offering herself this way she was exhibiting a deep, enormous trust in him as a human being, taking it on faith that even though he possessed the strength to hurt her badly, if he were cruel or careless, he would instead treat her tender flesh and heart with the care they deserved. She stood motionless in the bright morning sun, yet she was a statue with warm, supple skin, and the coursing warmth of her life's blood gave her a faint, rosy glow. Her eyes were deep pools of midnight blue, beckoning him, enticing him to enter the world of sensuality and love that was waiting for him.

He was still stretched out on the bed, but every muscle in his body was taut, the tight fabric of his jeans doing more to outline his arousal than conceal it. Burning color had flared on his high, chiseled cheekbones, and his tongue edged along his lower lip in an unconscious move, as if he were already tasting her sweetness. Finally he began to move, sitting up in slow motion, his eyes never leaving her body, glittering hotly as he explored every inch of her with visual hunger. He reached down to take off his boots and socks, tossing them to the side, where the boots landed with muffled thuds. Then he stood, unfolding his tall frame to tower over her. All moisture left her mouth. Without her shoes, she was suddenly aware of the differences in their sizes, their strength, the very shape and texture of their bodies. He was male, powerful, and aggressive. She was completely feminine, soft and satiny, yet capable of taking all of his aggression and power and turning it into an expression of love. She hoped, oh, how she hoped!

His lean hands were pulling at his belt buckle, releasing it and stripping the belt free of his pants with one firm tug. When he moved to unsnap his jeans, Susan came to life and reached out to cover his hands with hers. "Let me," she whispered. His arms fell to his sides, and he sucked in another deep, shuddering breath.

Slowly, drawing the time and the moment out, she released the snap and slid down the zipper, her tender hands moving inside the opened garment to trace his hipbones, explore the tight little cavity of his navel, then move around to palm the hard, taut roundness of his buttocks. Gently she ran her hands down his thighs, taking the jeans with her, delighted as she realized that he wore no underwear. When the jeans were below his knees, he moved suddenly, as if his patience had abruptly worn out. He stepped out of the entangling denim and kicked it away, seizing her simultaneously and falling back on the bed with her in his arms, cradling her against his chest.

Like a willing sacrifice on his sensual altar, she entwined her arms around his muscled neck and lifted her lips to his, her body writhing against him in a slow, delicate dance. His mouth closed over hers with hard, fierce possession, and he pulled her more fully onto him, mingling his legs with hers as he mingled his breath with hers, his tongue with hers, his taste with hers. The tartness of desire lay like a heady wine on his lips, and she sipped it eagerly. She was alive, soaring, her entire existence focused on him and exulting in the intensity of her being. She trembled in his arms, her entire body quaking.

He released her mouth to slide his lips like a burning brand along the curve of her jaw, then down the soft column of her neck. As if he'd discovered a rare treasure, he pressed his face into the tender hollow of her shoulder. His tongue darted out and tasted her, and Susan shivered in blind delight, her fingers lacing into his hair and pressing him to her.

"My God," he muttered thickly, nipping at her flesh with his sharp white teeth, leaving little stinging points of sensation that stopped short of pain and instead raised her internal temperature by several degrees. "You make me crazy. Sometimes I think I'd kill to get to you, even knowing that Preston has had you."

For a moment pain so intense that it blinded her tore at her insides, and she inhaled sharply. Then she managed to push it away, accepting that she would have to prove to him that he could trust her, in all things. She moved against him in a way that wrenched a groan from his lips. With a lithe, powerful twist of his body, he rolled and placed himself above her, his muscled legs controlling hers.

With one shaking finger, he outlined the small circles of her nipples, watching as the velvet flesh puckered into succulent buds. "Sweet Susan," he breathed, and lowered his head to offer homage with his mouth. Like fire, his lips burned over the soft mounds of her breasts, and he teased the quivering slopes with his devilish tongue. Susan moaned, a sound unnoticed except perhaps by the deeper, primal instincts of the man who bent over her. Her insides were molten, her body liquid with the flow of desires that urged her relentlessly onward. He suckled strongly at her breasts, and the moans became whimpers, little sounds of pleading.

But he lingered over her, as if determined to enjoy everything about her. With hands and mouth he explored her, discovering the different textures and tastes of her body, searching out her most sensitive places with probing fingers and a curious tongue. She writhed under his touch, her hips undulating as she arched higher and higher toward the sun, her skin breathing the perfume of passion. She cried out in hoarse, mindless reaction when his hand moved with sure, heartstopping intimacy to discover the degree of her readiness, and he sucked in a deep breath. "Now," he said with fierce intent, his hand moving her thighs apart, opening her legs to him. Susan obeyed the demanding touch instantly, unable even to think of not doing so, opening herself to him like a vulnerable flower, chaining him with her trust more surely than he could chain her with his strength.

He moved over her, his eyes feverish with desire, his strong body shaking as he covered her softness with the hard power of his own frame. He slid his hands under her, cradling the satin curves of her buttocks in his palms and lifting her up to his thrust. Susan whimpered softly, wanting him so much that she was aching with it, and she arched invitingly. He took her with a powerful surge that drove him deeply into her, sheathing himself completely in the searing velvet of her flesh. The whimpers in Susan's throat caught as a shock wave thundered through her body, her chaste body that hadn't known a man's passion since Vance's death. A reflexive cry of pain slipped from her lips, and her fingers dug into his biceps, feeling them bulge with the strain as he reached desperately for control.

He hung over her, staring down at her with astonishment freezing his expression. "My God," he muttered hoarsely.

Her lips were parted, her breath moving swiftly in and

out between them, as her body struggled to accept him, adjust to him. "Cord?" she gasped, asking for reassurance, a little frightened with an instinctive, feminine fear.

He held himself very still. "Do you want me to stop?" he asked. "I don't want to hurt you."

"No, no! Don't stop! Please, don't stop." The words turned into a moan as they trailed out of her mouth. She felt as if she would die if he left her now, as if a vital part of her would be torn away. But he didn't pull away; he lay motionless atop her until the tension had eased out of her body and he felt the inner relaxation, until she began to move under him with little instinctive undulations of her hips. She clung to him, her arms around his neck, her legs locked around his waist when at last he began to answer her movements with his own. He was slow and gentle, taking incredible care of her, making certain that she was with him every step of the way as he pushed his body toward satisfaction. His hands and mouth buried her conscious thought under a flurry of hot caresses that intensified the fire in her loins, pushing her out of control, past any semblance of serenity or decorum. In his arms she wasn't the quiet, demure Susan Blackstone; she was a wild thing, hot and demanding, concerned only with the riptides of pleasure that were sucking her out to sea. She clutched at him with damp, desperate hands, and her heels dug into his back, his buttocks, the backs of his thighs. He was no longer gentle, but driven by the same demons that drove her, pounding into her with a wild power that had only one goal.

"I can't get enough of you," he gritted, his teeth clenched. It was a cry that erupted without conscious thought, and he heard it but scarcely realized that he'd said it. But it was true; he couldn't get enough of her. He couldn't get deeply enough into her to satisfy the burning need that was torturing him; he wanted to blend his flesh with hers until the lines of separateness faded and he absorbed her into himself. He wanted to bury himself so deeply within her that she could never get him out, that her body, the very cells of her flesh, would always have the imprint of his possession.

While he was branding her with his touch, Susan branded him with hers. She'd never realized how incomplete she felt until this moment when she knew the shattering satisfaction of being whole. She tried with her hands, her mouth, the undulant caress of her body, to show him how much she loved him, giving him everything she had to give, declaring her love with every movement, mingling herself with him in an act of love that transcended the physical.

There, on a sun-washed bed, she gave her heart to an outlaw and found a heaven that she hadn't known existed.

In the silent aftermath of passion they lay together with their bodies slowly cooling, their pulses gradually resuming a normal rate. Time drifted past, and still they lay together, reluctant to move and break the spell, reluctant to face the moment when their flesh would no longer be joined. Her fingers threaded through the tousled softness of his dark hair, stroking gently, and he settled his full weight on her with an almost soundless sigh of contentment. Susan stared at the ceiling, so happy that she felt she might fly into a million little pieces of ecstasy. Her lips trembled abruptly, and the image of the rough, timbered ceiling blurred. She bit her lip to stifle the sob that rose in her throat and demanded voicing, but she couldn't prevent the identical tracks of moisture that ran out of the corners of her eyes and disappeared into the hair at her temples. He was relaxing into sleep and she tried to keep from disturbing him; it was silly to cry because the most wonderful thing in her life had just happened to her!

But he was a man who had stayed alive by paying attention to his senses and gut instincts, and perhaps he felt the fine degree of tension in her body. His head lifted abruptly, and he surveyed her brimming eyes with sharp attention. He levered himself up on one elbow and lifted his hand to wipe at the tears with his thumb, the callused pad rasping slightly across the sensitive skin of her temples. He was frowning, the dark, level brows lowered over narrowed eyes that searched her delicate features so intently that she felt he could see inside her mind.

"Is it because I hurt you?" he rumbled.

Quickly she shook her head and tried to give him a smile, but the stretching of her lips wobbled out of control and vanished. "No. You didn't really hurt me. It was only at first . . . I wasn't expecting . . ." She couldn't get the words out, and she swallowed, forcing her will on her voice. "It was just so . . . so special." Another tear escaped her eye.

He caught that one with his lips, pressing an open-mouthed kiss to her temple and darting his tongue out to cleanse the salty liquid from her skin. "Susan," he breathed almost inaudibly, saying her name as if he could taste it, as if he savored the sound of it. "I want you again."

Golden sunlight washed the room with brightness, allowing no shadows to hide their passion, and no shadows at all on her heart. Her lips trembled again, and she reached for him, drawing him into the tenderness of her embrace. "Yes," she said simply, because she couldn't deny her heart.

Chapter 7

THE RE WERE ISOLATED MOMENTS, DURING THE HOURS that followed, when she was able to think, but for the most part she was overtaken by the unstoppable tidal wave of desire. He knew just how to touch her, how long to linger, how to bring her time and again to the heart-stopping peak of pleasure. His hard hands learned every inch of her as he taught her to accommodate his desires, and she gave herself to him without reserve. She was incapable of holding any part of her heart back, all thoughts of protection left behind in the dust of the past. She had to love him with all the strength and devotion she could, because she could give no less. He'd known too much coldness, too much pain, and she sought to heal him with the soft, searing worship of her body. He was wild, hungry, sometimes almost violent, but with her love she absorbed the bitterness from him, soothing away the loneliness of his isolation. A combination of many things had made him a loner, a man without hearth or home, who lived on the razor's edge of danger and stayed alive by his wits and his finely honed body. Without words she accepted his passion and gentled it with her unquestioning trust. She tried to show him that he was safe with her, that he had no need for the wall that he'd built to keep himself apart from the rest of the world.

The sun was past its zenith and sliding down to the horizon when he relaxed abruptly and fell asleep, as if a light had been clicked off. Susan lay beside him and almost cried again, this time in thankfulness. He *did* trust her, at least a little, or he wouldn't have been able to sleep in her presence. She somehow had a mental image of him taking his pleasure with innumerable women, faceless and nameless; then, when they slept sated in his arms, he would slip away from them to find his solitary bed. She watched him as he slept, his powerful body sprawled across the bed, his mouth softened under the black silk of his moustache. He had long, curling lashes, like a child's, and she smiled as she tried to imagine him as a toddler, with his cheeks still showing the chubby innocence of a baby.

But the innocent child had grown into a hard, wary man whose body was laced with scars, evidence of the battles he'd fought just to stay alive. He'd told her about Judith, but other than that he'd kept his past locked away in the depths of his mind. Other men would have had tales to relate of their adventures, or at least mentioned the different cultures and lands they'd seen, but not Cord. He was a silent warrior, not given to rehashing past battles, and when he was wounded, he crawled away to lick his wounds alone.

The thought of him being hurt made her heart clench painfully. She couldn't bear it if he were ever hurt again; just knowing that he had already borne wounds was almost beyond bearing. She leaned forward in blind desperation and touched her mouth lightly, tremblingly, to the round, silvered scar on his right shoulder. His skin twitched under her touch, but he didn't awaken, and she drifted to the long, thin line that ran down under his left arm, trailing her lips along the length of the scar, with aching tenderness trying to draw from him even the memory of those wounds. She found every scar on his body, licking and kissing them as she crouched protectively over him, guarding him with her slender, delicate woman's body, healing him. She felt him quiver under her mouth and knew that he was awake, but still she roamed over his body, her gentle hands caressing him. He began to shake, his body taut and ready.

"You'd better stop," he warned hoarsely. She didn't stop, instead turning her loving attention to a scar that furrowed down the inside of his thigh, then moving on to a newer, still-angry scar that snaked down his abdomen. He groaned aloud, his hands clenching on the sheet. She lingered, more intent now on the tension that she could feel building in him, intensifying to a crescendo, wanting to make him writhe with need as he had done to her.

He endured her loving torment until he was a taut arch on the bed, then his control broke and he reached for her, a primal growl rumbling in his throat as he swept her over him, thrusting up to bury himself in the sweet comfort of her body. His movements were swift and impatient, his hands grasping her hips so tightly that tiny smudged spots would mark the placement of his fingertips for a week. He held her still for his sensual assault, rotating his hips in a manner that drove her to a fast, hard culmination, then followed her while she was still submerged in the powerful waves of satisfaction.

Afterward he cuddled her against his side, and she curled into his hard, strong body with a sigh that reflected her bone-deep exhaustion. His hand stroked over her hair, smoothing it away from her damp face. "I'm sorry I hurt you, that first time," he murmured, his thoughts turning lazily to the morning, remembering the shock he'd had at how *virginal* she'd felt. "But I'm glad as hell that Preston hasn't had you."

So he'd realized what her difficulty in accepting him had signified. She wished that he had trusted her enough to take

her word in the matter, but he'd learned the hard way not to
trust anyone, and it would take time for her to teach him
that he didn't always have to guard his back. She ran her
hand through the dark curls on his chest in an absent
manner. "Since Vance—" She stopped, then continued so
softly that he had to strain to hear her. "You're the only
one."

She didn't look up, so she missed the expression of
almost savage satisfaction that crossed his hard face. She
knew only the momentary tightening of his arms before his
embrace relaxed and he shifted his weight, coming up on
one elbow to lean over her. His hand settled proprietarily on
her soft stomach, a little gesture that said a lot. "I don't
want you going anywhere else with him," he informed her
in a voice so darkly menacing that she looked up at him in
quick surprise.

She hesitated, wondering if she dared presume that this
day of naked passion had established any sort of stable
relationship between them. Very steadily she asked, "Are
you offering your services as an escort if I need one?"

A guarded look came over his face, and he stroked his
jaw in a restless manner, as if missing his beard. "If I'm
available," he hedged.

Susan slowly extricated herself from his arms and sat up,
feeling a little chilled by his answer. "And when will you
be unavailable?" she queried. "When you're with
Cheryl?"

Surprise pulled his brows together, but she couldn't tell if
it was the thought itself that surprised him, or that she'd
thought she had a right to ask the question at all. Then his
face cleared, and amusement began to sparkle in his pale
eyes. Very deliberately he let his gaze wander over her,
noting the tumbled dark hair, the soft flush that his
lovemaking had left on her creamy skin. Her lips were
swollen and passionate-looking, and he remembered the
way they'd drifted over his body. Her breasts, high and

round, fuller than he'd expected, also bore a rosy glow from his caresses and ardent suckling, and as he stared at them he noticed that her pert little nipples were hardening, reaching out as if for another kiss. Swiftly he glanced at her face, and his amusement deepened when he saw the way she was blushing. How could she still blush? For hours she'd lain naked in his arms, totally unselfconscious, allowing him the complete freedom of her body, yet now it took only a slow, enjoyable visual tour of her nakedness to have her blushing like a virgin.

Then he had still another surprise as he felt the lower hardening of his body in response to her. How could he even think about sex again right now? Five minutes before, he'd thought that the day had been fantastic, the most sexually satisfying day of his life, but that he probably wouldn't be able to respond again for a week. Now his body was proving him a liar. He wanted her, again and again. The sensual pleasure he felt with her was staggering, but no sooner had his pulse calmed than he began to feel the nagging need to possess more of her. From the moment he'd seen her, he'd wanted to lie on her tight and deep, immerse himself in her tenderness. He'd never been jealous of a woman in his life, until he'd met Susan. It knocked him off balance, the fury that filled him whenever he thought of her dancing with Preston, kissing Preston, letting him put his arms around her. He'd wanted to hurt her because it drove him crazy to think of Preston making love to her. Now he knew that she'd been chaste, yet still there was the possibility that her loyalty was to Preston. Women were hard to read, and a treacherous one was deadly. If he were smarter, he'd keep this one at a distance, at least until everything was settled and he wouldn't have to watch every word he said to her, but he couldn't force himself to say the words that would send her away, just as he hadn't been able to resist her rather innocent striptease that morning.

Susan watched him, waiting for his answer, but his eyes

had gone opaque and his face was a blank wall, his thoughts hiding behind it. She was aware that he was becoming aroused by looking at her body, so why should he suddenly lock himself away? Was it because he didn't think she had any right to question him about his relationships with other women? Well, if he thought she'd sit quietly home while he danced the night away with Cheryl Warren, he'd just have to think again! She balled her fist and thumped him on the chest.

"Answer me," she demanded, her blue eyes darkening with fire. "Will you be out with Cheryl? Or any other woman, for that matter?"

He jack-knifed to a sitting position and swung his long legs off the bed. "No," he said shortly, getting to his feet and leaning down to scoop his jeans from the floor. "I won't be with any other woman."

Did he resent having to give her that reassurance? Suddenly she felt embarrassed at her nakedness, and she snatched up a corner of the tumbled sheet to hold it over her breasts. Until then she had felt protected by the closeness she'd shared with him, but now he was suddenly a stranger again, and her bareness seemed much more vulnerable.

He gave the sheet a derisive glance. "It's a little late to try to protect your modesty."

Susan bit her lip, wondering if it would be better simply to get up, get dressed, and leave, or if she should try to talk him out of his sudden ill-temper. Had she gotten too close to him today? Was he reacting by trying to push her away with hostility? Looking at him worriedly, she thought that he looked uncomfortable, the way a man looks when a woman is making a nuisance of herself and he doesn't know how to get rid of her. She paled at the idea.

"I'm sorry," she heard herself say in swift apology, and she scrambled off the bed, abandoning the flimsy barrier of the sheet in favor of dressing as quickly as she could. Without looking at him, she grabbed up her panties and stepped into them. "I didn't mean to push you. I realize that having sex doesn't mean anything—"

"Whoa, lady!" Scowling, he dropped his jeans to the floor and grabbed her arm, pulling her upright as she bent to retrieve her dress, then drawing her into the circle of his arms. Her soft breasts flattened against his chest, and she quivered with enjoyment, her thoughts instantly distracted. How could she want him again? Her legs were distinctly wobbly after the day's activities anyway, and she was already feeling achy in various places, but she knew that if he wanted to tumble her back on the bed again, she would tumble gladly and worry about her aches tomorrow.

He frowned down at her. "Don't try feeding me that free-and-easy hogwash, because that isn't you, and I know it. I'm just feeling uneasy. Things are getting complicated all of a sudden." He stopped without explaining any further and cupped her face in his warm fingers. "Are you sorry it happened?"

She put her hand over his, rubbing her cheek against his palm. "No, I'm not sorry. How could I be? I . . . I wanted it, too." She'd started to say, "I love you," but at the last moment she'd choked the words back and substituted others that were true, but lacked the depth of what she felt. He didn't want the words, didn't want to be burdened with her emotions, and she knew it. As long as she didn't say the words aloud, he'd be able to ignore the true depth of her feeling, even though he had to know how she felt after these past hours spent in his arms, when she had given herself to him completely in a way that only a woman in love could give. He had to know, yet until the words were spoken, the knowledge didn't exist.

"I don't want you to get hurt," he muttered.

She leaned against him, wrapping her arms around him. He was warning her, letting her know that she shouldn't expect anything permanent from him. Pierced by a stiletto pain at the thought of one day watching his back as he

walked away, she was also grateful for his honesty. He
wasn't going to hit her with a blow from behind. And
maybe, just maybe, she could change his mind. He wasn't
used to being loved, and it was obvious that, even unwill-
ingly, he felt more for her than he was comfortable with.
She had a chance, and she would risk everything on that.

"Everyone gets hurt," she murmured against his warm
skin. "I'm not going to worry about what might or might
not happen some day in the future. I'll worry about
someday when it gets here."

Someday she might have to do without him, a little bit of
her dying every day of emotional starvation. But that was
someday, and she had today. Today she was in his arms,
and that was enough.

Later that night, facing Imogene across the width of the
kitchen, she tried desperately to hold on to the memory of
what she'd shared with him. Imogene's first words to her
had been of concern, but that had quickly faded when Susan
told her flatly that she wasn't going to play spy. "I told him
what your plan was," she confessed remotely. "Then I told
him to make certain he didn't tell me anything, so he
couldn't think I was with him just to whore for information."

Imogene whitened with fury. She drew herself up to her
full height, her anger making her seem six feet tall.
Imogene in a rage was a formidable sight, but Susan stood
her ground, her soft mouth set in a grim line, giving back
stare for stare.

"Susan, my God, are you a fool?" Imogene shouted.
"Haven't you realized yet that we stand to lose everything?"

"No, I haven't realized it! Cord hasn't made any move at
all, other than threatening to press charges if the ridges
aren't leased to him. I've agreed to that, and he's waiting

for the geological surveys. Stop painting him as the devil, Imogene!''

''You don't know him like I do!'' Suddenly Imogene realized that she was yelling, and she drew a deep breath, visibly forcing herself back under control. ''You're making a big mistake if you take him at face value. He's planning something; I *know* it. If I just had some inkling, so I'd know what to protect! You could have found out,'' she said bitterly. ''But instead you've let him turn your head and make you forget about where your loyalty lies.''

''I love him,'' Susan said quietly.

Imogene gaped at her, her eyes going wide. ''You . . . what? But what about Preston? I thought—''

''I *do* love Preston, as a friend, as Vance's brother.'' Susan groped for the words that could explain. ''But Cord . . . makes me feel alive again. He gives me something to live *for*.''

''I hope you're not banking too much on that! Susan, where's your common sense? He'll willingly take you to bed, but if you expect more from him than that, you're a fool. When he gets tired of you, he'll drop you without thinking twice about it, and you'll be left to face everyone you know. You'll always be Cord's leftovers.''

''If I'd gone along with your plan, I would have been, anyway,'' Susan pointed out. ''I won't stab him in the back, even if it means I lose everything I own, but I don't think he means to do anything else at all. I think all he wanted was the oil leases.''

''You're not the only one who's involved here! You're not the only one who's at risk. Preston and I also stand to lose everything. Doesn't that mean anything to you?''

''It means a great deal to me. I simply don't think he's a threat to you.''

Imogene shook her head, closing her eyes as if in disbelief at Susan's blindness. ''I can't believe you're so blind where he's concerned. You love him? Well, that's just fine! Love him if you have to, but don't be fool enough to trust him!''

Susan went white. "I have to trust him. I love him too much not to. I'd trust him with my life.''

"That's your decision, I suppose,'' Imogene snapped sarcastically. "But you're also trusting him with ours, and I don't like that at all. He must really be something in bed, to make you so willing to turn your back on the people who love you, knowing that all he'll ever offer you is sex.''

Susan felt as if she were staring at Imogene from a great distance, and a faint buzzing sound in her head warned her that she might faint. Dizzily she groped for one of the kitchen chairs and almost fell into it. They were tearing her apart! The awful thing was that she could see Imogene's side of it. Imogene fully expected Cord to take some sort of revenge against her, and she was frightened, as well she should be. Imogene was lashing out, reacting to a driving need to protect her own, and in her desperation she was willing to hurt people if they got in her way.

Imogene hesitated for a moment, staring at Susan's pale, damp face as she slumped in the chair; then her face twisted, and for a moment tears brimmed in her pale gray eyes. She blinked them back fiercely, because Imogene Blackstone never wept, and moved swiftly to the sink, dampening several paper towels and taking them to Susan. She slid her arm around the young woman and gently blotted her face with the cool, wet towels. "Susan, I'm sorry,'' she said, her voice steady at first, then wobbling dangerously. Imogene never apologized. "My God, he's got us fighting among ourselves.''

The damp coolness of the paper towels banished Susan's momentary dizziness, but it couldn't banish the ache in her heart. She wanted to run to Cord, to throw herself into his arms and let his kisses make her forget that there was an outside world. But despite the hours she'd spent in his bed, she wasn't entitled to dump all her worries on his shoulders, even though all her worries centered around him.

She clasped her hands on the table, entwining her fingers so tightly that they turned white. "I haven't turned my back on you or Preston," she said with hard-won steadiness. "I simply can't do something that's so completely against the things I believe in. Please don't try to make me take sides, because I can't. I love all of you; I can't stab any of you in the back."

Imogene touched Susan's bent head briefly, then let her hand drop. "I only hope Cord has the same reluctance to hurt you, but I can't believe it. I don't want you to be caught in the middle, but it seems that you'll have to be, if you won't take sides. He'll smash anything that gets in his way."

"That's a chance I'll have to take," Susan whispered. She'd already accepted the risk she had to face in loving Cord; what else could she do?

The next morning she went to church as usual, but she couldn't keep her mind on the sermon. Imogene, sitting beside her, was quiet and withdrawn, not entering into conversation before the services began, her gaze fixed on the minister, but Susan felt that Imogene wasn't really concentrating on the sermon either. Preston had shadows under his eyes, and to Susan's concerned eye he seemed to have lost a little weight, though she'd seen him only two days before. The strain was telling on him, but he managed to smile and greet everyone as normal. Susan wondered if Imogene had told him anything that had been said the night before, then decided that it wasn't likely. Imogene was too reserved to cry on anyone's shoulder, even her own son's.

Susan declined Imogene's invitation to Sunday dinner and went home to prepare a light meal of a crisp salad and potato soup. The spring day was too beautiful to sit inside, so she took her needlepoint out on the patio and worked on it for a couple of hours. She was outwardly serene, but she was aware of the coiling tension inside her as she sat and listened for the sound of a car coming up her long driveway. Would Cord drive over today? The thought made her breath catch. He would take her upstairs to her bedroom, to the bed where no man had ever slept, and on the cool, pristine sheets he would blend his body with hers.

She closed her eyes as desire built in her, making her lower body feel heavy and tight, and painfully empty. Surely he would come; surely he could hear her silent call for him.

Stately, towering thunderheads began to march in from the west, and the wind developed a brisk chill, but still she sat there until the first fat raindrops began to splatter on the patio tiles. Gathering her needlework, she ran for the sliding doors and slipped inside just as the weather broke and the rain became a downpour, filling her ears with a dull roar. A sharp crack of thunder made her jump, and she hastily pulled the curtains over the glass doors, then moved around and turned on lights to dispel the fast, early dusk.

It was after eight o'clock that night before she admitted that he wasn't going to come, so she locked up the house and readied herself for bed. The storm had passed, but the rain continued to fall, and she lay awake for hours listening to the hypnotic patter, wishing that he was in bed beside her, warm and virile. The big house was silent and empty around her, emptier even than it had been after Vance's death, and that was strange, because Vance had lived here, and she had memories of him in every room. But Vance was gone, and Cord's personality was too strong to fight.

Because the day was so muted and gray when she woke up in the morning, and because she felt so depressed at not having seen Cord, Susan made a determined effort to cheer herself up. She chose a dark red silk sheath for work, and belted it with a snazzy wide black belt that she'd never worn before. A short black jacket pulled the outfit together, and Susan arched an inquiring eyebrow at her own reflection in the mirror as she leaned forward to put on her earrings. The sharply stylish woman in the mirror didn't quite look like Susan Blackstone, who usually preferred more conservative garments. But then, the Susan Blackstone who had looked in that mirror the Friday before had never spent the day making love with Cord Blackstone. She was gambling for the first time in her life, and the stakes were higher than she could afford. A woman who would risk her heart, knowing from the outset that the odds in her favor weren't too good, couldn't be as staid and conventional as Susan had always thought herself to be.

She kept her cheerful demeanor in place all day long, but after she got home and had eaten the dinner Emily prepared, after Emily had gone to her own house, she waited hopefully until long after dark, but still she didn't hear anything from Cord. A chill began to tighten her muscles. If the day they had spent together had meant anything to him at all, why hadn't he made any effort to see her again? Had it just been a . . . a convenience for him? A casual sexual encounter that he wouldn't think of again?

She thought of driving out to Jubilee Creek, but the lateness of the hour and the steady rain dissuaded her. Surely tomorrow she'd hear from him.

But she didn't, and the hours dragged past. She called Information to see if he'd had a phone installed, but they had no listing in his name. She could no longer even keep up the pretense of being cheerful, and her face was tight with strain, an expression that was duplicated on Preston's face. Susan knew that he had extended himself to the limit, liquidating assets to replace the money in Cord's account, and she wanted to ask him if he needed help, but an intimate knowledge of Blackstone pride kept her from making the offer. He'd refuse, and even if he later changed his mind, if things became desperate enough that he would want to accept her help, he wouldn't mention it to her.

Thursday afternoon she drove out to Jubilee Creek, but

there was no sign of Cord. She looked in the windows and could see no lights, no dirty dishes, no clothing strewn about. She tried both the front and back doors, and found them securely locked. The thought that he might have gone permanently made her sag against the door, and bitter tears of regret seared her lids before she forced them back; not regret for what had happened, but regret that she'd had only that one day in his arms. She should have had more! It wasn't fair to give someone a brief glimpse of heaven, then draw heavy curtains over the scene! Where Cord was concerned, she wanted it all: all of his smiles, his kisses, his company every day. She wanted to be the one to calm his anger or incite his passion. She wanted to wake up beside him every morning and look at his sleepy, beard-stubbled face, and at night she wanted to lie close against his tall, hard body.

Of course, she could just be borrowing heartache; the cabin hadn't been emptied, so she had to assume that he would be returning. It was just . . . Why couldn't he have let her know that he was leaving, or when he would be back? Would a phone call have been so difficult for him to make?

But those were the conditions she'd set: He wasn't to tell her anything. Her eyes widened in realization. What if his absence had something to do with Imogene and Preston? They were convinced that he was scheming against them, and though she had defended him, suddenly she was unsure. What did she know about him, other than that he was so exciting and dangerous that he made her heartbeat lurch out of rhythm every time she saw him? He was a hungry, demanding lover, but considerate in controlling his strength and handling her carefully. He danced with wild grace, and his body was laced with the scars that a warrior collected over the years. She loved him, but she was painfully aware that he kept most of himself hidden away. If he had lived by the law of fang and claw, could she expect him to do anything other than strike back at people who had wronged him? Was she a fool to trust him? She'd always thought that a trainer who walked unarmed into a cage with a snarling tiger was extremely foolish, but she had been just as foolish. Suddenly she knew that Cord was more than capable of taking revenge; he could raise it to the level of fine art.

The next day Preston came into her office and dropped tiredly into the comfortable chair next to her desk. "Well, I've done it," he said in a voice hollow with exhaustion. "I've stretched myself to the limit, but Cord has been repaid in full."

She was overcome with sympathy for him, looking at the dark shadows under his blue eyes. "I wish you would let me help—"

"No, thanks, sugar." He managed a slow smile for her. "It wasn't your doing, so you shouldn't have to pay. Now that the debt is covered, if you don't want to lease the ridges to him, you don't have to. I've pretty well blocked any move he can make to cause trouble about the money; I've even paid him interest."

"I wish you could talk with him and settle your differences," she said wistfully. "It's not right for a family to tear itself apart like this. All of that happened so long ago; why can't you put it in the past?"

"There's too much resentment, on both sides," Preston replied. He stretched his long legs out in front of him and crossed them elegantly at the ankle. "We never got along, for one reason or another. That thing with Judith Keller just topped it off, as far as he was concerned. And as far as I'm concerned . . ." He gave her a direct look. "As long as you're interested in him, I have to hate his guts."

Susan blushed, distressed at causing him any pain. "Don't feel like that, please. Don't add to the trouble. I can't stand the thought of being a bone of contention between the two of you."

"But such a sweet, lovely bone," he teased, his blue eyes lightening momentarily. He really was an extraordinarily good-looking man, she realized with some surprise, slim and elegant, with a smooth style that sometimes made him seem misplaced in this century. But Preston wasn't out of place; he was supremely suited for his occupation. He was cool, level-headed, and fair in his practices. He was also completely out of his league in fighting Cord, because he lacked the ruthlessness that had kept Cord alive in a lot of dim back alleys.

The light had already faded out of Preston's eyes. "Do you see him often?" he finally asked, his tone gruff as he struggled to hide his emotions.

It was only the painful truth when Susan replied, "No, not often at all." In moments of mental detachment she was astonished at the way she had given herself to a man whom she didn't know that well, hadn't seen that often, and who was a direct threat to her way of life. Then the memory of the heat of his kisses would banish her detachment, and she would no longer wonder at the way she had lost herself in his arms. He wasn't a man who inspired a sedate love; he evoked the deepest, wildest passions a woman's heart was capable of feeling.

Preston sat there, a frown puckering his brow as he thought. After a moment he said, "I'd like for him to know that the money has been repaid. Will you tell him for me?"

"If I see him again," Susan agreed steadily. "I don't know where he is." The bald confession stabbed her as she realized anew how empty she felt at the thought that she might not see him again.

Preston sat upright. "Has he left town?"

"I don't know. But I haven't seen him for a week, and he's not at the cabin."

"He's either gone again, or he's making some sort of move against me," Preston muttered absently, tapping his fingertips on the top of Susan's desk. "Let me know if you hear from him.'' He got up and left her office, still preoccupied with the news that Cord had dropped out of sight.

After a moment Beryl appeared with an armload of correspondence to be signed, pulling Susan away from the chasm of loneliness, but inside herself she was aware that she had only stepped back, not walked away from it entirely. It was still there, cold and black in its yawning emptiness, a bleak, bottomless pit where she would fall forever, locked away from the fire of the man she loved.

Chapter 8

JUST AS SHE TURNED INTO HER DRIVEWAY A SWIFTLY moving thunderstorm swept in from the Gulf, and it threatened to drown her as she dashed the short distance from her car to the covered side patio. Emily met her at the door with an enormous towel, having seen her drive up. Just as Susan stepped out of her soaking shoes and wound the towel around her hair, the rain stopped as swiftly as it had come, leaving only the cheerful dripping of water from the trees and the eaves of the roof. A split second later the thundercloud was gone and the sun was shining merrily on the wet landscape, making the raindrops sparkle like diamonds. Susan gave Emily a rueful look. "If I'd waited in the car for a minute, it would've been over with and I wouldn't have gotten soaked."

Emily couldn't suppress a chuckle. "If you wanted predictable weather, you'd live in Arizona. Go on upstairs and get dried off, while I finish your dinner."

Fifteen minutes later Susan was downstairs again, helping Emily put the finishing touches on the small but tasty meal she'd prepared. Emily watched her set a single place on the table, and the older woman's protective instincts were aroused. Putting her big spoon down with a thunk, she braced her hands on her hips. "I'd like to know why you've been eating alone every night, instead of letting Cord Blackstone take you out."

Susan flushed, not certain how to respond. Because it was what she feared most, she finally said, "Just because he passed out on the couch and spent the night here doesn't mean he's interested—"

"Baloney," Emily interrupted in exasperation. "I've got eyes, and I saw the way he was looking at you the next morning. You were looking back at him the same way, and don't try to deny it. Then he went upstairs with you, and it was quite a while before he came down."

"I don't know where he is," Susan admitted helplessly, staring down at the table. "He's not at the cabin. He hasn't called; he didn't even tell me he was leaving, or where he was going. For all I know, he won't be back."

"He'll be back, mark my words." Emily sniffed. "He's not used to accounting for himself to anyone, but if he had it in mind to leave for good, he'd have let you know."

"You knew him when he was a boy," Susan said, looking up at Emily with the hunger to know more about him plain in her eyes. "What was he like?"

Emily's care-worn features softened as she looked at the pleading face turned up to her. "Sit down," she urged. "I'll tell you while you're eating."

Susan obeyed, automatically eating the tiny lamb chops and steamed carrots that were one of her favorite meals. Emily sat down at the table across from her. "I loved him as a boy," she said, turning her mind back over twenty years. "He was always ready to laugh, always up to some prank, and it seemed like he was more relaxed at my house. He never fit in with the people his parents expected to be his friends, never really fit in here at all, and that just made him wilder than he naturally was anyway, which was wild enough. He was always ahead of everyone else, stronger than anyone else his age, faster, with better grades, more girlfriends. Even the older girls in high school were after him. Everything came so easy to him, or maybe he made everything come to him; I've never seen anyone more stubborn or determined to have his way. Thinking back on it, I know that he had to be bored. Nothing challenged him. He pulled off every wild stunt he could think of, but he had a golden touch, and everything always worked smooth as silk for him. I've never seen anything like his luck.''

Susan's breath caught at the image Emily had given her, of a boy growing up too fast, without any limits to guide him. He wouldn't accept any limits, she realized. He'd been propelled by the extraordinary combination of genes and circumstance that should have made him the prototypical Golden Boy, with all the comforts and privileges of wealth and class: handsome, unusually intelligent, athletic, gifted by nature with charm and grace. But his restless, seeking mind had soared beyond that, driven him to test the limits of chance. He had pushed and pushed, seeking a boundary he couldn't push beyond, until he'd gone too far and been driven away from his home.

There had been dark years in Cord's life, times when he'd been close to death, when he'd been cold and hungry, but she couldn't imagine him ever being frightened. No, he'd face everything that came his way, the mocking twist of his lips daring everyone and everything to do their worst. The remaining vestiges of the Golden Boy had been obliterated by the harshness of the life he'd led. Perhaps he had money now, perhaps he lived comfortably, but it hadn't always been so, and his senses were still razor-sharp. She thought of the scars on his body and her heart twisted.

"Everyone acts as if he's a wild animal," she said painfully. "Why are they so afraid of him?"

"Because they don't understand him. Because he's not like they are. Some folks are afraid of lightning; some think it's beautiful. But everyone's cautious around it."

Yes, he was as wild and beautiful as a bolt of lightning, and as dangerous. She stared at Emily, her eyes glistening with tears. "I love him."

Emily nodded sadly. "I know, honey. I know. What are you going to do?"

"There's nothing I can do, is there? Just . . . love him, and hope everything works out."

A foolish hope, doomed from the start. How could it work out? It was impossible to hold a bolt of lightning.

He was gone, and every minute seemed to drag by, rasping on her nerves. An hour was a lifetime; a day, eternity. No book, no gardening, no sewing, could ease her bone-deep sense of yearning. All she could think of was Cord, overwhelming her with his reckless charm and the impact of his forceful sensuality.

If only he was with her! In his presence she wouldn't care about Preston, or Imogene, or whatever was going on. In Cord's arms, she wouldn't care about anything. She could lose herself in him, and count the loss well worth the cost in pain. She loved him simply, completely, and she had to follow only the dictates of her emotions.

She slept restlessly that night, and was jerked out of sleep a little after midnight by a boom of thunder that rattled the windows. Susan lay snugly in her warm bed, listening to the lightning crackle; then a hard, driving rain began to pound against her windows and the wind picked up. Deciding she'd better turn on the radio and get a weather report, she sat up and turned on her bedside lamp. When she did, another pounding reached her ears and she paused, a small frown touching her brow. Then it was repeated, and she jumped out of bed. Someone was trying to beat her door down.

She grabbed her robe and raced down the stairs, turning on lights as she went. "Who is it? What's wrong?" she called as she neared the door.

A deep laugh answered her. "The only thing that's wrong is that you're on that side of the door and I'm on this one."

"Cord!" Her heart jumped into her throat and she fumbled hastily with the lock, throwing the door open. He sauntered in, as wild as the night, and as dangerous. The wind had tumbled his dark hair into reckless waves, and his pale eyes were glittering. He brought the fresh scent of rain in with him, because the wind had blown a fine mist of moisture over him. He was dressed in a conservatively cut, dark business suit, but the coat was hanging open, his tie was draped around his neck, and his shirt was open to the waist. The suit couldn't disguise the desperado that he was, and her mouth went dry with longing.

Unthinkingly, she clutched at his sleeve. "Where have you been? Why haven't you called? I've been so worried—" She stopped, suddenly realizing what she was saying, and stared up at him with eyes full of vulnerability.

"Uh-uh," he crooned softly. "No questions, remember? I'm not telling you anything, not where I was, or when I'll be going again." A savage enjoyment lit his face as another crash of thunder reverberated through the house, and his teeth flashed in a grin. "I like storms," he murmured, taking a step toward her and lacing his arm around her waist in an iron embrace. "I like making love while it rains."

Something was wrong; she couldn't quite catch her breath. She stared up at him dazedly, and she clutched his lapels for support. "I was just going to turn on the radio to get the weather report," she stammered.

He grinned again. "Thunderstorm warning, with possible high winds," he said, pulling her closer until she was pressed full against him. "Who cares?"

The gleam in his eyes was still interfering with her

breathing. "When . . . when did you get back?" she asked, hanging suspended over his arm, her feet having somehow lost touch with the floor. "Or is that another off-limits question?"

"Tonight," he answered. "I was driving home, thinking about how dead tired I was, and how good it would feel to fall into bed. Then I thought how much better it would feel to fall into bed with you, so here I am."

"You don't look tired," she observed cautiously. He didn't. He looked as if he could rival the storm for energy. He was almost burning her with his touch.

"Second wind," he said, and kissed her. His approach was direct and without hesitation, and he kissed her for a long time. She clung to him, first to his lapels; then her clutching fingers somehow found their way to his shoulders, and finally her arms were locked around his neck. He lifted her and started up the stairs, leaving all the lights on behind him, because that was the last thing on his mind.

He set her on her feet in her bedroom and watched her with lazily hooded eyes as he stripped his tie from around his neck and tossed it carelessly over a chair. The tie was followed by his coat; then his shirt was pulled free of his pants and discarded. When he kicked off his shoes and leaned down to pull his socks off, Susan swallowed at the sight of his half-naked body, so sleek and powerful, and she untied the sash of her robe and removed the garment, folding it over the chair. She could feel his eyes on her, on the ice pink nightgown that half revealed her body.

He dropped his pants and left them lying on the floor. His only remaining garment was a pair of jogging-style shorts, dark blue silk with white edging, which did nothing to hide his arousal. A thunderbolt of excitement raced through her as he nonchalantly stepped out of his underwear and came toward her, as naked and powerfully beautiful as an ancient god.

Quickly she raised the hem of the nightgown over her

head and drew it off, the silk whispering over her bare skin. His look of hunger became almost fierce as he reached for her. When he placed her on the bed, Susan reached out for the lamp and he halted her, his hard fingers closing around her wrist.

"Leave it on," he instructed in a voice gone gravelly rough. "I thought of this all the time I was gone. I'm not going to miss seeing one minute of it."

She couldn't help the blush that tinted her breasts and spread upward to her cheeks, and he found it fascinating. Without a word he took her in his arms.

Their loveplay extended as he explored her body as thoroughly as if he'd never made love to her before, had never spent a lovely sun-drenched day sprawled across a bed with her. When she was writhing against him in frantic need, he paused for a moment to reach for his pants, and Susan realized what he was doing. Without a word, he assumed responsibility for their lovemaking. Then he turned to her and swiftly moved between her legs, sliding into her so powerfully that moans of pleasure were wrenched from both of them. His patience was at an end, and he thrust strongly, his rhythm hungry and fast. Susan wound her legs around him and absorbed the power of his thrusts with her eagerly welcoming body, so dizzy with pleasure at being in his arms again, kissing him, giving herself to him in the most intimate act between man and woman, that he couldn't leave her behind in his relentless quest for pleasure. The powerful coil that had been tightening within her was released suddenly, and her entire body throbbed with the pulsating waves that raced down her legs to curl her toes and spread upward through her torso in a splash of heat. She heard the wild cries that were ground out through his clenched teeth, felt him arch into her helplessly; then it was suddenly quiet again as the storm passed and he let himself down to lie on her in contented exhaustion.

After a moment he sighed and carefully eased himself

from her, rolling over on his side. Susan touched him, her fingers gentle. "This might not have been necessary," she murmured. "I . . . I'm not sure I can get pregnant. Vance and I never used any protection, but I never got pregnant. I'm very . . . erratic."

He closed his eyes and a tiny grin touched his mouth. Relaxing, he threw one arm behind his head. "Somehow, that's not very reassuring. I get the feeling that if there's any man walking this earth who could get you pregnant, I'm him. We took a big chance last week, but we'll be more careful from now on." He opened one eye a slit and pinned her with the narrow ribbon of his gaze. "Let me know if it's too late to be careful, or if we hit it lucky. As soon as *you* know."

"Yes," she agreed, sinking down onto the pillow and closing her eyes as contentment claimed her. It felt so natural to be in bed with him, talking about very intimate things, feeling the heat of his body so close to her. She nestled closer to him and rubbed her face against the hair of his chest, feeling the soft curls catch at her eyelashes.

He drifted into sleep with her lying against his side, but woke when the storm, forgotten in their own storm of loving, renewed itself with a snap of lightning so close that the thunder was simultaneous, and Susan sat upright in bed at the unmistakable sound of a limb splitting away from a tree and crashing to the ground. Before she had time to voice her alarm, he seized her from behind and tumbled her back to the mattress.

"Just where do you think you're going?" he growled with mock roughness.

"The trees—" she began, and just then the lights flickered and went out.

"Oh, hell," he said into the sudden darkness. Another bolt of lightning flashed to earth and the eerie blue-white light illuminated the room. He was sitting up, too. "Where's a flashlight and the radio?"

"There's a flashlight in the top drawer of the night-stand," she said, pulling the sheet up around her as the damp chill of the air reached her. "The radio is downstairs in the den."

"Battery?"

"Yes." She listened as he fumbled around in the night-stand, finally locating the flashlight and clicking it on, the beam of light dispelling the darkness. He swung his long legs out of the bed.

"I'll bring the radio up here. Sit tight."

What else could she do? She pulled her knees up and rested her chin on them, her eyes on the storm erupting right outside her windows. It was loud and magnificent, full of fury, but she mourned the damage to the enormous old trees that surrounded the house. If one of the trees came down, it could take the roof of the house off and crush the walls.

Cord came back into the room, the battery-powered radio in his hand. He had it turned to a local Biloxi station. Placing the radio on the nightstand, he clicked off the flashlight and got into bed with her, pulling her down to nestle in his arms.

In only a few moments the amused drawl of the radio announcer was filling the room. "The thunderstorm warning for the Biloxi area has been canceled. I guess those folks at the weather bureau haven't looked out their windows lately. Now, this is what I call *rain*. There aren't any reports of any serious damage, though several power outtages have been reported, and there are some signs blown down. Nothing major, folks. We're in touch with the weather bureau, and if it turns serious—"

Cord stretched out a long arm and turned the radio off, silencing the announcer in mid-sentence. "It's already passing," he murmured, and she noticed that the lightning was indeed less intense, the thunder growing more distant.

The lights suddenly blinked back on, blinding both of them with their unexpected brilliance.

He laughed and sat up. "I was going to stay with you as long as the power was off," he said, getting out of bed and reaching for his underwear.

Bewildered, Susan sat up too, staring at him. He pulled on his underwear, then his pants, before she spoke. "Aren't you staying?"

"No." He slanted her a look that was suddenly cool and remote.

"But—it's so late, anyway. Why drive to Jubilee Creek—"

"Three reasons," he interrupted, a harsh note entering his deep voice. "One, I like to sleep alone. Two, I really need the sleep, which I wouldn't get if I stayed here with you. Three, Emily didn't turn a hair at finding me asleep on your couch, but finding me in your bed is something else entirely."

A hard, cold pain struck her in her chest, but she looked at him and saw the way he'd closed himself off, and she summoned all of her strength to give him a smile that wavered only a little. "Are you worried about your reputation?" she managed to tease. "I promise I'll take the blame for seducing you."

Her attempt at lightness worked; he smiled, and sat down on the side of the bed to cup her soft cheek in his palm. "Don't argue," he murmured. But when he was that close he could see her pain, though she was doing everything she could to hide it, and his level brows pulled together. He wasn't used to explaining himself, or talking about his past at all, but he found himself trying to explain his actions for the first time in years. The urge to take the uncomprehending pain out of those soft blue eyes was almost overwhelming. "Susan, I don't feel comfortable sleeping with another person, not anymore. I've spent too many years guarding

my back. I may doze off after making love, but I don't fall
into a deep sleep. Some part of me is always alert, ready to
move. I can't rest that way and I'm really tired tonight; I
need some sleep. We'll go out for dinner tomorrow night
. . . make that tonight, since it's almost morning. Seven-
thirty?''

"Yes. I'll be ready."

He winked at her. "I won't mind if you aren't dressed."

As he finished dressing, Susan watched him and hugged
the sheet up over her nudity. She bit her lip, trying to force
her own feelings away so she could consider his. She'd
sensed that he was uneasy about allowing himself to relax
when anyone else was with him, and she knew that her
vision of him leaving his women alone in their beds had
been an accurate one. *His women.* She had joined them, that
long line of women who had held him in their arms for a
taste of heaven, then lain weeping in their cold beds after he
had gone. Yet she wouldn't have turned him away, wouldn't
have missed her own chance at heaven. If she could turn
time back, she would go with him that first night she'd met
him, and not waste one moment of the time she had with
him.

He completed dressing and reached for his coat, then
leaned down to give her a swift kiss. Susan dropped the
sheet and rose up on her knees, entwining her arms around
his strong neck as she lifted her mouth. He paused, looking
down at her gentle mouth, already pouty from his kisses;
her eyes were serene pools, with thick black lashes drooping in a drowsy, unconsciously sexy manner. She was a
naked Venus in his arms, soft and warm and feminine, and
his hands automatically sought her curves as he kissed her
long and hard, his tongue deep within her mouth. Despite
his weariness, desire hardened his body, and it was all he
could do to pull away from her.

"You're going to be the death of me," he muttered,
giving her a look that she couldn't read before he left the

room. Susan remained on her knees until she heard the sound of the front door closing; then she sagged down on the bed, fighting the hot tears that wanted to fall. For a moment she'd sensed that he'd been tempted to stay, but only to slake the urges of his amazingly virile body, not because he trusted her, not because he felt he could sleep in her arms. She knew that she could have touched him, wriggled herself against him, and he would have tumbled her back down to the mattress, but that wasn't what she wanted. That hot, glorious madness that seized her at his lightest touch was wonderful, but she wanted more. She wanted his love, his trust.

The tiger is a majestic beast, savagely beautiful and awesome in its power, but it's locked alone in its majesty. The beautiful tiger is solitary, hunting alone, sleeping alone. A tiger mates, and for a time is less alone, but the moments of physical joining are soon gone, and the tiger once again roams in solitude. Cord was a tiger in nature, and after mating he had gone to seek his bed apart from every other creature on earth, because he trusted no other creature.

She pounded her fist on the mattress in mute frustration. Why couldn't she have fallen in love with a man who *liked* cuddling up and falling asleep, a man who hadn't spent years of his life kicking around the globe in a lot of God-forsaken places, who did all the normal things like going to work during the week and cutting the grass on weekends? Because, she interrupted her own thoughts fiercely, a man like that wouldn't be Cord. He was wild and beautiful, and dangerous. If she had wanted a man who wasn't all of those things, she'd have fallen in love with Preston long ago.

She lay awake, her eyes on the ceiling as the hours slid past and dawn came and went. Part of her was hurt and humiliated that he had come to her for sex, then left as soon as he was satisfied, but another part of her was glad that he had come to her at all, for any reason. Certainly, if he made love to any woman, she wanted it to be herself. She wanted to believe that he felt something for her besides physical desire, but if he didn't, she would try to use that desire as a base to build on. As long as he came around at all, she still had hope.

She was taken by surprise the next afternoon when sudden cramps signaled that their reckless day of lovemaking hadn't borne fruit; she'd been feeling listless all day, but credited that to her lack of sleep the night before. She was further surprised when she burst into tears, and it wasn't until that moment that she realized she'd been unconsciously hoping that Cord's seed had found fertile ground. She almost hated her body for being so unpredictable, so inhospitable; she wanted his child, a part of him that would be hers forever. She wouldn't use a pregnancy to chain him to her, ever, if he wanted to go, but how she would love a baby of his making! Her arms ached at the thought of holding an infant with soft dark hair and pale blue eyes, and their emptiness haunted her.

She was pale and shadows lay heavily under her eyes when Cord arrived to take her to dinner; she told him immediately that he had no need to worry about a pregnancy, and almost winced at the relief he didn't bother to hide. Despite that, they had a pleasant dinner, and after eating they danced for a while to some slow, dreamy forties-style music. He'd taken her to a restaurant in New Orleans where she'd never been before, and she liked the place-out-of-time atmosphere. He knew that her energy level was low, and she thoroughly enjoyed the way he coddled her that evening. She drank a little more wine than she was accustomed to, and was floating slightly above the earth as he drove her home in the sleek white Jaguar that he had arrived in, though she had expected the red Blazer. The man has style, she thought dreamily, stroking her fingers over the leather of the seats. In the light of the dash his face was hard and exciting, the virile brush of his moustache outlining the precision of his upper lip. She reached out and let her fingers lightly trace his mouth, causing his brows to arch in question.

"You're so beautiful," she murmured huskily.

"Feel free to admire me any time you like, madam," he invited formally, but the wicked, sensual glint in his eyes was anything but formal as he glanced at her. She was a little high, her eyes filled with dreams, and he knew that she would come willingly into his arms if he stopped the car and reached for her right then. He shifted uncomfortably in his seat as his body reacted to his thoughts. He wanted her, but he knew that she didn't feel well, and he wanted her to enjoy their lovemaking as deeply as he did, not just allow her body to be used for his pleasure. He thought of how she looked in the throes of passion, and desire slammed into his gut so hard that he jerked in his seat. When this was over, when he had accomplished all that he wanted, he promised himself that he'd take her on a long vacation, maybe a cruise, and he'd make love to her as much as he liked. He'd satisfy his craving for her once and for all, sate himself on her slim, velvet body that was so surprisingly sensual. Her sensuality was so unconscious, so natural, that he sensed she wasn't even aware of it. A perfect lady, he thought, until he took her in his arms; then she turned into a hot, sweet wanton who took his breath away.

He didn't plan any further into the future than that; Cord had learned not to make long-range plans, because they inhibited his ability to react to circumstances. When some people formed plans in their minds, they locked their thoughts on course and couldn't deviate from them, couldn't allow for unforseen interruptions or detours. When Cord plotted his course of action, he didn't tie himself down; he always allowed for the possibility that he might have to jump to the left instead of to the right, or even

retrace his steps entirely. That flexibility had kept him alive,
kept him in tune with his senses. In that way, he was a
creature of the moment, yet he always kept his goal in
mind, and changing circumstances only meant that he
would have to reach that goal by a different route. He was
usually prepared for anything and everything, but when
he'd returned to Biloxi he hadn't been prepared for the
primitive desire he would feel for a woman who had one
foot in the enemy camp and seemed determined to keep it
there. To the victor belonged the spoils, and he looked at
Susan with hard determination; when he had won, she
would be his, and he would force all thoughts of her in-laws
out of her head. He wouldn't allow her any time to think of
anyone but him. The savagely possessive need he felt for
her had forced him to adjust his actions, but in the
end . . . in the end, everything would be just like he'd
planned it, and Susan would be his, on his terms.

Susan sensed the control he exercised when he kissed her
lightly and left her at her door; she was too tired, too sleepy
from too much wine, to try to understand why he left so
abruptly. She only knew that she was disappointed; she
could have made a pot of coffee and they could have sat
close together and watched the late news, just as she and
Vance had often done. . . .

But Cord wasn't Vance.

Susan stood in the darkened foyer and looked around at
the beautiful, gracious home Vance had built for her. The
light she had left on at the head of the stairs illuminated the
pale walls and the elegant floor-to-ceiling windows, the
imported tiles of the foyer. Her home was warm and
welcoming, because it was a home that had known love, but
now she stood in the darkness, surrounded by the things
that Vance had given her, and all she could think of was
another man. Cord filled her days, her nights, her thoughts,
her dreams. His pale lodestone eyes compelled her, like the
moon silently controlling the tides. She tried to visualize

Vance's face, but the features refused to form themselves in her mind. He had taught her about love; his tender care had helped shape her into a warm and loving woman, but he was gone, and he had no more substance for her than that of the drifting mist. *Vance, I really did love you,* she called out to him silently, but there was nothing there. Vance was dead, and Cord was so vitally alive.

Instead of going up to bed she went into the den and turned on the lights, then walked unerringly to the precise spot in the bookshelves that held a small album, though it had been at least four years since she'd looked at it. She took down the leather-bound volume and opened it, staring at the pictures of Vance.

How young he looked! How fresh and gallant! She saw the familiar mischievous sparkle in his blue eyes, the rather crooked smile, the strong Blackstone features. She traced the lines of his face with one gentle finger, seeing the resemblance he bore to Cord. He looked much the way she imagined Cord would have before experience had worn away his youthful wonder at the world, before all his ideals had been blasted out of existence. "I loved you," she murmured to Vance's smiling face. "If you could have stayed, I'd have loved you forever."

But he hadn't, and now Cord had stolen her love like the renegade he was.

Gently she replaced the album and left the room, walking slowly up the stairs to her empty bed, her mind and her senses filled with the memory of the night before when Cord had swept in with the rain, wild and damp, the air about him almost crackling with the heat of his passion. She hadn't even thought of denying him, even though he'd disappeared for a week without a word of warning. She'd simply undressed, so eager for his touch that she wouldn't have protested if he'd taken her there in the foyer.

She creamed the makeup off her face, closing her eyes slightly to combat the faint giddiness caused by the wine.

How passionate he'd been the night before, and how considerate he'd been this evening. She tried to convince herself that he cared for her, but the thought kept coming back that he hadn't wasted any time getting away from her after driving her home. And the night before, he'd left after making love to her. He only wants me for sex, she silently told her reflection, and shut her eyes tightly against the words. It had to be more than that, because she wasn't sure she could keep from falling apart if it wasn't.

Chapter 9

BY THE TIME ANOTHER WEEK HAD COME AND GONE, SUSAN
was convinced that she knew nothing about Cord. He was
the most enigmatic man she'd ever met; just when she'd
decided that he was only using her as a convenient sexual
outlet, he confounded her by taking her out every evening,
wooing her with wine and good food, and dancing with her
into the wee hours of the morning. Dancing with him was
special. He was the most graceful man she'd ever known,
and he enjoyed dancing. Between them, rituals of dancing
were both flirtation and foreplay. She could feel his
powerful body moving against her, sending her senses
tumbling head over heels, and the unabashed response of
his body told her that he was reacting the same way. Held in
his arms, she felt secure, protected, locked away in their
private world. She could have dreamed her life away in his
arms.

He was a gentleman in every sense of the word, tenderly
solicitous of her, courting her in a manner so old-fashioned
that it stunned her even though she deeply enjoyed every

moment of it. He gave her the grace of a few days' privacy, then brought his abstinence to an end with hungry impatience; instead of kissing her gently good-night, as he had been doing, he picked her up and carried her to her bed. When he left several hours later she lay sprawled nude on the tangled sheets, too exhausted to get up to find a nightgown or even pull the sheet over herself. She slept with a heavenly smile on her passion-swollen mouth.

The nights that followed were just as passionate, and she should have been wilting from lack of sleep, but instead she was radiant, full of energy. She sailed through the hours at work, too immersed in her own happiness to really pay attention to Preston's growing depression, knowing that when the night came she would be in Cord's arms again.

Her happiness made the blow, when it came, just that much more cruel. She was going over a productivity report from the small electronics plant they owned when Preston appeared at her office door. Susan looked up with a ready smile, but the smile died when she saw the taut expression that had made his face a gray mask. Concern snapped her to her feet, and she went across the room to him, taking his arm. "What is it?"

He stared at her for a minute, and she silently reproached herself for not having paid more attention to him this past week. She'd known that something was bothering him, but she hadn't wanted anything to dim her happiness. Her selfishness made her writhe inside.

Wordlessly, he extended the papers in his hand. Susan took them, her brow wrinkling as she stared at them.

"What is this?"

"Read it." He moved over to a chair and lowered himself into it, his movements slow and jerky, strangely uncoordinated.

She flipped through the papers, reading slowly. Her eyes widened, and she read them over again, hoping that she hadn't understood correctly, but there was no way to misunderstand. The meaning of every word was perfectly clear. Cord had bought up an outstanding loan against the Blackstone Corporation and was calling it in. They had thirty days to pay.

Almost suffocated by the thick sense of betrayal that rose in her throat, she dropped the papers to the top of her desk and lifted her stunned gaze to Preston. She couldn't speak, though she wet her lips and tried to force her throat to form the words. How could he have done that?

"Well, now you know where he went on that mystery trip," Preston said bitterly, nodding toward the papers. "Dallas."

She braced one hand flat on the desk, trying to support herself as acid nausea rose in her throat. She conquered the moment, but she couldn't conquer the pain that threatened to bend her double. Why had he done it? Didn't he realize that this hurt her as much as it did Preston? This wasn't just Preston he was striking at; he was threatening the entire corporation, her livelihood as well as the livelihoods of thousands of workers who depended on their jobs to put food on the table. He had to know, so the only supposition she could reach was that he simply didn't care. After the week she had spent with him, the passion she'd shared with him, the brutal realization that it all meant nothing to him was like a slap in the face, and she reeled from the impact of it.

"I thought we were protected against this sort of thing." Lifelessly, Preston stared at the floor. "But he found a way, and he's bought up the loan. He's called it in. God knows where he got the money to buy it up, or even how he knew where to go—" He broke off suddenly, his blue eyes narrowing as he stared at Susan with bitter accusation.

For a moment she didn't read the expression on his face; then her eyes flared with understanding. She went even whiter than she had been. How could he so readily believe that she would betray them to Cord, after all she had done to try to convince Cord not to seek vengeance? But why not? Why should Preston trust her? Cord didn't trust her, despite the passionate devotion she revealed every time she gave herself to him.

"How can you believe that?" she choked. "I haven't told him anything."

"Then how did he know?"

"I don't know!" she shouted, then stopped, pressing her hands against her mouth, aghast at her loss of control. "I'm sorry. I didn't tell him; I swear I didn't."

His blue eyes were suddenly sick, and he drew a deep, shaking breath. "My God, he's got us fighting each other," he said miserably, getting to his feet and coming around to her. He took her in his arms and held her tightly to him, rocking back and forth in a comforting motion. "I know you didn't tell him; you don't have a deceptive bone in your body. I'm sorry for being so stupid. I'm rattled. Susan, he's trying to bankrupt us."

The evidence lay on her desk, so she couldn't even try to deny it. She pressed her face into Preston's shoulder, vaguely aware that she was shaking. The awful thing was that, even with her knowing that Cord was capable of being so ruthless and devious, the aching, burning love she felt for him didn't diminish at all. She had known the chance she was taking in mating with that human tiger.

How long they clung together like frightened children trying to comfort each other, she didn't know. But gradually she calmed, and their embrace loosened.

There were things to do, strategies to plan. "How badly will we be weakened?" she asked in a voice that was flatly calm.

Preston's arms dropped away completely, and he turned to drag a chair around so he could sit beside her at her desk. "Dangerously. He couldn't have timed it better. At the moment, our cash flow is restricted because we've invested so heavily in projects that won't begin paying for at least another year, possibly two years. You handled the paper-work on the laser project in Palo Alto, so you know how much we've sunk in that one project alone.''

She did. "Then what about our personal assets? If we liquidate, we can raise enough money to cover the loan—''

He was shaking his head to stop her, and he smiled wryly at her. "How do you think I raised the money to repay him for the money we used?''

She sat back, stunned. How neatly Cord had boxed them into a corner! He must have been planning this all along. First he had threatened to bring charges against Preston for stealing, then he had sat back and done nothing, giving Preston time to replace the amount taken, knowing that Preston would have to stretch himself thin to cover that much at one time. He had maneuvered them like pieces on a chessboard.

Still, she cast around for a solution. "Imogene and I can cover it. We have stocks we can sell, and property in prime locations—''

"Susan, stop it," he said gently. "Mother and I were both involved in using Cord's money, and we both had to sacrifice to replace it. She's stretched as thinly as I am, and you can't handle this all on your own. You wouldn't have anything left if you did.''

Susan shrugged. The thought of being penniless didn't bother her. "If we can hold on for a year, two years at the most, then the corporation would be safe. That's what matters.''

"Do you really think I'd let you sell off everything Vance gave you? From the moment he married you, he worked to make certain you'd always be comfortable, no matter what happened. He cherished you, and I won't let you undo all of the things he did for you.''

"If we can stay out of bankruptcy, everything can be replaced.''

"Covering this loan won't guarantee that. What if he

buys up another one? He's obviously got money behind him, enough money to destroy us if he wants to keep pushing. If he buys up another loan, we end up in the bankruptcy courts, even if you do sell everything you own to cover this one."

Preston's logic was irrefutable, and she went cold to the bone. "Then there's nothing we can do?"

"I don't know. We're going to have to consider everything. The damnable part of it is, he has a stake in this corporation himself, and that isn't stopping him. He'll take that loss in order to get back at me. I can't believe he went this far. I know he hates me, but this is . . . this is crazy!"

It was unnerving to think of someone so determined, so ruthless, that he would go against his own best interests in his quest for revenge. He was tightening the screws, pushing, enjoying tormenting Preston. He'd said that he wanted to make the other man squirm. He might have reason enough for the way he felt; she could only guess at the hellholes he'd been in since he'd been turned away by his family, though she had seen the marks they had left on his body. But no matter what the past had been, it was time the senseless hurting was ended. It had gone on long enough, tearing families apart, creating bitter enemies of the same blood. She wanted to take Cord by the neck and shake him until he'd regained his senses, and for a moment she could almost smile at the image of herself shaking someone who was almost a foot taller than she was, and who outweighed her by about a hundred pounds.

She was exhausted when she went home that day. They had spent the hours poring over financial statements, marshalling their forces to meet this challenge. Preston was a superb corporate tactician, but she'd never before realized the extent of his subtlety and expertise. He knew exactly how much they could sacrifice without dealing themselves a mortal blow, and he'd set the wheels in motion to liquidate the assets he thought the corporation could spare.

She was late getting home, but Emily was waiting for her with a hot meal, which the older woman made certain she consumed. Somehow, Emily always knew when Susan was tired or depressed, and she would dispense an extra measure of coddling, but not all her tender concern could erase the tension from Susan's face that night. Thinking that all of her nights out with Cord might be tiring Susan out, Emily asked, "Are you going out with Cord again tonight?"

Susan started at hearing the name that had been reverberating in her thoughts. "Oh . . . I don't know. He said he might be over later tonight. He had to drive to New Orleans to take care of some business." She felt sick at the thought. What sort of business? Finding another nail to drive into the coffin of Blackstone Corporation?

"Well, I think you need to get more sleep than you've had this past week," Emily scolded. "You look like a dishrag. Send him home early if he does come over."

Somehow, Susan managed a smile for the woman, grateful for her concern. "Yes, I will." She loved him, but right now she couldn't be with him. She had the feeling that if she looked over her shoulder, she'd be able to see the handle of the knife that was sticking in her back.

Perhaps he wouldn't come. She hoped he wouldn't. She was too tired, too hurt, too raw from the knowledge of his betrayal. But why kid herself? He wouldn't see it as a betrayal, because he'd never promised her anything. All he had given her was the coin of physical passion, not a hint of commitment beyond the moment.

She hoped he wouldn't come, yet she wasn't surprised later that night to hear the rumble of the red Blazer that he used for his casual driving. She'd begun to think that she was safe for the night; it was after nine o'clock, and she'd been thinking about taking her bath and going to bed. But now he was here, and she stood in the den, her heart beginning to pound in apprehension. She felt sick; her hands were cold and clammy, and she pressed them against her skirt. How could she face him? Why couldn't he have waited until tomorrow, when she might be calmer?

The doorbell rang, but still she stood rigidly in the middle of the floor, unable to force her legs to move. Cold dread rippled down her spine. Seconds ticked past, and the doorbell began an insistent peal as he jammed his finger onto it and held it there. It wasn't until he began to pound on the door with enough force to rattle it on its hinges that she managed to move, her legs shaking. She crept into the foyer and released the bolt on the door.

The door crashed open under the impact of his fist, narrowly missing knocking her down. Cord loomed over her, his face dark and savage. He seized her by the arms, his fingers biting into her soft flesh. "Are you all right?" he bit out. "The lights were on, but when you didn't answer the door I thought something must be wrong. I was going to go around and break out the glass in the sliding doors—" He never finished the sentence, instead pulling her to him with one iron arm locked around her waist, his other hand cupping her chin and turning her face up to him. He bent his head and his mouth closed over hers, hard, hungrily, and for a moment she forgot everything. She was swamped by the exciting maleness of his scent, the coffee taste of his mouth. She clung to him, her fingers digging into the heavy muscles of his back as she rose on tiptoe to fit herself to him.

His desire rose swiftly, launched from the perfect condition of his superb body. Before she could think, he had lifted her off her feet and started up the stairs, after kicking the door shut. Feeling the last vestiges of control slipping away from her, Susan freed her mouth from his and gasped, "Wait! I don't—"

He caught her mouth again, his tongue plunging deep inside, stifling her desperate words as he placed her on the bed. If he had released her then, stepping back to remove his clothes, she might have had a chance, but he stayed with her. He covered her, his mouth taking hers with hard, deep kisses, while his hands delved under her skirt and peeled away her underwear. Stunned by his urgency, after a moment she forgot about the rift between them and held tightly to his neck, her slender body arching to him as he parted her thighs and fit himself between them. He paused a moment to adjust his clothing and insure her protection, then thrust deeply into her, the impact of his body making her jerk.

She wasn't the only one taken by surprise by his urgency. Cord had been unpleasantly surprised by the desperation that had knotted his stomach when she hadn't answered the door, and he'd had a vision of her sprawled lifeless at the foot of the stairs. Or someone could have broken in on her, and raped her before killing her. That last thought had made the hair on the back of his neck lift up, and he had been snarling silently as he pounded on the door. Then it had opened and she'd stood there, pale and silent, but obviously healthy, and his desire had bloomed with his relief. He had to have her right then, bury himself in her and satisfy his body as well as his mind that she was still there, still healthy, and still his. The taste of her, the silken feel of her under his hands, the intimate clasp of her body, were all that could drive the fear from his mind. He luxuriated in his possession of her, feeling her response building and the tension in her growing tighter, and the knowledge that she wanted him, that he could satisfy her, was a pleasure as great as that he was taking from her soft flesh.

Susan heard the soft little whimpers in the back of her throat, but she was powerless to stop them, powerless to control her body. She reached blindly for satisfaction, her fingers clenched in his hair, her body arching up to meet his. He was crushing her, yet she didn't feel his weight; his heavy shoulders and chest were holding her down, yet she was soaring high and free, everything forgotten except for this moment in time. She was completely physical, yielding to his rampant masculinity and demanding that he give her all of himself.

He caught her legs, pulling them high to coil them around his back, and the whimpers turned into sharp, breathless cries. Deliberately he paced his movements, keeping her on the edge but not allowing her to go over it, not wanting the act to end. His strong hands on her hips controlled her, guided her, held her when she would have taken over the rhythm he'd set. She clenched her teeth on the agony of pleasure that boiled in her; then suddenly it was too much to be held in, and she heard the words of love that she gasped, the words that she'd always longed to say but had held inside.

A rumble in his chest and the tightening of his hands on her flesh signaled the end of his control, and he began to thrust hungrily into her. Instantly an incredible heat exploded inside her, washing through her with ever-widening waves, making her shudder beneath him. She sank her teeth into his shoulder in an effort to control the sounds she was making, and the primitive, sensual act pushed him over the edge. Short, harsh cries tore from his throat as his satisfaction thundered through him, and he clasped her to him with a wild strength that made her gasp for breath, as if he could meld her flesh with his for all time. When he'd finished, he slowly relaxed until he lay limply on her, his body still quivering with small aftershocks. She smoothed his sweat-damp hair, her fingers gentle on his moist temple. His hot breath seared her throat, and she felt the flutter of his eyelashes against her skin as he began to doze.

But he lay there for only a moment before rousing himself and gently moving from her. He rolled heavily onto his back and lay there, one brawny forearm thrown over his eyes.

Susan lay beside him, tension and dread growing in her again now that the appetites of her body had been satisfied. She should never have let that happen, not tonight, not when she had so much on her mind. And she had told him that she loved him. He couldn't have misunderstood her; it seemed to her that the words still lingered in the air, echoing with ghostly insistence. Would he say anything, or would he just ignore what she'd said? He hadn't asked for any commitment from her any more than he'd offered one. He probably wasn't even surprised; it couldn't be the first time that a woman in his arms had cried out that she loved him.

Caught in her misery, she was only half-aware when he left the bed. The sound of running water caught her attention, and she opened her eyes to look at him through the open door of the bathroom as he stood drinking deeply from a glass of water. His strong brown throat worked as he appeased his thirst. He'd already straightened his clothing, she saw, and her hands clenched into fists. He'd be leaving now that his sexual appetite had been satisfied.

He came back and stood over her, his level dark brows lowered over eyes so pale and fierce that she almost flinched from them. "You scared the hell out of me," he said flatly. "Why didn't you answer the door?"

Restlessly, she sat up, and flushed wildly when she saw that her skirt was still tangled above her waist. Quickly she fumbled with the cloth, straightening it and pushing it down to cover her nakedness, an act that sparked a flash of fury in his eyes. But when she darted a glance up at him, she saw only the same iron implacability that had been there before as he waited for an answer. Pushing her tumbled hair back from her face, she said in a dull tone, "You bought up a loan against us and called it in."

Silence lay thickly between them for a long moment; then he sliced it by saying harshly, "You're not involved in that."

A laugh broke from her throat, a laugh that was almost a sob, and she got quickly to her feet, leaving the bed where she had given herself to him so thoroughly. For a moment she feared her legs wouldn't hold her, but after an initial wobble she regained control of them and moved a few paces away from him. "I have to be. You know that everything is tied together. If you attack them financially, you're attacking me financially. If you bankrupt them, you bankrupt me."

"You don't have anything to worry about. I'll take care of you."

The cool arrogance of his words almost made her choke, and she whirled on him in disbelief. "Is that supposed to make it all right? You'll reduce me to a . . . a kept woman, and I'm supposed to be grateful?"

One dark eyebrow quirked. "I don't see your problem," he said, and added with casual cruelty, "after all, you said that you love me."

She winced, unable to believe he'd attacked her so soon, even though she'd put the weapon in his hand. Suddenly she was too close to him, and she put the width of the room between them, withdrawing from him as far as she could. She bent her head, unable to look at him and face the contemptuous knowledge that she knew must be in his eyes. "Would you . . . would you actually push us all into bankruptcy just to get back at Preston? Even knowing that a lot of other people are involved, that they'd lose their jobs?"

"Yes." His voice was hard, as hard as he was, and the last vestige of hope died in her. Until then there had been one small shred of faith left; she had been able to hope that he was only punishing Preston and would stop before things went too far.

"You'd be hurting yourself!" she cried. "How can you do this?"

He gave a negligent shrug. "I've got other things to fall back on."

She'd begged before, with no result, but now she was reduced to doing it again. "Cord, stop this! Please! Don't push it until it's gone too far. When will you be satisfied?

After you've ruined us all, then what? Will it have brought Judith back for you?''

His face turned into stone, and his eyes narrowed. Wildly, goaded by her own pain, she lashed out at him, sensing that she'd found a way to wound him. ''You're just trying to ease your own guilt about Judith, because of your part in what happened to her—''

With a growl he strode across the room, seizing her before she could dart to the side and avoid him. His hands bit into her shoulders and he shook her lightly. ''Shut up about Judith! I made a mistake in telling you about her, but you'll be making an even bigger one if you ever mention her to me again. For the last time, stay out of this.''

''I can't. I'm already in it.'' She stared up at him with eyes so huge that they eclipsed her entire face, eyes so filled with pain that any other woman would have been weeping uncontrollably. They were going to destroy each other, Cord and Preston, and she was helpless to stop it. There could be no winners in this family war, because when the bond of common blood goes bad, it causes a rift that can never be healed. She saw the chasm that was already widening between herself and Cord, and she wanted to scream out in desperate protest, but there was nothing she could do. She held herself rigidly in his painful grip, trying to control the shrieking agony that was tearing her heart apart.

His grasp on her eased, and he stroked his thumbs over the fragile ridges of her collarbones. ''You're too soft for this,'' he murmured to himself; then he eased her back into his embrace, shifting his arms to hold her against him. She was silent, letting herself rest against him because she hadn't the strength to deny herself what she feared might be the last time he'd hold her like this. He bent his head to press his warm lips into the sensitive curve where her neck met her shoulder, and a delicious shiver ran over her body. Just like that, with only a casual caress, he was able to make

her want him again. She loved him too much, too dangerously, because she could hold nothing of herself back.
There was no way she could protect herself.

"Don't go back to work," he instructed softly, brushing
his lips against her hair. "Stay at home, and stay out of this.
Vance left you secure, and whatever happens to Preston
won't affect you at all." His big hands stroked slowly over
her back and shoulders, their effect on her hypnotic. "You
said that you love me; if you do, you won't take his side
against me."

For a moment, for a weak, delicious moment, she wanted
nothing more than to do just as he said, to let his hard
embrace protect her and make her forget all other considera-
tions. Then she stiffened and slowly pushed herself away
from him, her face taut and pale.

"Yes, I love you," she said quietly, because there was no
use in trying to hide it from him any longer. How could she
deny it, when her body told him the truth every time he
touched her? "But I have to do whatever I can to stop you
from bankrupting the family."

His eyes narrowed. "You're choosing him over me?"

"No. But I think you're wrong in what you're trying to
do, and if you won't stop, then I have to help him fight
you."

Black fury gathered in him, sparking out of his pale eyes,
but he held it in. "Is it asking too much for you to trust me
in this?" he rasped, watching her carefully.

"The same way you trust me?" she shot back. "You told
me yourself, just a moment ago, that you're trying to
bankrupt us! Is that supposed to reassure me?"

He gave a derisive snort, the fire in his eyes turning to
ice. "I should've known! You spouted that garbage about
loving me, *then* you asked me so sweetly to ease up on
Preston. You're good in the sack, baby, the best I've had,
but you don't have that kind of a hold on me."

"I know," she whispered blankly. "I've always known

that. But I wasn't trying for any emotional blackmail. I think . . . I think you'd better go.''

"I think you're right.''

As he moved past her, she blinked at him with eyes suddenly blurred by a film of tears. He was going, and she knew he wouldn't be back. "Goodbye,'' she choked, feeling herself shatter inside.

He gave her a grim look. "It's not goodbye, not yet. You'll be seeing me around, though you'll wish you weren't.'' Then he was gone, lightly taking the stairs with graceful bounds. Slowly she followed him, and she reached the door in time to watch the red flare of the Blazer's taillights disappear as he rounded a curve. She shut the door and locked it, then methodically moved about and made certain the house was secure for the night. She even sat down and watched the late movie until it went off, then realized that she hadn't absorbed any of it. She didn't even know the name of it, or the names of the actors. She hadn't been thinking of anything, just sitting there, her mind numb. She wanted it to stay numb, because she knew that when the numbness wore off, she was going to hurt more than she could bear.

She went through the motions of going to bed; she showered and put on her nightgown, moisturized her face, neatened up her bedroom and put her discarded clothing in the laundry basket. Then she lay in bed until dawn, her eyes open and staring at the ceiling. He was gone.

He was gone! It was a litany of pain that echoed through her endlessly, an inner accompaniment to the gray, dreary days that followed. The sun could have been shining; she simply didn't know. But she couldn't see any sunshine, and she functioned only through instinct and sheer grim determination. She'd kept going after Vance's death, and now the same steely determination kept her upright even when she wanted nothing more than to collapse in a corner of her bedroom and not ever come out again.

She'd had to accept the bleak truth of Vance's death because she had seen his lifeless body, had buried him. It was worse with Cord. He was gone from her, yet he seemed to be everywhere. They met at several functions, and she had to act as if it didn't almost double her over with pain to see him. He was usually with Cheryl, of course, though she heard that he wasn't limiting himself to the other woman. She had to see him, had to listen to him say all the polite things while his icy eyes cut her, had to watch him slide his arm about Cheryl's waist, had to imagine him kissing the other woman, touching her with his hot, magic fingers, drawing her beneath him in his big bed at the cabin.

To stay sane she drove herself at work every day, working longer and longer hours, working frantically with Preston in an effort to raise enough cash to pay off the loan without seriously weakening the corporation. It was an impossible task; they both knew that if Cord chose to attack them again, they wouldn't be able to meet his demands.

Quietly, without letting Preston know, Susan sold some prime property in New Orleans that Vance had left her and added the proceeds to their cash fund. Preston would have died rather than let her sell off any of her personal property, though she knew he'd been heavily liquidating his. Sometimes, when she thought about the fact that Cord was deliberately forcing them to sell off land that had been in the family for generations, she hated him, but always that hate was mingled with love. If she hadn't loved him so much, she wouldn't have felt so betrayed by his actions, wouldn't have been so deeply angry when she saw Preston, without complaint, destitute himself personally in order to keep the corporation out of bankruptcy.

This had shaken Imogene, too, to the very basis of her foundations. Since the night she and Susan had argued so violently, she had been a little quieter, as if some of the spirit had gone out of her. Perhaps she had sensed then that she couldn't fight Cord, that by the very act of returning he had won. Always before, Imogene had been actively involved in any corporate decisions, but now she let Preston and Susan carry the weight. For the first time she was showing her age.

At last it was done. They had enough to cover the loan, and though Susan and Preston shared a moment of relief, it wasn't without worry. They had used every ounce of spare reserve they had, and another blow would be too much. Still, the relief was strong enough that they celebrated in the French Quarter that night, in a far noisier restaurant than the one Cord had taken her to. But she was glad of the noise and distraction, and for once she ate a good meal. In the time since Cord had sauntered out of her house she'd lost several pounds that she hadn't been able to spare. It was as much overwork as depression, or so she told herself every morning when she frowningly examined herself in the mirror, noting that her clothing was too loose to fall correctly on her increasingly slender body.

On the drive home Preston startled her by apologizing. "You've broken up with Cord because of this, haven't you?"

There was no denying it, no use in concocting a lame excuse that they simply hadn't gotten along, so she simply murmured, "Yes," and let it go at that.

"I'm sorry." He cast her a frustrated glance. "I should be glad, because I didn't like you being with him, but I'm sorry that you've been hurt. I didn't want you in the middle like this."

"I made my decision. He insisted that I choose sides, and I simply couldn't watch him cost a lot of people their jobs without trying to do something about it."

"I hope he knows what he's lost," Preston said violently, and returned his attention to his driving.

Even if he knew, he wouldn't care, Susan thought dully. He certainly wasn't pining away for her; he looked better every time she saw him, his hard, dark face becoming darker as the late spring sun continued to bronze him. Had he finished clearing off the land down by the creek? Was he doing any more work on the cabin?

When he had pushed her out of his life, he had left her lost and desolate, without any emotional focus. She wondered if the rest of her life would be like this, a dull misery to be endured as she went through the motions of living.

Chapter 10

IF SHE HAD KNOWN WHAT AWAITED HER WHEN SHE walked into the office three days later, she would never have gone. Beryl was already there and had a fragrant pot of coffee brewing. "Good morning, Beryl. Is Mr. Blackstone in yet?"

"No, not yet. Do you want a cup of coffee now?"

Susan smiled at the young woman. "I'll get it. You look like you have enough to handle right now," she teased, nodding at the stacks of paperwork that littered Beryl's desk.

Beryl nodded ruefully. "Don't I, though? Mr. Blackstone must have worked until midnight last night. He left all of this, and enough tapes on the dictaphone to keep me typing through the weekend."

"Really? I didn't know he'd planned to come back to the office last night. He left when I did, and I can't think of anything that would have been so urgent."

She poured herself some coffee and carefully balanced the cup as she went into her office, keeping a cautious eye on the sloshing liquid. She placed the cup on her desk and walked around to pull the curtains open, letting the brilliant morning sunlight pour into the room. The day was hot already, with a sultry feel to it that had dampened the back of her neck with perspiration even before she'd left the house that morning. She was beginning to think of taking a vacation, finding a beach somewhere and doing nothing more strenuous than lying in the sun. Somehow, sweating on the beach didn't sound nearly as hot as sweating at work.

After fingering the blossoms of her favorite geranium, she went to her desk and sat down. It wasn't until then that she saw the thick manila envelope lying there with her name printed on it in big block letters. Frowning, she opened the sealed envelope and pulled out a sheaf of papers. On top was some sort of legal document, and she turned it around to read it.

Immediately she went deathly white, not having to read further than the front page to know it for what it was. Cord had bought up another loan and called it in.

My God, he was going to do it. They couldn't weather this. They couldn't pay, and the shock waves he was going to make would reverberate throughout the corporation and the banks they were involved with. Their credit would be ruined. They simply couldn't pay this and keep operating.

Where was Preston? She wanted to run to him, wanted to hear him say that he would be able to work another little piece of magic and somehow come up with the money they needed. It was selfish of her, and she controlled the urge. He would have to know, yes, but let him have a few more hours of peace, of not knowing.

How had the envelope gotten on her desk? The office was always locked when they left, and Preston had worked late the night before. . . .

Then she knew, and she felt sick. Preston already knew about the loan, and he'd left the envelope on her desk.

She flipped through the legal document, and behind it she

found a letter to her, in Preston's handwriting. His usually elegant style was a scrawl as if the letter had been written in agitation, but the writing was unmistakably his. She read the letter through carefully, and when she was finished she let it fall to the floor, tears searing her eyes.

If Cord had wanted only to defeat Preston, he'd won. Preston had gone. His letter was both defeated and desperate. He'd done all he could, but he couldn't fight Cord any longer. Perhaps, if he left, Cord would let up. By taking himself out of the picture, Preston hoped that Cord would cease his vengeance.

Cord had had the legal paperwork delivered to Preston at home, by special messenger, an act that chilled Susan with its calculated cruelty. Preston had then returned to the office, methodically finished all the work currently on his desk, left the letter for Susan, and disappeared.

She couldn't blame Preston for leaving; she knew that it was his last-ditch effort to save the corporation, to keep Cord from putting it under. He hoped that when Cord found that Susan was running the corporation he wouldn't call in the loan, knowing that his prime target had fled and that now he was attacking only a woman he'd previously been very interested in.

As if that would stop him! Susan thought despairingly. Then her spine stiffened. As if she would run crying to him now, asking him to have mercy on her!

She'd begged him before, for Preston's sake, for everyone's sake, and he'd turned a cold shoulder to her. She wouldn't beg him for herself now.

Susan didn't recognize the fierce anger that seized her, but she wasn't going to just give up. If she had to fight him until she didn't have a penny left, then that's what she would do.

She picked up the telephone and quickly punched out a number. She wasn't surprised when Imogene answered herself.

"Imogene, do you know where Preston is?" she asked directly, not wasting time with polite greetings.

"No. He only told me that he was going." Imogene's voice sounded tired and a little thick, as if she'd been crying.

"Do you know why he left?"

"Yes. I tried to talk him out of it, but he wouldn't listen. He just wouldn't listen," she sighed. "He thinks that this is the only way he can get Cord to stop. What . . . what are you going to do? Are you going to see Cord?"

"No!" Susan said violently. She inhaled swiftly, searching for control and finding it. "I'm not going to tell him anything. I'm going to fight him with everything I have, and I need your help."

"Help?" Imogene echoed blankly. "What can I do?"

"You've been involved with this corporation for years. You have a lot of contacts, and you know everything that's going on even if you don't come to the office. There's too much to do on an everyday basis for me to handle it by myself and fight Cord, too. Will you come? Do you want to fight him?"

There was a long silence on the other end of the phone, and Susan waited tensely, her eyes closed. She really needed Imogene's help. She didn't fool herself that she'd be able to carry on for long by herself. The burden would break her. But Imogene hadn't been herself, and she wasn't sure what her mother-in-law would do.

"I don't want to fight him," Imogene finally said softly. "This insanity has gone on long enough. If I thought it would stop him, I'd sign everything I own over to him this minute just to bring peace to our family. I have to share in the responsibility for this mess, and I'm not proud of it. I shouldn't have turned on him; he's family, and I forgot that. I regret it so much now, but regrets don't do any good."

Susan's heart sank. "You won't help?"

"I didn't say that. I'll be there as soon as I can get myself ready and make the drive. But it's not to fight him, dear. It's to help you, and to do what I can to keep the corporation out of bankruptcy. That's the only important thing now, and when it's over, I'll crawl on my hands and knees to Cord if that will satisfy him and stop this war.''

The thought of proud Imogene being willing to humble herself in such a way left Susan fighting tears again. "I'll be waiting,'' she whispered, and hung up the phone before she embarrassed herself by sobbing into it.

If she had worked before, it was nothing compared to the way she drove herself now. She arrived in the office shortly after dawn and often remained until nine or ten in the evening. On the surface, it didn't seem possible that she would be able to meet Cord's demands, but she didn't give up. Imogene was on the phone constantly, calling in favors, trying to arrange a loan that would keep them going. But even old friends were suddenly wary of the Blackstone Corporation, for the business grapevine was remarkably sensitive, and word had filtered through that they were on shaky financial ground. Their common stock was trading hands rapidly, and in desperation Susan put some of her own stock up for sale. Preston and Imogene had already sold some of their stock in order to replace the money they'd embezzled from Cord, hoping to buy more when their cash flow had improved. But Cord had kept them on the ropes and hadn't let the pressure ease at all. At least the price of the stock was holding up, due to the brisk trading, but Susan knew that she had to take even more desperate measures.

She had stock in other companies, blue-chip investments, and ruthlessly she turned them into cash. She kept it secret from Imogene, knowing that Imogene would be as horrified at the idea, as Preston had been. Imogene was holding up wonderfully, attacking the work with increased vigor, and as she settled into it she began to display a wonderful panache for the job. Susan didn't want to do anything to throw the older woman back into the mild depression that had held her in its grip lately. She knew that Imogene worried about Preston and fretted over the absence of her only living son; that burden was enough.

Every morning when Susan looked in the mirror she realized anew that she was living on her nerves, and sometimes she wondered how much longer she could keep going. The shadows under her eyes seemed to have become permanent fixtures that she carefully disguised with make-up. She always left the house now before Emily arrived, and she was too tense to prepare breakfast herself and eat it. There was always a meal left for her when she got home at night, needing only to be warmed, but more often than not Susan was too exhausted to eat it. She was existing on pots of coffee and hasty bites taken out of sandwiches, sand-wiches that were seldom finished and instead left to grow stale while she worked.

The steamy weather further sapped her strength, the heat and humidity weighing her down like a smothering blanket. She couldn't sleep at night, even with the air-conditioning on, and she would lie watching the flash of heat lightning, hoping that the bursts of light meant thunderstorms and rain, but the clouds never came and each day dawned hotter than the one before.

Lying on her bed in the thick, humid nights, the light cover kicked down to the foot of the bed because even a sheet was too oppressive, she thought of Cord. During the day she could resent him, hate him, fight him, but when the nights came she could no longer hold the memories at bay, and she would hug her pillow to herself, keening her pain almost soundlessly into the pillow. He had been on that bed with her, his dark head on the other pillow; he had wrapped her graceful legs around him, linking her to him with a chain of flesh while he drove deeply into her body and her heart. She wanted him so much that her entire body ached, her breasts throbbing, her thighs and loins heavy with need.

She wanted just to see him, to watch his beautifully shaped mouth quirk into one of those devastatingly wicked smiles. Whenever she dozed she dreamed of him, and she would jerk herself awake with a start as she reached out for him. Sometimes the impulse to go to him was almost too strong to ignore, and in the hot, heavy nights she suffered alone.

She heard, through the grapevine of gossip that always yielded an astonishing amount of information, that Cord was gone again, and this time she didn't wonder if he'd ever come back; now she wondered what new weapon he was readying to use against her. No, not against *her* personally, but against them all in general. Though she wasn't able to pinpoint the exact date when he'd left, she knew that it was about the same time Preston had gone; it was possible that he didn't know Preston had bowed out and left the corporation in her lap. As far as all their acquaintances were concerned, Preston was on a business trip. That was the tale she and Imogene had decided to put out, rather than trigger a flood of gossip that would grow larger and wilder with every turn.

Despite everything, when the grapevine informed her that Cord had returned, she didn't feel the dread that should have overwhelmed her. For a sweet moment of insanity she was simply glad that he'd returned, that he was once more close by geographically, if not emotionally. Somehow she felt that if he was at least in Mississippi, then it wasn't all over. When it was finished for good, he'd leave for good.

If she hadn't been so tired, so desperate, pushed beyond common sense, she'd never have considered the idea. But late one afternoon she thought again of the ridges. She hadn't slept at all the night before, with her thoughts whirling around in her mind like a rabid squirrel in a cage, until she felt as if her very skull were sore from being banged from within. The air conditioner couldn't handle the heat and humidity, and her lightweight tan suit clung to her sticky skin. She'd already shed the jacket, since it was late and everyone else had already gone home, but even the thin cotton camisole top she'd worn with the suit seemed to be restricting her. A distant rumble of thunder held out the hope of rain to a parched region, but Susan had ceased believing in the thunder's promise. It had proved to be deceptive too often lately.

She had done everything she could think of, and still she hadn't managed to scrape together enough cash to pay off the loan. She'd liquidated a large portion of her stock in Blackstone Corporation, all her stock in everything else, and had disposed of all of the property Vance had accumulated for her . . . all of it except for the land the house stood on, and the ridges.

The ridges. The thought of them was like a jolt of electricity, straightening her in her chair. *The ridges!* With their promise of oil or natural gas, they were a gold mine, and she'd had it under her nose all the time. The money she could get from leasing them would be enough to finish covering the loan, and in her exhaustion she thought that it would be only fitting that the money from the ridges be used to defeat Cord; after all, it had been the ridges that had brought him back to Mississippi in the first place.

In the back of her mind she knew it was odd that Cord hadn't pressed her about signing the lease, but she simply couldn't follow his reasoning. She loved him, but even after weeks of agonized wondering, she couldn't understand him.

The thought of the ridges gave her a spurt of strength, rather like a marathon runner's last desperate burst of speed. She would drive out to the cabin and offer the lease to Cord, and he could take it right now or leave it. If he didn't take it, then she'd lease the land to the first oil company she could interest in it, but she was going to give him the first chance at it. She knew that her excuse was flimsy, but suddenly she had to see him. Even if he were an enemy now, she had to see him.

Without giving herself time to reconsider, she locked the office and left the building. If she thought about it, she'd begin to worry, and she'd let the doubts change her mind. Her hands were trembling as she guided the Audi out of Biloxi. A distracted glance at the fuel gauge warned her to stop for gas, but even that small interruption in her progress was too much to tolerate. She thought she'd have enough gas to get home, and that was all she cared about at the moment. She'd worry about getting to work later.

The radio volume was low, but even the background noise was rasping on her nerves, and she snapped the radio off with a quick, irritable movement. It was so hot, and she felt so weak! A moment of dizziness alarmed her, and she turned the air conditioning vents so the cold air was blowing right on her face. After a moment she felt better, and she urged the Audi to greater speeds.

The Blazer was parked under one of the giant oak trees that kept the fierce sun away from the front of the cabin, and the front door stood open. Susan guided the Audi to a hard stop in front of the porch, and as she opened the door to get out, Cord strolled lazily out of the cabin to lean against one of the posts that supported the porch roof. He had on boots, and jeans so old that one of the pockets was missing, and that was all. She looked up at him and her heart stopped for a moment. He'd begun to let his beard grow again, and the several days' growth of whiskers on his jaw made him look like an outlaw out of a Western. His hard, muscled torso was darkly tanned, his hair longer, and if anything, his pale eyes were even more compelling than she'd remembered. Her mouth went dry, and her legs wobbled as she went up the steps, clinging with all her strength to the rough railing.

She'd tried to imagine what his first words would be, and her imagination had supplied any number of brutal things that would wound her. She braced herself for them as his narrowed gaze went over her from head to foot.

"Come on in and have a glass of iced tea," he invited,

his rough, callused hand closing on her elbow and urging her inside the cabin. "You look like you're about to melt."

Was that it? She had to swallow an almost hysterical giggle. After all her panic, he calmly invited her in for iced tea!

Somehow she found herself sitting at his table while he moved around the kitchen. "I was just about to eat," he said easily. "Nothing hot in this weather, just a ham sandwich and a tossed salad, but there's plenty for two."

She started. He wanted her to eat? "Oh, no, thank you—"

He interrupted her refusal by sliding a plate in front of her. She stared down at the ham sandwich, wondering if she could possibly swallow a bite of it, and his hand entered her field of vision again, this time placing a chilled bowl of salad beside the plate. A napkin and cutlery were placed by her hand, and a big glass of beautiful, amber tea over ice finished her instant meal. When she lifted her stunned gaze, she saw that he'd set the same for himself, and he draped his tall frame into the chair across from her.

"Eat," he said gently. "You'll feel better after you do."

When had she last had a meal, a real meal? The days had merged into one long, steamy nightmare, and she couldn't recall her last meal. Half-eaten sandwiches, coffee, and an occasional candy bar had constituted her diet since Preston had left. She began to eat slowly, and the crisp, fresh flavor of the salad, only lightly coated with tart dressing, was suddenly the best thing she could imagine eating. She savored every bite of it, and the cold tea seemed to cool her from the inside out. Because she'd been eating so little she was unable to eat all of the sandwich, but Cord made no comment on the half left on her plate. Instead he swiftly cleared the table, placing the dishes in the sink before coming back to the table and refilling her glass with tea.

"Now," he said, dropping into his chair again, "you

don't look like you're going to pass out at my feet, so I'll listen to whatever you came to say."

Susan held the frosty glass between both hands, feeling the refreshing chill on her hot palms. "I want to talk to you about the ridges," she said, but her mind wasn't on her words. She was staring at him, her eyes tracing the lines of his features as if etching them permanently on her memory.

"So talk. What about them?" He folded his arms across his chest and leaned back, bringing his booted feet up and propping them on the chair beside him.

"Do you still want to lease them?"

His lids dropped down to hood his eyes. "Get to the point, Susan."

Nervously, she took a sip of tea, then fidgeted for a moment with the glass, returning it to precisely the same spot where it had been before, making certain that it matched the ring of water that marked its position. "If you want them, then lease them now. I've decided not to wait for the report from the survey. If you don't want the lease any longer, I'm going to lease them to some other company."

"Oh, I still want them," he said softly, "but I'm not going to give you any money on them right now. You'd run all the way to Biloxi to give the money to Preston, and I'll be damned if I'll give you a penny until this is all over. The money from the ridges is for you, to keep you in your accustomed style after Preston doesn't have a penny left." He gave her a cynical grin, one full of wry amusement at himself. "I'll keep you in silk underwear, honey."

Susan choked and jumped to her feet, her cheeks scarlet. "Then I'll lease them to someone else!"

"I don't think so," he drawled, swinging his long legs to the floor and getting to his feet, moving gracefully to put himself between her and the door. "If you think I've used every club I have against Preston already, then you're mistaken. If you lease that land to anyone else, I'll crush him, and you can bet your sweet little life on that.''

Susan drew back from him, stumbling a little as she tried to circle the table without turning her back on him. She was slowed by her exhaustion, and totally unable to react when he moved suddenly, cutting her off. His hands closed on her fragile waist, and he felt the slenderness of her under his fingers. His black brows snapped together in a forbidding frown. "How much weight have you lost?" he demanded curtly, glaring down at her.

Despite the tremors that quaked through her insides, Susan held herself stiffly. "That's none of your business." Her fingers dug into his biceps as she tried to push him away, but he was as immovable as a boulder.

He held her with one arm and swept his other hand over her body, exploring her newly frail contours. He slid his hand over her hips and buttocks, her slender thighs, then up to rub gently over her breasts, making her cry out and writhe in a desperate attempt to escape him. He held her easily, his eyes blue with fury. "What in the hell has he done to you?"

Shards of pain pierced her, and she twisted suddenly, a gasping cry breaking from her lips. She managed to break his grip, and she shoved herself away from him, her face pale, her hair straggling out of its once-tidy knot. She hurt so much, and she was so desperate, that she screamed at him, "He hasn't done anything to me! You've done it; you've done it all! You're not crushing him, you're crushing *me!* He left—'' Horrified at what she was saying, she stuffed her hand into her mouth to stop the mad tumble of words, her eyes huge and so dark they were almost black as she stared at him.

If he had been angry before, he exploded now. Hammering his fist on the table with a force that upset her glass of tea, he roared, "What do you mean, 'He *left?*' That damned weasel!''

"He's not a weasel!" She'd been pushed too far to be wary of his temper, to even consider the questionable wisdom of defending Preston to Cord. "He left because he hoped you'd stop when you saw that you weren't hurting him any longer! He's trying to save the corporation, save thousands of jobs—"

"You mean he thought you'd come running to me with the information that you were trying to do it all on your own, and I'd back off. Damn you, Susan, why didn't you do just that? Why have you driven yourself into the ground like this?"

"Because I think you're wrong! Preston isn't using me as a sacrificial lamb; if you'd stop hating him long enough, you might see that he's not the same person he was years ago. You can try to ease your own guilt by making him pay, but you're wrong to do it!"

"Is that why you've run yourself half to death, to show me how wrong I am?"

He was never going to listen to reason. The realization slapped her in the face, and she reeled from the force of it. "No," she whispered. "I've run myself half to death trying to keep a corporation alive. I don't sleep because I lie awake trying to think of a way to raise money, and I don't eat because I don't have the time to spare." She'd gone completely white now, her eyes blazing at him. "I've sold everything I own, except my house and the ridges, trying to stay afloat. Do you want them, too? Or maybe the keys to my car? Or how about my record collection? I've got some real golden oldies—"

"Shut up!" he thundered, reaching out a hand to catch her.

She twisted away, unable to bear his touch. "Leave me alone," she said rawly, then almost ran out of the cabin and tumbled into the Audi. Slamming the door, she savagely turned the key in the ignition and the engine caught immediately, but when she put the car in gear it gave a shuddering jerk and died. "Don't do this to me," she said through gritted teeth, turning the key again. The motor turned over but didn't catch, and in horror her eyes flew to the fuel gauge, where the needle bumped against the E. "Damn you!" she shrieked at the car. "Don't do this to me!" She began to pound on the steering wheel with both fists, screaming, "Damn! Damn! Damn!" with every impact, and tears burst from her eyes.

"Susan!" The door was wrenched open, and Cord caught her wrists, hauling her out of the car. "Susan, stop it! Settle down, honey, just settle down. Don't fly apart like this. Let me see if I can get the car started."

"You can't," she blurted, pulling her hands free to bury her face in them and weep uncontrollably. It was just too much. She, who always controlled her tears no matter how much she hurt, had dissolved into sobs because she had run out of gas. "The gas tank is empty."

He slid into the driver's seat, keeping one long leg on the outside of the car, as he turned on the ignition and checked it for himself. Sighing, he got out of the car and closed the door. "I'll drive you home."

"I don't want you to drive me home!" She turned to walk down the slope and he made a grab for her, hauling her back just as an enormous clap of thunder shook the earth. She jumped, startled, looking up at the horrendous black cloud that had suddenly taken over the sky. A brisk wind had begun blowing, but she hadn't noticed it until then. As they both looked up, the first enormous raindrops splattered them in the face with stinging force, and Cord put his arm around her, hustling her up on the porch just before the heavens split open and dropped a deluge so thunderous that they had to shout to make themselves heard.

"You can't walk home in this," he yelled, bending down to put his mouth close to her ear. "We'll wait until it lets up; then I'll take you home."

Despairingly, Susan looked at the gray curtain of rain.

Already it had turned the area around the cabin into a shallow river as the water ran down the slope, rushing downward to the creek. She knew that it would splash up to her ankles, and gave in to his opinion that she couldn't walk home. But neither could she stay here, so close to him, in the cabin where they'd made love the first time. Her nerves were at the breaking point. "I want to go home!" she half screamed at him. "I'm not going to stay here! I simply won't!"

A look of savage impatience twisted his face; then he brought himself under control by sheer effort of will. He caught her arm and dragged her into the cabin, slamming the door shut in an effort to close out the roar of the rain.

"All right, all right!" he snapped. "We're going to get soaked just getting into the Blazer, you know."

"I don't care." Obdurately she stared at him, and he stared back at her in frustrated fury, but evidently he saw something in her face that made him hesitate. She had no idea how frail she looked, or how deeply the shadows of exhaustion lay under her eyes. He shoved his hand through his too-long hair, making the silky strands tumble down over his forehead.

"I'll pull the Blazer up as close to the porch as I can," he muttered. "There's a newspaper on the table in front of the fireplace; put it over your head and make a run for it. But I warn you, it's not going to do much good against this downpour." He stalked to the cabinet and pulled out a plastic trash bag, then disappeared into the bedroom. Susan remained where she stood, feeling icy chills race over her body, too dispirited to wonder what he was doing. He came out a moment later wearing one of those disreputable T-shirts that hugged his magnificent body so faithfully. He had the trash bag folded and tucked under his arm, and a battered khaki-colored baseball-style cap was jammed on his head. He looked as stormy and furious as the cloud outside.

Without speaking to her, he went out on the porch, and she followed him. He didn't bother with the steps; he walked to the end of the porch nearest to the Blazer and paused a moment to stare in disgust at the pounding rain. Then he leaped off the end of the porch, and was in a dead run by the time his feet hit the ground. As depressed as she was, Susan watched him in admiration, admiring the speed and grace of his powerful strides. He looked like a linebacker closing in on a pass receiver, every movement purposeful and deadly.

A bolt of lightning, blindingly white, snapped to the ground close to the creek, and the ear-splitting crack made Susan shriek and jump back as the entire earth shook. The tiny hairs on the back of her neck lifted at the electricity that hummed through the air, and suddenly she realized how powerful this storm was, how dangerous it was to be out in it. The limbs of the giant oaks were waving back and forth as the trees bent before the onslaught. She wanted to call Cord back, but he was already in the Blazer; she heard the engine roar into life, and the headlights came on. She stumbled back into the cabin to get the newspaper he'd indicated, only to find that the storm had blotted out the lingering twilight and it was so dark inside the cabin that she had to switch on a lamp to find the newspaper.

Her fingers trembled as she turned the light off again. As Cord maneuvered the Blazer up close to the porch, inching it between her car and the steps, the headlights threw twin beams of light through the open door, illuminating the wet floor where the gusting wind had blown the rain across the porch and into the house. She touched her hair and found it was damp, and her clothes were equally damp; she hadn't even noticed that she'd been getting wet.

He blew the horn, and she started. Why was she standing there in the dark? Quickly she crossed the room and struggled out onto the porch, the wind making a strong effort to push her back inside. It took all her strength to tug the door closed, and the newspaper she held over her head was blown uselessly to one side. She grabbed it with both hands and held it; without giving herself time to think, she dashed down the steps, splashing in icy water that was over her ankles. She was soaked through to her skin immediately, and she gasped at the iciness of the rain. Cord had leaned over to open the door of the Blazer for her, but when she let go of the newspaper with one hand to reach for the hand that he extended to her, the paper was promptly whisked away and the deluge struck her unprotected head. The Blazer sat so high on its huge wheels that she couldn't jump up in it, so she caught the edge of the seat in an effort to haul herself up. Cord cursed, the word drowned out by the pounding rain, and leaned over to catch her under the arms. He lifted her bodily inside, then leaned in front of her to slam the door shut.

"There're a couple of towels in the trash bag," he informed her curtly, sliding back under the steering wheel and putting the vehicle in gear.

She pulled one of the towels out and patted it over her bare arms and shoulders, then blotted her dripping hair. That was the best she could do, and she stared in dismay at the soaked seats and floorboards of the Blazer. "I'm sorry," she choked, realizing now that they should have remained at the cabin until the storm had passed.

Rain still glistened on the rock-hard planes of his face, and drops were caught like liquid diamonds in the black silk of his beard. He pulled the soggy cap from his head and dropped it on the seat between them. In silence she offered him the towel, and in silence he took it, rubbing it over his face and head with one hand as he eased down the driveway.

The headlights caught the swirling, muddy waters of Jubilee Creek as they crossed the small bridge, and she was frightened at how high the water had risen in the short time it had been raining. Cord gave the water a grim look. "I hope I can get back."

He had to keep both hands on the wheel to hold the Blazer steady against the gusts of wind that pushed at it; one particularly strong gust pushed them so far to the side that the two left tires left the road and dug into the soft earth on the side. Cord wrestled them back onto the roughly paved secondary road, but they could proceed at nothing more than a crawl. The headlights did no good against a blinding curtain of rain, and the windshield wipers, though going full speed, couldn't keep the windshield clear.

Making a sudden decision, he glanced at her and pulled the Blazer over onto the side of the road, then cut the ignition. As the engine died, the roar of the rain hitting the metal top sounded even louder. He'd turned off the headlights but left the dashlights on, and in the dim glow she turned frightened eyes on him.

"I can't see to drive," he explained. "We're going to have to wait until this blows over."

She nodded and clasped her hands tightly in her lap, staring out through the windshield. She couldn't see anything; the darkness was absolute, the rain cutting them off from everything else, isolating them in the small sanctuary of the Blazer.

Seconds ticked past and became minutes; if anything, the rain fell harder. Cord turned on the radio, but the static was so bad that they couldn't make out what the announcer was saying, and he snapped it off again. Out of the corner of his eye, he caught her shivering, and he reached out to touch her chilled arm.

"You should have said something," he scolded, and started the motor, then flipped the heater switch to high.

The blast of warm air felt good on her feet and legs, and she slipped her icy feet out of her soggy shoes to stick her toes up close to the vent.

Silence thickened and grated on her nerves. "It's been a long time since I've seen it rain like this," she ventured, if only to break the quiet.

He drummed his fingers on the steering wheel.

She controlled a shiver. "Why did you start letting your beard grow again?"

"Because I don't like to shave."

The curt sentence slapped at her, and she winced. So much for conversation. She hugged her arms around herself, for the first time thinking of the suit jacket she'd left in her car, as well as her purse. She'd been acting like a wild woman, so desperate to get away that she hadn't given a thought to anything else.

A metallic sound began to reach her ears, just barely detectable above the pounding of the rain. She sat up straighter and cast a puzzled glance in Cord's direction, to find that he was listening too. "What is it?"

"Sleet."

No sooner were the words out of his mouth than the sound of the sleet began to intensify. He turned off the motor, his eyes alert and wary.

"The thunder and lightning are further away," Susan said hopefully, not admitting until that moment that she was a little frightened.

"Shhhh," he cautioned, his head turned slightly in a listening position. He reached out and caught her hand, his hard fingers wrapping securely around hers. Susan caught her breath and listened, too, becoming more uneasy as she realized what they were listening for. The sleet stopped, then abruptly the rain stopped, leaving behind a silence that was broken only by the dripping of water from the battered leaves of the trees.

It was the silence, the utter stillness, that was so unnerving. There was a tense, heavy waiting quality to the air, making it difficult to breathe, or perhaps she was simply too frightened to draw in a deep breath. She was clinging so hard to his hand that her nails were sinking into his flesh. "You can see to drive now," she said nervously.

He slid across the seat until he was pressed warmly against her, his body heat making a mockery of the soggy condition of his clothes. He put his arm around her shoulders in a comforting gesture and briefly pressed his lips to her temple. "We'll wait a while," he told her mildly. "We won't be able to hear it coming if the motor is running."

Susan shivered and closed her eyes. "I know." Her every muscle was tight, her heart pumping faster. The quiet before the storm wasn't just a cliché, it was a reality. As a native of the warm southern climes where the heated Gulf bathed the region in warm moisture, triggering wild and magnificent storms whenever a cooler system from the west swept in to collide with that warm, damp blanket of air, Susan knew all too well the lethal power of the twisting tornados that were spawned out of the towering thunderheads. She knew all the signs, the warnings, and as a child had been drilled in school in the best way to survive a tornado. The Number One Rule: Don't get caught by one.

"If we think we hear something, get out of the truck as fast as you can," Cord instructed quietly. "There's a small ditch on the left of the road; it's probably full of water, but that's where we'll go anyway."

"Okay." Her voice was strained but calm, and she rolled down her window a little, making it easier to hear. Only the dripping of the water, splattering down on the undergrowth, reached her ears.

The first hailstone hit the windshield of the Blazer with such force that they both jumped, and Susan bit back a shriek. Cord uttered a short, sharp expletive, then anything else he might have said was drowned out as golfball-size hail began to pound the Blazer, ripping the leaves of the trees to shreds, taking small saplings completely down. The din was incredible. Susan felt that they were on the inside of a giant drum, with some maniac beating wildly on it. She tore her hand from Cord's grip and pressed her palms over her ears.

Then it was gone, racing away, leaving the ground covered with shimmering balls of ice, a deep rumble following after it.

With a quick, hard motion Cord reached over her and shoved the door open, then used his body to force her outside. He grabbed her around the waist, keeping her from falling as her feet hit the ice and skidded out from under her. She was barefooted except for her stockings, and the ice was unbearably cold, bruising her soft feet, but she knew that she had better traction without her shoes anyway. High heels would have been more than useless, they would have been dangerous, unsafe for picking her way across a road covered with ice balls. Heedless of the pain, she ran, hearing the rumble come closer, feeling the earth begin to tremble beneath them.

They splashed into the ditch, the freezing water taking her breath. There was an eerie yellowish cast to the sky, an absurd lightening of the night sky, and she was able to see the taut lines of Cord's face. With one hand on her shoulder he forced her to lie down in the ditch, and the rushing stream of water splashed up in her face, filling her mouth with the taste of mud. She spat it out and looked up at him, her eyes burning. If she had to die, then thank God it was with him. Then he was covering her, pressing her down deeper into the foul water, putting his body between her and the fury of the storm that was thundering toward them.

Somehow, it didn't seem quite real. Inside she was terrified, but on the outside she was not only calm but oddly detached. She felt the wind buffeting their bodies, so fierce and strong that the tumbling water was blown out of the ditch to splash across the field in tandem with the gargantuan rain that had begun slashing down out of the abruptly inky sky. It had been raining hard before, but that was

nothing to the way it rained then. The water that had been
blown out of the ditch was instantly replaced by the
downpour. Her skin was bruised and stinging in a thousand
places as small stones and debris were hurled through the
air, and she could hear nothing but the roar of the
enormous, thundering monster as it tore across the earth.
She clung to Cord, her slender arms wrapped about his head
in an effort to give him as much protection as she could, and
her desperate strength was so great that he couldn't dislodge
her arms to tuck her more securely under him.

A deep, bull-throated bellow of destruction assaulted her,
and she screamed, a sound that went unheard in the greater
scream of the storm. Cord's grip on her increased until she
thought her ribs would snap under the force of it, and he
pressed her harder, deeper into the ditch. She fought for
breath, but couldn't drag any oxygen into her lungs, as the
monster's suction pulled all the air away into its rotating,
twisting maw. Her only thought was, I'm glad I'm with
him.

She must have fainted, though she could never be sure.
Certainly she was dazed by the storm, her senses scattered.
One moment she was suffocating, feeling as if any moment
the tornado would come down on them, and the next the
world was strangely normal, even serene. It was still
raining, but it was a normal rain, as if the violence of a
moment before had belonged to another world. There was
no lightning, no thunder, no hail . . . and no wind. Cord
was still lying heavily on her, his chest heaving as he too
sucked in much-needed oxygen, his arms outspread and his
fingers sunk into the mud as if he would physically anchor
them to the earth with his own body. They remained like
that for several minutes, lying in the ditch with the rain
slanting down on them, as they tried to assimilate the fact
that they were not only alive, but relatively unscathed.

Susan moved beneath him, turning her face into the
hollow of his throat, and her fingers moved through his hair.

He rolled off her and sat up, his arm behind her as he eased her into a sitting position. "Are you all right?" he demanded hoarsely.

"Yes," she said, and was surprised to find that her throat was sore, her voice so husky that she could barely form the word.

They stumbled to their feet, clinging together, and Susan heard Cord swear quietly as he peered through the darkness and the rain, searching for the Blazer. "I'll be damned," he muttered. "It's turned completely around, and pushed off the road on the other side."

Susan put her hand over her eyes to keep the rain out and was finally able to make out the black bulk of the Blazer, further away now than it had been when they'd jumped out of it so long ago . . . or had it been only a few minutes ago? Cord must have eyes like an eagle, she realized, because she could tell only where the Blazer was, not what direction it was facing.

"It missed us," he said suddenly, with hoarse jubilation. "Look where it came across the road."

Following his pointing hand, she could make out a twisted, broken mass that was evidently an enormous tree, lying across the road. There was an odd, flashing illumination, so bright and blue white that it almost hurt the eyes to look at it. The falling trees had taken down the power lines with them, and now a live wire was lashing back and forth just above the ground, throwing sparks like a Fourth of July celebration. The tornado had dipped down to earth and exploded everything in its path, by passing them by no more than fifty yards.

Seeing her pick her way, limping, across the hailstones, Cord turned to her and swung her up against his chest. Susan felt as if she'd used her last reserves of strength, and she was just as glad to let him carry her; wearily, she let her head fall against his shoulder, and his arms tightened momentarily about her. He carried her to the Blazer, placing her inside it before walking around and vaulting into the seat behind the steering wheel. He turned the key in the ignition, and to her amazement the engine started immediately. He flashed her a quick grin. After the last hour it was a pleasure to have something going right. He changed gears, easing the Blazer along, the big tires churning in the mud until they gained the hail-slick surface of the road.

"We're going back to the cabin," he said, letting the truck move slowly to keep it from skidding on the ice. "I can't get you home until morning, when I can see how to pick my way around those trees and power lines that are down."

Susan didn't say anything, merely clung to the edge of the seat. She was certain the power would be off at the cabin, but he could build a fire, and the thought of being warm and dry again seemed like heaven. Her muscles were still tense, and she found she couldn't relax, her gaze fixed on the stabbing beams of the headlights as they probed through the gray curtain of rain.

They reached the crest of the gentle incline that led down to the creek, and Cord brought the Blazer to a halt. "I'm going down to check the bridge," he said, and left the truck before she could cry out that she wanted to go with him. Somehow, she didn't want him out of her sight for even a moment.

He came back in only a few minutes, his face harsh in the blinding glare of the headlights. He got back into the Blazer. "The water's over the bridge; we can't chance crossing it. We have to spend the night in the truck."

Chapter 11

SUSAN BIT HER LIP, THINKING OF THE FIRE THAT HAD BEEN warming her in her imagination. She was silent as he shifted into reverse and turned the Blazer around, then drove a little further back the way they'd come. Finally he pulled to the side of the road and parked.

She had been so frantic to get away from him, she thought dimly, but now she was glad that he was here, that he was all right. They had come so close to death . . . but what if only she had been spared? The thought of him lying dead from the brute force of the storm was unbearable.

Her shaking hand went to her dripping hair, and her fingers combed through it. The driving rain had evidently washed the mud out, but she found a few twigs that she pulled out and dropped to the floorboards. But what did it matter, anyway, if her hair was a mess? She began to laugh.

Cord's head jerked around at the sound, and he reached out to touch her shoulder. Susan covered her mouth with her hand, trying to stifle the unwilling mirth, but she couldn't. "Baby, it's all right," he murmured, sliding out from under the steering wheel and taking her in his arms. "It's over; you're all right."

The hard strength of him surrounded her, and Susan burrowed into it, her arms lacing around his waist. The strained laughter turned into choking, dry sobs, then slowly diminished as he continued to hold her, talking to her in a quiet, gentle voice, his hand stroking her head.

But her shaking didn't diminish, and finally his hand moved down over her bare shoulder and arms. "My God, you're freezing," he muttered, taking his arms from around her. He found the two towels that he'd brought when they'd dashed through the rain from the cabin to the Blazer, and wrapped one around her hair. "Get out of those wet clothes," he ordered, but in a voice so calm and matter-of-fact that she didn't balk. "There's a blanket in the back; I'll wrap you up in it." He turned the heater on high.

Susan looked at him, her eyes enormous. "You need to get out of your clothes, too; you're not impervious to cold, either."

The normal tone of her voice reassured him, and he flashed her a grin that shone against the darkness of his growing beard. "I'm warmer than you are, but I'll admit that wet jeans are damned uncomfortable." He peeled his T-shirt off over his head and wrung the excess water out, then draped it over the steering wheel.

The sight of his bare, powerful torso agitated her, and she jerked her gaze away, beginning to unbutton the flimsy camisole top while he struggled to take off his boots in the limited space they had. Her cold fingers wouldn't cooperate, and she had managed to get out of only the camisole and the strapless bra she'd worn under it by the time Cord had completely stripped and was wiping himself down with the other towel.

When he'd finished, he came to her assistance, pushing her shaking hands aside. He dealt with her skirt, pantyhose and panties in short order; then he dried her vigorously, the rough fabric of the towel speeding her circulation and driving some of the chill away.

He reached in the back for the blanket, unfolding it and draping it across the seat. He sat in the middle of it, then scooped her up and placed her on his lap, and wrapped the rest of the blanket around both of them like a cocoon.

Blessed warmth enveloped her, and Susan gave a blissful sigh, cuddling against his amazing body heat. She felt suddenly peaceful; they were completely alone and isolated from the world, at least until morning. They were naked together, rather like Adam and Eve, and for the moment she wanted nothing except that they be warm and dry. Everything else could wait until morning. For now she was in his arms, and the feel of him was heaven. The scent of his skin, of his warm masculinity, both soothed and aroused her, and she turned to press more fully into the hair-softened contours of his hard chest.

Cord held her, his hands on her satin curves, his face troubled. "I've never in my life been as scared as I was tonight," he admitted in a rumble, his words startling Susan.

She lifted her head from his shoulder, her eyes wide with astonishment. "You?" she demanded, her voice rising in disbelief. "*You* were afraid?" That didn't seem possible. He had nerves of ice, an imperviousness to danger that both alarmed and reassured her.

"I kept thinking: What if I couldn't hold on to you? What if something hit you? If anything had happened to you—" He bit his words off, his face growing darker.

Susan was stunned. "But you were in danger too."

He shrugged, utterly indifferent to his own fate. Perhaps that was how he faced all dangers, with complete unconcern, and perhaps that was why death hadn't found him yet. He didn't fear it, and therefore it didn't seek him. But he had been afraid for her. . . . Her mind stopped, almost afraid to take the thought any further. She simply pressed close to him once again, her hands clinging to his neck.

He rubbed his bristly cheek against her forehead, his hands tightening on her. "Susan."

She loved the sound of her name on his lips. With unconscious sensuality, she moved her breasts against him, the hair on his chest feeling like rough silk against her sensitive nipples. "Ummmm?" she murmured bemusedly.

"I want to make love to you. Will you let me?"

The thought, the rough thread of need in his voice, made her shiver in delight. She lifted her mouth to him, simply and without reserve, and he took it with a tender fervor. He kissed her for a long time, their tongues meeting in mutual need, while his hard fingers found her breasts and stroked them until they hardened and thrust out for his touch.

He lifted his head and gave a low, shaky laugh. "Is that a yes?"

"That's a yes." Despite the weeks they'd been apart, the anger between them, she wasn't shy with him. She was his, in the purest sense, and always in his touch she had perceived his genuine pleasure, the care and concern he gave her. His passion might border on roughness in his urgency, but he never hurt her, and she knew that he never would. Her trust in his physical care of her was so great that despite the rift between them, she knew that she had nothing to fear from him. And for this moment, there was no rift, no pain or disagreement; all of that had retreated, and would arrive with the sunrise, but for now there was only the sweet fever between them.

She could have fought him, could have insisted that he preserve the distance between them, but in the aftermath of the storm, none of their reasons for argument seemed very important. She loved him; she didn't want to fight him. After what they'd just been through, she wanted only to hold him and feel his hard, warm flesh against her, reassure herself that he was unharmed. He was so infinitely precious to her that she didn't want to waste a moment of this time they had together by holding him off. She'd worried herself sick about their situation anyway, and it hadn't changed anything. Let the sunrise bring its troubles; she had the nighttime, and for now that was enough.

He was slow, and exquisitely gentle, using his kisses and the boldness of his stroking fingers to bring her to fever pitch before he stretched her out on the seat, his hard hands controlling her even when she reached for him, trying to pull him down to her. Susan writhed in blind delight, small cries escaping from her throat, her eyes tightly closed as her head rolled slowly back and forth. He was suckling leisurely at her breasts, his tongue curling around each of her aching nipples in turn, a caress that sent bolts of ecstasy shooting through her body. She was no longer cold, but burning with a radiant glow, her body arching up to his.

Deftly he moved her, rearranging her legs, and his mouth left her breasts to trail down her stomach, his beard softly rasping her satin flesh and making her gasp at the rough pleasure. His tongue found her navel and he kissed her, paying homage to her for a long, sweet moment before moving on to a richer treasure.

A startled cry tore from her when he claimed her with his mouth, kissing her deeply, making lightning forays with his tongue that pushed her toward the edge so swiftly she couldn't breathe. Then she forgot about breathing as her fingers tangled in his damp hair; he was killing her with pleasure, stabbing her to death with his devilish tongue, and she rushed to meet her small death. He held her securely until she was calm again, lying peacefully in his arms; it was several moments before she realized he was doing nothing but holding her.

"Cord?" His name was an expression of bewilderment. "What about you?"

"I'm all right." Very gently, he tilted her face up and

kissed her. "It's just that I'm unprepared; I don't have any way to protect you."

His unselfish consideration jolted her, but the ecstasy he'd just given her wasn't enough. She didn't want just simple release; she wanted him, with all his delicious masculinity, his driving power, the very essence of the man. She reached out for him, her soft hands touching his face. "I want *you*," she said in a low voice. "Would you mind, very much, if we took the chance?"

A shudder rippled through him, and he moved swiftly to lie over her, parting her thighs and taking her, a groan of pleasure breaking from his lips. He held nothing back from her, his urgency communicating itself to her. He was shaking in a way she'd never seen before, and she tried to soothe him with her yielding softness. All too soon he was hoarsely crying out his satisfaction; then he sagged against her to rest.

After only a moment they were both shifting uncomfortably. During the heat of their lovemaking, neither had noticed their awkward positions or cramped limbs, but now they seemed to be fighting a tangle of gear shift, steering wheel, and door handles, all of which were in uncomfortable places. Cord chuckled as he tried to untangle himself from her and still manage not to maim himself.

"I think we'll be more comfortable in back; God only knows why we didn't get in back anyway."

With the back seat folded down they had considerable space, though still not enough for Cord to stretch out his long legs. He'd cut the motor, so they had to depend on the one blanket and each other for warmth, but now that Susan was dry she didn't feel the chill so much. They lay on half of the blanket, and he pulled the other half around them. Susan nestled in his arms, quietly happy. "I'm so tired," she murmured, then smothered a yawn. She didn't want to sleep, didn't want to waste any of the time they had together, but her body was demanding rest. The stress of the past weeks, the emotional tension and fear she'd experienced today, had all taken their toll. Her limbs felt as heavy as lead, and her eyelids simply would not stay open.

She yawned again, her eyes slowly closing. She put her hand on his chest, where she could feel the strong, steady beating of his heart. He was so big and tough; she felt infinitely safe and protected when she was with him. "I do love you," she told him quietly, not needing anything now beyond the telling of it. She'd just wanted to say the words aloud this once, when there was peace between them. It was a gift, a simple gesture from her heart.

"I know," he whispered against her temple, and held her while she slept.

He hadn't expected to sleep at all; his senses were too raw. He had been sure that he would feel the restlessness that always seized him if there were anyone else about while he slept. But the rain kept drumming on the roof of the Blazer, and the darkness enclosed them like a cave; he was warm and dry, and his body pleasantly satisfied. She was soft in his arms, small and delicate, so completely feminine that from the moment he'd met her he'd found himself tempering his strength lest he accidentally hurt her. This afternoon, when she'd been crying and beating on her steering wheel, he'd felt as if he'd taken a punch in the chest; she simply wasn't the weepy type, yet he'd hurt her enough to make her cry, and he hadn't meant to. He'd been infuriated to hear that Preston had run off and left her to shoulder everything, that instead of Preston knuckling under and sacrificing, it had been Susan. He had to end this, as soon as he could, for Susan's sake. She was at the end of her rope, physically and emotionally.

She loved him. Once a woman's offering of love would have made him impatient, restless to be gone. He couldn't offer anything in return, and he hadn't wanted the complications of clinging hands, teary scenes, or the incredible plots of revenge some women could concoct when they felt they'd been wronged. Judith's death had scarred him deeply, left him so wary of being wounded like that again that he'd instinctively protected himself . . . until Susan. She'd gotten in under his guard, and because she didn't demand anything of him, he found himself giving more.

Still, he hadn't realized, until she'd practically ordered him out of her house and out of her life, just how close she'd gotten to him. He'd felt lonely, and he was a man who treasured his solitude. His healthy body had burned for sexual release, but other women seemed unattractive in subtle ways he'd never noticed before. He didn't want other women; he wanted Susan, with her serenity like a halo around her. Susan, who became a sweet, loving wanton for him, only for him.

Now she was in his arms again, pressed against his heart, just where she belonged. He moved drowsily, seeking a more comfortable position, and she moved with him, her soft hands holding him even in her sleep. It was the most uniquely satisfying experience of his life, and a slight smile touched his hard mouth as he went to sleep.

As often happens after a storm, the next day dawned sunny and warm, but without the suffocating humidity that had been weighing down on everyone. It was as if nature were pleased by the destruction it had wrought. Cord's eyes blinked open, and for a moment he stared at the expanse of innocent, deep blue sky. The interior of the Blazer had already heated under the morning sun, and a trickle of sweat ran down his side, tickling him. He twitched, and Susan stirred, stretching. He rolled to his side and watched as she slowly came awake, her eyelashes fluttering. The blanket fell away, revealing her slender bare body, her full, pretty breasts and succulent nipples. His loins tightened, and he put his hand on her hip. "Honey, we have to leave soon," he said huskily. "Before we go . . . ?"

Susan heard the question, the intent in his voice, and she

turned to him. "Yes," she said drowsily, reaching out for him.

He took her gently, slowly, holding the world at bay while they loved each other. When it was done he leaned over her, his weight supported on one elbow, his eyes very clear and demanding. "Stay with me. Don't go back to the office. I'll take care of you, in every way."

Tears blurred her eyes, but still Susan managed a smile for him. As the salty liquid seeped from the corners of her eyes, she said shakily, "I have to go back; I can't just turn my back and walk away from everyone who's depending on me."

"What about me? How can you turn your back on me?" His words hit her hard, and she flinched.

"I love you, but you don't *need* me. You want me, but that's entirely different. Besides, I don't think I have what it takes to be a mistress." She reached up and stroked his bearded cheek, her mouth trembling. "Please, take me home now."

Silently they dressed in their damp, incredibly wrinkled clothing, and Cord began the torturous drive, detouring time and again as their way was blocked by fallen trees or downed power lines. They passed utility crews who were hard at work, trying to get new lines up, and in some cases new poles. The sounds of chain saws split the peaceful morning air as men began cleaning up the debris. What was normally a fifteen-minute drive took well over an hour, but finally Susan was tumbling out the Blazer's door into Emily's arms. The older woman's worn face was tight with concern.

"My lands, just look at the two of you," she breathed, and tears sparkled in her eyes.

Cord managed his devilishly casual smile. "I think we look pretty good for two people who've been lying in a ditch." Actually, every muscle in his body was protesting, not only from sleeping on a hard, cramped surface, but from the beating he'd taken from the hailstones. For the first time he saw a bruise high on Susan's cheekbone, and he reached out to touch it with his thumb. She stood very still under his touch, her eyes filled with pain and longing.

Emily wiped her tears away, and hustled them both inside, bullying them shamelessly now that she knew they were safe.

"Both of you get upstairs right now and take a hot shower, and toss those filthy clothes out so I can wash them—"

"I'll be leaving in a minute," Cord interrupted her. "I've got to see if I can get to the cabin and check for damage. But if you have any coffee brewed, I'd appreciate some."

She brought him a cup and he sipped it gratefully, the hot liquid sending new life into his body. Susan stood watching him, her arms limp at her sides, wanting to do as he said and go with him, forget about everything. Without knowing that she had moved, she found herself in front of him, and without a word he set the cup aside and folded her tightly in his arms. He kissed her roughly, almost desperately, as if he would imprint his possession on her mouth, and as Susan clung to him she felt the acid tears burning down her cheeks.

"Shhhh, shhhh," he soothed, lifting his lips at the salty taste. With his fingertips, he wiped her cheeks dry; then he framed her face between his big hands and held it turned up so he could see into her drowning eyes. "Everything will be all right. I promise."

She couldn't say anything, so he kissed her again, then released her. He gave Emily a swift hug and left, not once looking back.

Susan jammed her fist against her mouth, trying to hold back the sobs that shook her, but they burst out anyway. Emily led her upstairs and helped her undress, then took away her soiled clothing and laid out fresh garments while Susan stood under the shower and cried.

She knew there were a thousand things that needed doing, but she couldn't summon any interest in any of them. She wanted only to curl up on her bed and cry until she couldn't cry any more. It was all just too much; she couldn't fight any longer. It was a measure of her willpower that she had controlled her tears by the time she left the bathroom; she sat down and dried her hair, then applied a careful blend of makeup to hide the traces of her tears. After dressing in the casual slacks and shirt that Emily had put out for her, she went downstairs for the meal that she knew Emily would have ready. She wasn't hungry, but eating was a necessity that she'd been neglecting lately, all to no good. She wouldn't be able to keep the corporation from bankruptcy, even if she divested herself of everything she owned except her clothing, then held a yard sale to get rid of even that.

She sat on the patio all day, soaking up the sun, dozing, thinking, but her thoughts only went in circles and produced nothing. She called Imogene and explained why she wouldn't be at the office that day; she had no idea when Cord would be able to get the Audi back to her, but she found that it was the one bright spot she could see right now: She would be able to see him again when he did bring it to her.

She was probably a fool not to have taken him up on his proposition, she thought tiredly. She should just forget about tomorrow, about all the duties and obligations that she'd always served; she should go with Cord and take what love she could get from him. He cared; she knew he did. Perhaps he didn't love her, but she knew that he'd offered her more than he'd ever offered any other woman, except Judith. Poor, hurt, confused Judith, who was now the point of all this enmity years after her death. Because everyone had failed her, because she'd died, Cord was trying to make it up to her now, to get revenge for her, and for himself, perhaps, so he could be at peace.

She'd told him that she didn't have what it took to be a mistress, but what did it take, really, except a woman in love? She thought longingly of spending every night with him, of traveling around the world beside him. She'd always been a woman who was happy with her hearth and home, but for Cord she would learn to wander, and lay her head on a different pillow every night if that was what he wanted.

It was only a matter of time, anyway, before the life she knew was all over. She had failed; she couldn't pay the loan.

When Cord still hadn't brought her car back by the next morning, Susan called and asked Imogene to pick her up; there was nothing more she could do, but she would continue to handle the office and make the myriad decisions that still had to be made every day. The ship might sink, but she wouldn't make a confused mess of it. Dignity and grace in defeat, that was the ticket.

Giving herself pep talks didn't help much. She was agonizingly aware that she'd lost on both sides. She'd tried to heal the rift in the family, but instead it had grown deeper. Cord might want her, care for her, but how could he ever trust her? He'd asked her to stay with him, but instead she'd given her aid to Preston. Knowing that Cord was wrong didn't ease the hollow ache inside her.

She had to face everyone at the office, where they had all somehow heard that she'd almost been caught in a tornado. Several tornadoes had ripped through Mississippi that night, and one close to Jackson had hit a residential area, leaving two people dead, but her acquaintances and employees were only interested in the local one, which had missed all the populated areas and destroyed only trees and newly planted crops. She managed to be very casual about it, and her lack of detail soon killed their interest.

When she went home that night she found the Audi there, and disappointment speared her. Why couldn't he have brought it when he knew she would be home? But perhaps he was avoiding her. She stared at the car for a long moment before thanking Imogene for the ride.

Imogene reached over and patted her hand. "Is there anything I can do?" she asked. "Anything I can say to Cord? I know you're not happy, and I feel like it's all my fault."

"No, it's not your fault," Susan denied, managing a smile. "I made my own decisions, so I imagine I'll have to live with them."

Emily was still waiting, and she made a pretense of cleaning up the kitchen while Susan ate, but Susan had a feeling that she had caught on to Susan's habit of disposing of the food instead of eating it. As she dutifully ate the last bite, Emily nodded in satisfaction. "Cord told me to make certain you were eating. You're too thin. This business is tearing you apart, and I'm ready for it to end."

"It won't be long," Susan sighed. She hated herself for asking, but she had to know. "Did he say anything else?"

"He said he lost one of his trees, but it fell away from the cabin, and there's hail damage to the roof, but other than that everything came through the storm okay."

"That's good." It wasn't personal news, but it was better than nothing. She refrained from asking if he'd looked tired.

Emily had just left when Imogene phoned. "Susan, can you come over?" she asked, urgency filling her voice. "Preston's back, and he's found out something about Cord!"

"I'll be right there." Susan dropped the phone and ran to get her purse. Something about Cord? Her heart clenched. Had he done something illegal? Whatever it was, if there were any way, she'd protect him. No, it couldn't be anything illegal; he was far too visible, and he made no attempt to disguise his identity. It was far more likely that he'd crossed some powerful people. Preston might plan on using his knowledge against Cord, but she'd make certain that Cord knew all about his plans.

As she drove over to Blackstone House she was hardly aware of the turns she took, or the speed at which she traveled. Her heart was slamming wildly in her chest, hurting her ribs. She'd been longing for Preston to come back, but now that he had she could only fear that he'd try to hurt Cord in some way.

Preston looked surprisingly normal when he opened the door to her as she ran up the steps. He was casually attired; his tan was deeper, and he looked relaxed. He was startled when he saw her. "Good Lord, Susan, you've lost a good ten pounds. What've you been doing?"

She brushed his comment aside. "It doesn't matter. What have you found out about Cord?"

He ushered her into the den, where Imogene was waiting, and waited until she was seated before speaking. "I've been doing some detective work while I was gone," he explained. "I wanted Cord to think that I'd chickened out so he wouldn't make any attempt to cover his tracks. It worked, thank God. He must've thought he'd won without a real battle."

"I doubt that," Susan interrupted. "He didn't know until the day before yesterday that you'd gone."

He frowned. "But why? Didn't you tell him?"

Susan's eyes widened, and she sat up straight. "That's what you wanted me to do, wasn't it? You dumped all of that on me, thinking I'd run straight to him and beg for mercy. He said that was what you were doing, but I didn't believe him." She stared at him, her eyes clear and accusing, and he shifted uncomfortably.

"What else could I think?" he tried to explain gently. "Are you saying that I completely misread the situation?"

"I don't know; I haven't any idea how you read it."

He turned away from her distinctly chilly gaze. "Anyway, I went to New York. I'd noticed that the prices of our stock had remained high despite the rumors that had to be going around, so it followed that someone was buying. I suspected then, but I wanted to be certain. Cord has been buying up all the stock that came on the market. He's not pushing the company into bankruptcy; he's been pushing us into selling stock, which he's been buying. He's mounting a takeover!"

A takeover! For a moment Susan was dazed; then a spurt of admiration for Cord's nerve made her laugh. "A takeover!" she giggled, clapping her hands. "All of this for a takeover!"

"I don't see that it's so funny."

"Of course you don't! After all, *I'm* the one who's been selling stock in an effort to raise money to pay off that loan!"

Imogene went white. "Susan! Your own assets!"

Preston stared at her; then he swore quietly, and rubbed his eyes in a disbelieving manner. "Susan, we talked about that. I told you not to liquidate anything of yours."

"You also walked off and left me in a sink-or-swim situation," she pointed out. "I thought I had a company going under; I didn't know it was just corporate games! The stock isn't all that I've liquidated!"

He looked ill. "My God, you've done all that . . . and he had no intention of calling in that loan. He just wanted us to panic and sell enough to give him a majority. Susan, how much did you sell?"

"Nine percent."

"That still leaves you six percent. I have eleven percent, and Mother has eleven. Twenty-eight percent total. Cord has, I think, twenty-six percent. We still have a majority."

"If his takeover doesn't succeed, he may still collect on that loan," Imogene pointed out, but Preston shook his head decisively.

"No, that would be killing his own source of income. It didn't make sense from the beginning that he'd hurt himself financially just to get back at me, but I thought that maybe he did hate me that much. Then when the stock sold immediately whenever any shares went on the market, I began to think that it was something else entirely he was after."

"Why didn't you tell me?" Susan inquired. "Never mind; I know the answer to that. You didn't trust me because I was seeing Cord, and Cord didn't trust me because I was helping you."

"I'm sorry," he said softly. "I had no idea it would be this hard on you. I swear, I'll replace everything you sold."

She dismissed that with a wave of her hand. "It doesn't matter." She just wanted it over with.

Preston decided not to pursue the issue, because she was looking tired and dazed. "I drove out to see Cord as soon as I got in this afternoon," he continued. "I called a board meeting for ten in the morning, and this will be put to a vote. He'll have to take his chances on snapping up any more stock before we get to it, so he knows his game is up."

It had all been just a game. That was all she could think of that night. Just a game.

She didn't know how all of the shares had been originally divided; when she'd married Vance, she'd known only that the family had owned fifty-one percent of the stock, and the rest of it was in others' hands. Others owned chunks of shares, but with the majority in family hands it hadn't mattered. Imogene had owned fifteen percent, Preston fifteen percent, and Vance fifteen percent. Susan had inherited Vance's shares. That had left six percent of the family majority, which she had always assumed was scattered around to distant cousins. She hadn't known of Cord's existence until the day he'd come back; he'd been gone for so long that no one talked about him. But now it was evident that he'd owned the remaining shares.

Preston and Imogene had both sold four percent of their stock in order to cover what they'd used of Cord's money; that gave Cord fourteen percent, assuming that he'd bought it, which he must have done. She'd sold nine percent, giving him twenty-three percent. If he had twenty-six percent, he'd bought some common stock as well, and possibly had acquired voting proxies from other stockholders. Preston also had voting proxies. It was all just a game of numbers, nothing else. If anything, the corporation was stronger, since Cord had essentially paid off an outstanding debt. The family now owned fifty-four percent of the stock. Everything was just fine.

Now Cord's reassurances made sense. He'd known that the company was in no danger of bankruptcy, but he hadn't trusted her enough to tell her what was going on, just as Preston hadn't trusted her enough to tell her his suspicions. She'd tried to be a mediator, and instead had become the sacrificial goat.

She was glad that the morning would bring the end of it. She was tired of games. They seemed to be fine for everyone except the goat.

Chapter 12

OF THE FIVE PEOPLE IN THE BOARDROOM THE NEXT MORN-
ing, Cord looked the most relaxed. He was dressed impec-
cably in a summer-weight pin-stripe suit, the cut of which
had a definite European flair. His growing beard gave him a
raffish look that kept the suit from being *too* impeccable,
but then his rampant masculinity allowed him to wear
anything with elan . . . or wear nothing at all, her imagination whispered, conjuring up a vision of how magnificent he
was in the nude.

Imogene was calm, almost remote. Preston was all
business. Beryl looked as calm as ever. On the other hand,
Susan felt disoriented, and none of the familiar boardroom
rituals or words made any sense. She darted another glance
at Cord, only to find him watching her, and he gave her a
slow wink. Was he that unconcerned about the outcome?
Was that elaborate scheme nothing more to him than
another way of irritating Preston? If so, his practical joke
had been enormously successful.

She was so detached that she missed what they were saying. It wasn't until she caught a surge of anger that she was able to gather her senses and pay attention.

"This is my birthright," Cord was saying, his tone hard and his eyes cold. "It took me years to realize that, but I'm not giving it up. I decided to fight for it, and there won't be any compromising."

"That's your loss," Preston said crisply. "Shall we put it to the vote?"

"By all means."

Cord sat there, so confident, but then it wasn't in him to be any other way. He had to know that he hadn't enough to best their combined shares, but that knowledge couldn't be read in his face.

He'd been shoved out of the family circle. What was in his mind now, when victory danced before him? Thoughts of revenge? Or just a determination to be in that family once again, wanted or not? To assume responsibility for what was his, to finally settle in his home?

"I vote yes," Cord drawled easily, and Susan jerked her thoughts back.

Imogene sat quietly, not looking at either Preston or Cord, but how else could she vote? She wouldn't vote against her own son. "I vote nay," she finally said.

"I vote nay," Preston followed promptly. "Susan?"

He was sure of her, Susan realized. She looked at him, and found him watching her impatiently, the gleam of victory already in his eyes. What a shark he was! He was a perfect chairman, conscientious and bold, and able to use guerrilla tactics when they were called for.

There was nothing for her to read in Cord's eyes. He simply waited. He hadn't contacted her, hadn't tried to persuade her to vote in his favor. Why should he? She'd come down solidly on Preston's side in every skirmish. No wonder he didn't trust her! He would be a good chairman, too; he'd shown his expertise in gathering enough money to mount this campaign.

"Susan!" Preston prodded impatiently.

Trust has to start somewhere, she thought painfully. Cord was so used to guarding his back that it was second nature to him now. "I vote yes," she said in a low tone, and total silence descended on the room, except for the quick rasp of Beryl's pencil across the pad as she recorded everything.

Preston looked to be in shock; he was pale, his mouth compressed to a thin line that was bracketed on each side by grooves of tension. The meeting was quickly adjourned, but only Beryl left the room. Everyone else remained in their seats; perhaps even Cord was stunned by the turn of events. Susan's motives were too murky for her to explain them even to herself, but she was aware, deep inside, of a feeling that she simply couldn't fail him now. If he had lost, he wouldn't have returned to being an absentee board member, his shares automatically voted by Preston; Cord entered a fight to win. He would have gone on and on, and the conflict would have continued to tear the family apart and drain the company. Let it end, even if she made herself an outcast with Preston and Imogene. Why not? She was tired, too tired to really care, and she was doubly bitter at being played with so callously by both Cord and Preston. She'd just been a pawn in their games, moved around according to their whims, and kept in the dark by both of them.

Imogene leaned forward, clasping her hands on the table. "Let it end," she said quietly, looking from her son to Cord and back. "We were a family once; I'd like us to be one again. I was wrong for my part in it, and if you can possibly forgive me, Cord, I'll be very grateful." The steel that was an inherent part of her personality shone clearly out of her gray eyes, and in that moment Susan knew that she'd never liked or respected her mother-in-law more.

Without waiting for an answer from Cord, Imogene turned her determined regard to Preston. "I know this will be difficult for you; you've been an outstanding chairman, and it won't be easy for you to turn over the reins. But I'm asking you to do it without bitterness, and to do whatever you can to ease the transition. Cord is family; he's as much a Blackstone as you are. I hope you're big enough to let this end now, before it totally destroys us. People have already been hurt, and others will be if this continues. Susan was the only one of us with enough sense to realize that from the beginning. If you won't stop it for yourself, then stop it for me . . . and for her. God knows she's paid enough for your enmity."

Susan flinched, hating to have her feelings dragged out in the open like this. She sat very still and pale, her eyes focused on her hands. Now it was up to them to either settle their differences or draw new battle lines. Either way, she'd withdrawn from combat, retreated to lick her wounds. She was simply too tired to care any longer.

Preston sat with an abstracted frown on his brow, his gaze turned inward to long ago, when he'd first become enemies with his cousin. "I always envied you," he said absently, reviewing his memories. "Everything always came so easily to you. Vance was a hard act to follow, but with you . . . My God, when you were around, I became invisible. Everyone watched you."

Cord stared across the length of the table at his cousin, his dark face hard and expressionless. What he thought of Preston's admission was impossible to guess.

Giving an unbelieving little shake of his head, as if he couldn't quite take in how far their enmity had taken them, Preston straightened his shoulders and looked at Cord directly. "When I was sixteen I started dating Kelly Hartland, and I fell hard for her. You were just starting your sophomore year in college, and I suppose to a high school girl that was irresistible. You came home for a weekend, met Kelly at a party, and just like that she dropped me flat.''

A startled look flared in Cord's eyes. ''Kelly Hartland? A little strawberry blond cheerleader type? I can barely remember her. I dated her a couple of times, but it was nothing heavy.''

''It was for me. I hated you for taking her away from me when you obviously didn't care about her. At sixteen I thought she was the love of my life. When your affair with Judith blew up in your face, I saw a way to get back at you, and I took it. I'm not proud of it, but there's no way to undo it.''

Cord inhaled deeply, and even without looking at him Susan knew that the mention of Judith was lashing at him, uncovering the deep pain and guilt he felt at the way she'd been treated. Yet the bonds of common blood, weakened by years of bitterness and hatred, were reaching out again, and the two men looked at each other, seeing their common heritage in each other's face. The serrated edge of pain rasped in Cord's voice when he spoke. ''Judith was my wife. We were married after we left here; she died the next year. I could've killed you for what you did to her.'' A crystalline sheen was suddenly in his eyes. ''I'm guiltier than anyone else for what happened to her.'' Even now, he was bitterly angry at the way she'd died, her spirit gone, her laughter stilled.

Silence fell, and suddenly Susan couldn't bear any more. Without looking at anyone, she pushed her chair back and got to her feet, walking out swiftly before she could be called back. Her chest was aching, yet she didn't think she could cry. The time for that was past.

Her senses were dulled as she went to her office, walking past Beryl who looked up eagerly, full of questions, but Susan didn't see her. She felt chilled to the bone, so cold that she could never be warm again.

All of this had been because of women who had long ago faded into the mists of the past. There was a certain irony in her own situation; did either of them want her for herself, or merely because each thought the other wanted her?

She had barely moved away from the door after closing it when it was thrust open again, and Cord loomed behind her, so close that she felt oppressed by his size, and she moved instinctively away from him. At her action, his eyes narrowed, and he closed the door behind him.

"Why did you leave the meeting?" he asked evenly.

"I'm going home." Her legs felt wooden as she walked to her desk and retrieved her purse, tucking it under her arm. She avoided his gaze and moved to the side to step around him.

He took one stride and stood in front of her, blocking the door. "I need you here, Susan. You know it won't be easy, making the transition. Up until now only the family has been involved, but now everyone else will have to be informed and dealt with. I need your help. You can do more with a look than most people can manage with a baseball bat."

"If I hadn't thought you could handle it, I wouldn't have voted for you," she said tiredly. "Please, let me by."

"Why did you vote for me? Everyone else was as surprised as I was." He put his hand on her bare arm, the warmth of his fingers searing her, seeking a response, some sign of the quiet radiance he associated with her.

Susan couldn't give him one. She simply stared woodenly at the light gray fabric of his suit. "I'm tired; I want to go home," she repeated.

He looked at her pale, tense face, seeing the shadows around her eyes, and though all of his instincts screamed against letting her slip away now, it was obvious that she was almost at the breaking point. "I'll drive you home."

"No." Her reply was immediate, and firm.

He bit back a curse. "All right, if you don't want me to drive you home, I'm sure Imogene will—"

"I drove myself here; I can drive myself home. I'm not going to tangle with any power poles."

Forcing himself to compliance, he said, "All right. I'll come by tonight—"

"No," she interrupted, looking at him now, pain and betrayal plain for him to read in her eyes. "Not tonight."

It was a hard battle that he fought with himself, evident in the grim set of his jaw, the drumming of the pulse in his temple. "We have to talk."

"I know. Maybe later; I don't think I can handle it right now."

"When?"

She managed a shrug, but her lips were trembling. "I don't know. Maybe six or seven years."

"Hell!" he roared, his control shattered.

"I'm sorry, but that's the way I feel! Please, just leave me alone! I don't have anything else you want, anyway; you've already got my stock and my vote." She pushed past him, ducking her head to keep from looking at him. She just watched her feet, mentally commanding them to function. She left the building, and the hot Mississippi sun burned down on her, blinding her momentarily with its brilliance. She blinked and fumbled in her purse for her sunglasses, finally extracting them and sliding them on her nose. The sun felt good on her chilled skin, she noticed dimly. She would go home and sit on the patio in the sun, and sleep if she could. That was the most ambitious plan she could make at the moment, with her mind so dulled by pain.

She drove home slowly, carefully. Emily, bless her, didn't ask any unnecessary questions. Moving like an automaton, Susan shed her dress and slip, and peeled the hot pantyhose away from her legs. The freedom afforded her by an old pair of shorts that she usually wore only while gardening, and a plain white sleeveless blouse with the tails tied in a knot at her midriff, made her breathe easier for the first time in days. It was over. She had lost more than anyone else, but she could rest now.

She pulled a chaise longue out into the full strength of the sun and lay down, letting the heat begin the healing process in her exhausted body. Her eyelids each weighed a thousand pounds; she was unable to keep them up, and after a moment she stopped trying. She dozed in the sun, her mind blank.

Emily woke her once with an offering of iced tea, which Susan accepted gratefully. The chill was gone now, and she felt pleasantly hot, her skin damp with perspiration. She drank the tea, then turned over on her stomach and slept again. During the worst of the heat Emily came out and pulled the big patio umbrella into position to shield Susan, then went back in to finish the chores Cord had set for her.

Susan awoke late in the afternoon and wandered in to eat the light salad and stuffed tomato that Emily had prepared. Her eyes were still heavy, and she yawned in spite of everything she could do to prevent it.

"I'm sorry," she murmured. "I'm still so tired."

Emily patted her arm. "Why don't you go watch the evening news? Just put your feet up and relax."

"That's exactly what I've been doing for *hours*," Susan sighed, but it was still an outstanding idea.

It was inevitable that she'd go to sleep in front of the television. Her last memory was of a stalled low pressure system on the weather map.

She was stiff when she woke, and she stretched leisurely, trying to ease the kinks out of her back and legs. Her lashes fluttered open, and she stared straight into Cord's eyes.

With renewed energy she sat up abruptly. "What are you doing here?" she demanded, her eyes wide, the haunted look creeping back into them.

"Waiting for you to wake up," he returned calmly. "I didn't want to startle you. Now I'm going to do exactly what I wanted to do the first time I saw you."

She pressed herself back into the corner of the couch, watching him warily as he approached and leaned over her. "What was that?"

"Throw you over my shoulder and carry you off." He gripped one of her wrists, gave a gentle tug, and to her astonishment she found herself being hoisted over his shoulder. He settled her comfortably, one arm locked around her legs to hold her steady, while he patted her bottom with the other hand.

Dizzily she grabbed at his belt loops to anchor herself. "Put me down!" she gasped; then, as he moved deliberately around the room, switching off the television, turning off the lights, she said, "What are you doing?"

"You'll see."

It wasn't until he carried her outside into the warm, fragrant night air that she began to struggle, kicking futilely against the band of his arm. "Let me down! Where are you taking me?"

"Away," he answered simply, his boots crunching on the gravel of the drive. In an effort to see Susan braced her arms on his back and raised herself, looking over her shoulder. His Blazer was sitting there, and he opened the door, then very gently lifted her off his shoulder and placed her on the seat.

"Emily packed your clothes," he informed her, leaning in to kiss her sweetly astonished mouth. "I've already put them in the Blazer. Everything's taken care of, and all you have to do is ride. I still have that blanket in the back, if you'd rather sleep," he finished huskily, his tone telling her how clearly he remembered the last time he had used it.

Susan sat in dazed astonishment as he shut the door and walked around to the driver's side. He was really kidnapping her, with Emily's cheerful aid! She supposed she should feel more indignant, but she still felt slow and drowsy, and it just didn't seem worth the effort to protest.

When he slid under the steering wheel, she asked quietly, "How did you know I wouldn't try to run while you went around to get in?"

"Two reasons." He started the motor and shifted into reverse, turning to look over his shoulder as they backed up. "One, you're too smart to waste what little energy you have in a useless effort." He braked, then changed to first gear and smoothly let out the clutch, his powerful legs working. "Two, you love me."

His logic was iron-clad. She did love him, even though she was still trying to deal with the hurt he'd inflicted. She supposed that she could best describe her feelings as those of being ill-used, shuffled about with little regard in the high-stakes game he and Preston had been playing.

Cord slanted her a searching look. "No fervent denials?"

"No. I'm not a liar."

The simple dignity of her statement, coupled with her listlessness, shook him to the core. She loved, but without hope. He felt as if a flame that had been given into his care was flickering on the brink of extinction, and it would take tender nurturing to bring it back to full strength. His first thought, when she'd left the office earlier in the day, had been to give her time, let her rest and recover her strength, but as the day wore on he'd been seized by an urgent need to do *something,* to bring her back into the circle of his arms where she belonged. His arrangements had been hurriedly made, as he swept all obstacles and protests out of his path.

He'd thought she would sleep, but she sat very still and erect in the seat, her eyes on the highway. When he'd gone past every destination that she'd guessed, she finally asked, "Where are you taking me?"

"To the beach," he answered promptly. "You're going

to do nothing but eat, sleep, and lie in the sun until you gain back the weight you've lost and lose those smudges under your eyes.''

Susan pondered his answer for a moment, since they were evidently not going to the stretches of beach that she was familiar with. She sighed. "What beach?''

He laughed aloud, a rare sound. "I'll narrow it down to Florida for you. Does that help?''

She did sleep, finally, before they reached their destination. In the early hours of the morning Cord pulled the Blazer up to a darkened beach house and put his hand on her shoulder to gently shake her awake.

The house was right on the beach, and the luminescent Gulf stretched out before her as far as she could see. The white sand of the Florida panhandle looked like snow in the faint starlight. When she climbed from the Blazer, the constant wind off the Gulf lifted her hair, bringing with it the scent of the ocean mingled with the fresher scent of rain.

It was a basic Florida beach house, built of whitewashed cement blocks, with large windows and low ceilings. Following Cord as he moved through the house turning on the lights, she saw a small, cheerful kitchen in yellow and white, a glass table in an alcove, with a ceiling fan above it, and a living room with white wicker furniture; then Cord led her to a small white-painted bedroom. He brought in the single suitcase Emily had packed for her and placed it at the foot of the bed.

"Your bathroom is through there,'' he said, indicating a door opening off the bedroom. "I'll be in the room straight across the hall, if you need me for anything.''

Of all the things she had considered since he'd put her in the Blazer, that she would be going to bed alone wasn't one of them, yet that was exactly what happened. He kissed her on the forehead and walked out, closing the door behind him, and she stood in the middle of the room, blinking her eyes in astonishment.

But the bed beckoned her, and she took a swift shower, then crawled naked between the sheets, too tired to see if Emily had packed a nightgown for her.

Over breakfast the next morning, a meal that he cooked before awakening her, she commented, "You know, this isn't very wise behavior for a man who's just taken control of a firm. You should be in the office."

He shrugged and liberally spread his toast with jelly. "There's wise, and then there's wise. I think I have my priorities in the right order."

Pursing her lips, Susan carefully cut her toast into thin strips. She wasn't quite certain why he'd brought her to the beach, but her questions could wait. She'd slept until she was almost dopey, and consequently she was rested for the first time in weeks. She didn't think she could handle any personal questions right then, but there were a lot of things she wanted to know.

"You had it all planned out before you came back, didn't you?"

He glanced up, his blue eyes glittering as the morning sun fell on his face. "It all depended on the first step. When I put pressure on him, he had to sell off stock and weaken himself financially in order to replace the money that he'd taken in order for any of it to work. He literally financed my takeover; the money that he replaced was used to buy up the first loan. Then, when that loan was paid, I used the money again to buy up the second loan."

His nerve and gall were truly astonishing, leaving her shaking her head in awe. "You didn't have any other money to back you?"

"Of course, I have money," he snorted. "I'm a hell of a good gambler, regardless if it's cards, dice, horses . . . or oil. I've lost my shirt a few times, but more often than not I come out on top."

"Oil?" she asked blankly. "You wanted to lease the ridges yourself? You weren't acting for any company?"

He shrugged, his powerful shoulders rippling under the light blue polo shirt he wore. "The ridges were a smokescreen," he admitted. "They were a way to put pressure on Preston; I wanted him to refuse to lease them to me, giving me an excuse to use my lever against him."

Susan remembered feeling, at the time, that he'd deliberately pushed Preston into refusing; he'd manipulated them all like a master puppeteer, and they'd danced whenever he pulled the strings. "So there's no oil in the ridges? No wonder you weren't in any hurry to sign the leases!"

"I didn't say that." He reached out and put his hand on hers. "Stop butchering that slice of toast and eat it," he commanded. "Haven't you received the geological survey you ordered?"

"No, not yet."

"Well, the part about the oil is true, or at least there's a good chance of either oil or natural gas."

She ate a piece of toast, and fiddled with another one until she looked up and saw him glaring at her. She hastily took a bite, then put the remainder on her plate. "I'm really not very hungry. I'm sorry."

"That's all right. You'll get your appetite back soon." He rose and began to clear the table; when Susan moved to help him, he stopped her with a lifted hand. "Whoa, lady. Put that plate down. You're not to do any work."

"I'm fairly certain I'm still strong enough to carry a plate," she informed him mildly.

"Sit down. I think I'm going to have to explain the rules to you."

At the mock sternness in his voice, she sat down like a naughty schoolgirl, her hands clasped on her knees. He sat down in the chair opposite her and explained the situation to her slowly and carefully. "You're here to rest. I'm here to take care of you. I'll do the cooking, the cleaning up, everything."

"How long will heaven last?" she asked, and for the first time a tiny smile lit her face, catching his eye like a ray of sunshine after a storm.

"As long as it takes," he replied quietly.

He was serious. The next few days passed leisurely, even monotonously, but after the stress of the last weeks, that was exactly what Susan needed. Time was measured only by the rising and setting of the sun. At first she slept a lot, as much from mental fatigue as any physical tiredness. She didn't occupy her thoughts with tormenting questions of "What if?"; her mind was curiously blank, as if it were just too much trouble to think about anything. She rested, she ate, she slept, all under the mostly silent guardianship that Cord offered.

She not only slept alone, she was completely undisturbed, and as she regained her strength she began to wonder about that. It was a sign of her returning vitality that she wondered about anything, but she was young and healthy, and the coddling she'd been receiving was rapidly restoring her strength. Her depression and fatigue had been feeding on each other, and with the weariness banished, the uncharacteristic depression began to lift. It was almost like rebirth, and she quietly enjoyed it. But she knew that it was also obvious to Cord that she was feeling much better, and every night she expected him to come to her bed. When he didn't, she had the panicked thought that perhaps he didn't want her any longer; then she realized that he was waiting for her to make the first move, to indicate that she was ready to resume their relationship.

Uncertainty kept her silent. She wasn't certain that it was what she wanted; she still loved him, but there was still that lingering sense of betrayal that she couldn't shake, and she knew that as long as she had doubts about him she had to hold herself aloof. Nor did she want simply to resume an affair; she wanted far more from him than that. She wanted his love, his legal commitment, and, if possible, his children.

The fifth night they were at the beach house a thunderstorm blew in from the Gulf and dumped its fury on them, rattling the windows with its booming claps of thunder. Susan awoke with a start, a cry on her lips, as for a confused moment she thought a tornado was bearing down on her. Then she realized where she was and curled up under the sheet, listening to the drumming rain against the window. She'd never been frightened of storms in the past; in fact, she rather enjoyed the display of power and grandeur, as long as it didn't escalate into a tornado. She would forever have a healthy respect for those snaking, dancing storms.

Her door opened abruptly, and Cord stepped into the room, his nakedness revealed in the flashes of lightning.

Susan stared at him, feeling the tart taste of desire on her tongue, the slow, heated coiling in her abdomen and thighs.

"Are you all right?" he asked softly. "I thought you might be nervous, after the tornado."

She sat up, pushing her tousled hair away from her face. "I'm fine. I was a little startled when it first woke me, but I'm not frightened."

"Good," he said, and started to leave the room.

"Cord, wait!" she called, not planning to say the words, but they burst out of her anyway. He hesitated and turned back to her, standing silently, waiting. "I think it's time to talk," she ventured.

"All right." He moved his shoulders in a strange manner, as if bracing himself. "I'll go put on some pants and be back."

"No." Again she stopped him, holding her hand out to him. "There's no need, is there?"

"I didn't think so," he returned. "But I wasn't sure how you felt."

"I feel the same. . . . Please, sit on the bed." She moved to one side and pulled the covers about her waist, sitting up in the circle of them.

He dropped down to her bed, confiscated one of her pillows and stuffed it behind his back, stretched his long legs out on the mattress and turned on the lamp. "If we're going to talk, I'm going to be comfortable, and I want to be able to see you."

She tucked her legs under her Indian-style, trying not to stare at the wonderfully masculine form sprawled in front of her. She couldn't imagine a man made any more beautifully. Every time she saw him, she only admired him the more; he seemed to improve with age. But his body was distracting her, and she forced herself to look at his face. The small, knowing, infinitely pleased smile that lurked on his lips made her flush; then she laughed a little at herself.

"I'm sorry. You have a knack for making me blush."

"*I* should be blushing, if I'm reading your mind correctly."

He was, and they both knew it. She quickly sought control, and found it. This was far too important for her to let herself be sidetracked. "Before I say anything else, we might as well get one thing out of the way. I love you. If you can't deal with that, if it makes you uncomfortable, then we have nothing to talk about. You might as well go back to your own room."

He didn't move an inch from his comfortable position. "I've known for some time," he said, his eyes darker than she'd ever seen them before. "I knew the first time I made love with you. If you hadn't loved me, you never would have stripped for me like that, or put yourself in my hands so completely."

"But you couldn't trust me? You left me in the dark, knowing how much I was worrying, how it tore me apart to have to fight you?" A jagged edge of pain tore into her again just at the memory, and she drew a quick breath, fighting to keep from falling apart, but still the hurt was evident in her voice.

"In my defense, let me say that I hadn't expected you. You blindsided me, sweetheart, and I've been floundering ever since. Except for my parents, I can't say that I've ever known anyone I could trust until I met you, and so many years had passed since I'd been able to turn my back to anyone that I couldn't let myself believe it. You defended Preston so stubbornly, even though you said you loved me; how could I be sure you wouldn't run and tell him immediately if I let it slip that I wasn't trying to bankrupt the company, only to pressure him into selling enough stock for me to have the majority?"

"Don't you see?" she cried. "I defended Preston *precisely* because I thought you were trying to bankrupt him to get revenge for Judith!"

"No, I wasn't after revenge, though I wanted him to think so. I'm far too guilty myself to have any right to take revenge. But the way things were when I left . . . honey, you have no idea how bitter and violent it had become. I wanted to come back home, and I knew the only way I could do it was from a position of power. I didn't want to simply live in the area again; I wanted to be accepted, to be a part of what I'd had before, when I was too young and too hot-headed to appreciate it."

"And if you'd told me all of that, you thought I'd still ruin it for you?" she asked, blinking back tears.

He cupped her cheek in his palm, his fingers caressing her jaw. "Don't cry," he murmured. "I told you, I'm out of the habit of trusting people. I've spent a lot of time in dives and jungles and back alleys that—well, never mind. But, damn it, you know I never planned for you to be the one to sell! I never thought he'd dump it all on your shoulders, but he's a smart bastard, I'll say that for him. His idea almost worked. If I'd known that *you* were the one being beaten down, I'd have stopped on the spot. It was your own stubbornness in not telling me that kept things going for so long, that gave me enough time to buy the stock I needed."

"Along with my vote," she reminded him thinly.

"Yes, along with your vote." He watched her intently, reading the myriad expressions as they flitted across her lovely face. She looked incredibly sexy, he noticed, with her hair all tousled and her eyes still heavy-lidded, her skin softly flushed from sleep. The dark shadows were gone from beneath her eyes, and the soft curves of her breasts shone beneath the thin silk of her nightgown, with her small nipples pushing against the fabric in an enticing manner that made him want to lean forward and take them into his mouth, silk and all. He felt it again, that punch in his chest, and he realized anew that she lit his life like an eternal candle, pure and white. If that serene flame ever went out he'd be doomed to darkness for the rest of his life.

"I was wrong not to trust you," he said softly. His voice went even quieter, so deep that it rumbled in his chest. "I knew that you loved me, and it was almost too much for me to believe. I was afraid to believe. My God, Susan, don't you know? Don't you have any idea what you do to people? Everywhere I turned, there were people falling all over themselves to please you, to get you to smile at them, to have your attention for just a little while. Even Imogene would fight her weight in wildcats for you! If I'd let myself believe that sweetness was all mine, then found out that it wasn't, I couldn't have handled it. I had to protect myself by not letting you get too close."

Susan stared at him, bewildered by his words. "People fall all over themselves for me? What do you mean?"

She truly didn't know, he realized, had never noticed the effect her radiant smile had on people, or the almost inevitable softening that crossed their faces whenever they talked to her. My God, he had a treasure that men would fight for, possibly kill for, and she didn't even know her own power, which he supposed was part of her elusive, but hauntingly sweet charm.

"Never mind," he told her gently. She wouldn't believe him even if he told her. "The important thing is, do you love me enough to forgive me?"

"I have to," she replied obliquely, but the truth was plain in her eyes. She had to forgive him, because when she searched down to the deepest recesses of her heart, she loved him too much not to forgive him anything.

Very tenderly, he reached out and caught her waist, drawing her out of her tangle of covers and pulling her atop him, resting her weight on his chest. "I'm glad," he said gravely, his diamond-eyes so close that she could see her own reflection in the dilated blackness of his pupils. "Because I love you so much that I think I'd go crazy if you sent me away."

Susan's eyes widened, and her heart gave a great bound, then resumed beating with thuds that hammered against the delicate cage of her ribs. "I . . . what?"

"I said, I love you," he repeated, sliding his hands up her back in a slow, heated caress. She quivered, tried to speak, but her trembling lips couldn't form the words, and instead she gave up and dropped her head to his shoulder, her hands holding tightly to him. He folded her to him, pressing her soft, deliciously feminine body against his. Sudden tears, hot and acid, burned his eyes. He'd almost lost her, almost let her love slip away from him, and the thought tormented him.

"I love you," he said again, this time whispering the words into the dark cloud of her hair. The searing tears slid down his hard, sun-browned cheeks, but he wasn't aware of them. His world had narrowed to the wonder he held in his arms, the slim, delicate body that held such sweetness and gallantry, such an endless capacity for love, that he was staggered by it.

Susan drew a little away from him, her heart stopping when she saw the wet tracks on his face, and in that moment she knew beyond doubt that he loved her. He was looking at her with a deep, consuming love that he made no effort to hide. The last of his bitterness was drained away in the salt of his tears, the last grief and guilt he felt for Judith. She put her cheek against his, rubbing the wetness away.

Knowing that she would never refuse him, that what they felt burning between them needed to be consummated, had to be sanctified by their union, he rolled and deftly placed her beneath him, his legs parting her thighs. He rose to his knees and lifted her nightgown, then drew it over her head. After tossing it away, he regarded her slim beauty for a moment, then let his weight down on her. He kissed her fiercely, then drew back with masculine satisfaction stamped on his bearded features. "I'm going to marry you."

Again shock reverberated through Susan, but now it was a joyous shock, as at last she began to believe what was happening to her. She looked up at him, and suddenly a smile curved her lips. Just like that; it wasn't a proposal, a question, but a statement. He was going to marry her, and she'd better not try to argue with him about it!

"Yes," she said, then caught her breath as he entered her. Her moistly yielding body accepted him without difficulty, the sweet honey of her flesh welcoming him. He moved against her, probing slowly, and he groaned aloud in pleasure.

Then he raised himself on his elbow to look down at her, his gaze burning with desire. "It might be a good idea if we get married as soon as possible," he murmured. "After the night in the Blazer, you could well be pregnant."

"I know." She slid her hands over his shoulders to his neck, and smiled up at him. "I hope so."

An answering smile touched his lips. "Just to be on the safe side, let's do it again." He kissed her again; then their

bodies began to move in unison, with a passion that was
wild and tender and sanity-destroying, their love binding
them together with an electrically charged force field of
devotion. What had begun with a dance on a crowded
ballroom floor had become a sensual dance of love,
sanctified by the tears of a hard man who'd had to learn how
to cry.

Epilogue

CORD LAY HEAVILY ON HER, SWEETLY LIMP AFTER THE whirlwind of their lovemaking. Susan nibbled on his shoulder, and he put his hand in her hair to pull her head up. He began kissing her again, slow, drugging kisses that lit the fires between them again, fires that burned higher and hotter than ever after a year of marriage. Just as he began moving within her, a faint, fretful cry caught their attention, a cry that quickly escalated into an all-out bellow.

He cursed luridly as he slid off of her. "She's got the most incredible timing!" he grumbled as he stalked naked from the room, outrage evident in every line of his powerful body.

Susan pulled the sheet up over her nude body; she was cool without the heat of him next to her. A slow, gentle smile touched her lips as she envisioned the scene in the next room. Cord might grumble and grouse, but he'd melt as soon as he set eyes on his tiny daughter, who had just learned how to blow bubbles. As soon as she saw her father, she'd stop her bellowing, and her arms and legs would go into overtime as her entire body wriggled in delight. She'd treat him to her entire repertoire of accomplishments, from kicking to blowing bubbles, and he'd be lost in adoring admiration. Alison Marie was a four-month-old tyrant, and she had Cord wrapped completely around her dainty finger.

It was a good thing they'd gotten married so swiftly, because within a month it had become evident that Susan was indeed pregnant. Cord had teased her before Alison had been born, insisting that if the baby were a girl, he was going to name her Storm, and if it were a boy, it had to be called Blazer. She'd been a little worried at how he would accept fatherhood, but she'd worried over nothing. No man could have been more delighted over his child.

She prepared herself to nurse the baby, and in a moment Cord came back into the bedroom, cradling Alison in the curve of his strong arm and crooning to her as her plump little hands waved in the air, trying to catch his beard. "We're going to have to trade her in for a model that doesn't leak," he said, getting back in bed, still holding Alison, while Susan stuffed a pillow behind her back.

When she took the baby, he moved to put his arm around her, holding her so most of her weight rested on his chest. "Look at that little pig," he drawled, as the baby latched onto the milk-swollen nipple with starving ferocity. He was fascinated by everything about her, and had been from the moment he'd known of Susan's pregnancy.

Despite it being her first child, she'd breezed through the months with almost boring ease. She'd had little morning sickness, no cravings, and had carried the baby easily. Her biggest problem had been Cord, who had hounded her if she even tried to change a light bulb. She had Alison with a minimum of fuss, and Cord had been there to hold his daughter, who weighed in at a tiny five pounds and two ounces.

Now his big hand touched the small, round head, smoothing the black curls that covered it. She opened her eyes briefly, revealing pale blue irises surrounded by a ring of darker blue. She was his image, and he adored her. But the delights of her mother's breast occupied her at the moment, and she closed her eyes again, suckling vigorously.

Soon she slept again, and Susan's nipple slipped from the relaxed rosebud mouth. "I'm going to have to wean her soon," she sighed.

"Why?"

"She's starting to teethe."

He laughed softly, sprawling naked on the bed. "Dangerous, huh?"

"Extremely." She carried Alison back to the nursery, and stood for a moment holding the infinitely precious little bundle in her arms. The baby grunted as she was placed on her stomach, but a tightly curled fist brushed her mouth and she latched onto it in her sleep, sucking noisily on her knuckles.

He was waiting for her when she came back into their bedroom, and he drew her back down into his embrace. Susan curled against him, placing her head on the broad, hairy chest. Being married to him was better than she'd dreamed, because she'd never thought that her restless renegade would have been so content.

He and Preston had reached a truce, a working relationship that allowed peace between them. Preston remained as president of the company, because his experience and ability were too good to waste. Cord's own daring and verve had blended with Preston's attention to detail, and together they were creating a company that was innovative but not reckless, sure-footed but not too cautious. The challenge kept Cord fascinated, and at night he came back to her arms, which was all she'd ever asked of heaven.

He reached out and clicked off the lamp, yawning in the sudden darkness. He settled her in his arms, in their sleeping position, and she nuzzled her mouth against his flesh. Just as she'd dreamed months ago, sleeping with him every night was deeply satisfying. They talked in the darkness, sharing the things that had happened to them during the day, planning what they wanted to do together. His hand moved lazily over her soft body, then found her breasts and became more obvious in his attentions.

"Susan? Do you think she'll wake up this time?"

Susan laughed, winding her arms around his neck. Her beloved desperado, her darling renegade, still swept her away into his dark, magic world of love.

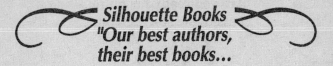

Silhouette Books
"Our best authors,
their best books...

DIANA PALMER
Soldier of Fortune in February

ELIZABETH LOWELL
Dark Fire in February

LINDA LAEL MILLER
Ragged Rainbow in March

JOAN HOHL
California Copper in March

LINDA HOWARD
An Independent Wife in April

HEATHER GRAHAM POZZESSERE
Double Entendre in April

**When it comes to passion,
we wrote the book.**

BOBQ1

He staked his claim...

HONOR BOUND

by
New York Times
Bestselling Author

previously published under the pseudonym Erin St. Claire

As Aislinn Andrews opened her mouth to scream, a hard
hand clamped over her face and she found herself face-
to-face with Lucas Greywolf, a lean, lethal-looking
Navajo and escaped convict who swore he wouldn't hurt
her— *if* she helped him.

Look for HONOR BOUND at your favorite
retail outlet this January.

Only from...

Silhouette®
TM

where passion lives. SBHB

Also available by popular author

LINDA HOWARD

Silhouette Intimate Moments®

| #07349 | DUNCAN'S BRIDE | $2.95 | ☐ |

Best of the Best™

| #48270 | ALL THAT GLITTERS | $4.50 | ☐ |
| #48271 | COME LIE WITH ME | $4.50 | ☐ |

Silhouette® Books

| #48240 | LINDA HOWARD 2-IN-1
-MIDNIGHT RAINBOW
-DIAMOND BAY | $4.59 | ☐ |
| #48243 | LINDA HOWARD 2-IN-1
-HEARTBREAKER
-WHITE LIES | $4.59 | ☐ |

(limited quantities available on certain titles)

TOTAL AMOUNT	$
POSTAGE & HANDLING	$
($1.00 for one book, 50¢ for each additional)	
APPLICABLE TAXES*	$_____
TOTAL PAYABLE	$_____
(check or money order—please do not send cash)	

To order, complete this form and send it, along with a check or money order for the total above, payable to Silhouette Books, to: **In the U.S.:** 3010 Walden Avenue, P.O. Box 9077, Buffalo, NY 14269-9077; **In Canada:** P.O. Box 636, Fort Erie, Ontario, L2A 5X3.

Name: _____

Address: _____ City: _____

State/Prov.: _____ Zip/Postal Code: _____

*New York residents remit applicable sales taxes.
 Canadian residents remit applicable GST and provincial taxes.

▼ Silhouette®